POISONED WEB
THE DEIZIAN EMPIRE: BOOK TWO

BY
CRISTA MCHUGH

Poisoned Web
Copyright 2013 by Crista McHugh
Edited by Rhonda Helms
Copyedits by Victory Editing
Cover Art by Sweet N' Spicy Designs

ISBN-13: 978-1-940559-99-5

1

A roar ripped through the city of Emona, slapping against the walls of the Imperial Palace and making them quake under the force of the noise. The members of the Legion stiffened, their fingers tightening around the hilts of their swords. And all but two of the slaves ran deeper into the inner confines of the palace.

Izana and Farros stood in the middle of the courtyard, refusing to shrink in fear like the other Alpirions.

She glanced at her fellow slave, meeting his gaze in a silent challenge before bolting toward the outer wall. Neck and neck, they raced, the sun beating down on their skin and the thin shimmer of sweat that coated it. Izana ducked under Farros's well-muscled arms when they reached the narrow staircase to the upper ramparts, using her smaller size to her advantage. She wanted to be the first person to see the newly engaged imperial couple enter the palace. She needed to see her mistress wearing the crown proclaiming her to be the future empress. And she prayed that this would be the first step in gaining freedom for her people.

Her lungs burned in protest as she ran into the wall, but her heart leaped with joy. Even though the carriage carrying

1

Emperor Sergius and his bride-to-be was over a mile down the road, the crowd still cheered outside the palace walls. The people loved Lady Azurha, loved that she had been one of them, that she had walked along these very streets before she found her way into the palace and won the heart of the emperor. By now, the whole city knew how she'd saved his life from Pontus, one of the emperor's cousins who coveted the throne for himself.

But very few knew the whole truth—that Azurha was the Rabbit, the most feared assassin in the empire. Varro had made those directly attending to the imperial couple swear to this a secret, but how quickly had the gossip spread before he made them take that oath?

Farros leaned against the wall beside her, his massive chest still heaving from their race. Did he know the truth?

"I think my lady's fears were for naught," she said, sweeping her hand toward the crowded streets below. "Look at how they cheer for an Alpirion empress."

His dark eyes glinted with cynicism. "They cheer now, but how long do you think it will last? How many Deizians will bend their knee to a former slave?"

"More than you think." But his words jabbed a sliver of fear into her chest. She chewed her bottom lip as she started counting the enemies Lady Azurha had made in the last three weeks. For starters, there was Governor Hostilius and his spoiled daughter, Claudia. Not to mention some other Deizians who believed the emperor was soiling the royal line by marrying a woman outside their race.

As though he knew what she'd been thinking, Farros gave a slow nod. "The Deizians may be few, but they hold all the power." The muscle rippled along his jaw before he added, "For now."

Nervous laughter bubbled up from her throat. "Are you suggesting someone is plotting to overthrow the emperor and his people?"

"Our people managed to withstand Deizian conquest for centuries."

The dark intensity of his statement quickened her pulse. She took a step back, studying the man beside her. Farros was built more for the gladiatorial ring than the imperial household, where he worked in the stables. The sleeves of his tunic rose high enough to partially expose a tattoo on the inside of his bicep. He stared at the procession below, the sun reflecting off his freshly shaven head and coppery skin, the corded muscles in his forearms flexing as he pumped his hands into fists. If he wanted, he could snap her neck in a matter of seconds.

He looked back to her, his face sliding into the flirtatious smile he normally wore around her. Only now, she knew it was a mask. She'd glimpsed the man behind it.

"Why do you look so worried, Izana?"

"Because you talk like a man destined for trouble."

Farros took her hand and pulled her back to the wall, caging her between his body and the stone bricks. The pounding of her heart drowned out the celebration below, but she still heard his low voice whispering in her ear, "As slaves, we've been told that as long as we obey our masters, we have nothing to fear. But that may not always be the case."

Her breath caught, giving her a few precious seconds to choose her words carefully. "You are not my master."

"Come now, Izana," he continued, his hot breath bathing the hollow of her neck where the mark of her former owner was still visible. "How many men have mastered you over the years?"

Fury sizzled through her veins, driving away her fear. She rammed her elbow under his ribs. The air whooshed out of his lungs, and his arms retracted to cradle his injury, allowing her to escape. She retreated until she was well out of arm's reach before replying, "I'm no longer engaged in that business, and unless you wish for me to tell my mistress everything, you'll keep your hands to yourself."

Her feet flew down the stairs in tempo with her pulse, never stopping until she was safely within the palace. Thankfully, Farros didn't give chase. He was probably still doubled over on the ramparts.

Varro, the palace steward, stood beside the locked doors leading to the emperor's private quarters. He pressed his hand against the plate as she approached, his brown eyes never missing a thing. "Is something wrong, Izana?"

She shook her head. "The sun was very warm today. I'm sure Lady Azurha will be ready for a dip in the tepidarium when she returns."

Varro nodded, even though his expression told her he didn't quite believe her. It didn't matter. Once she was behind those doors, she was safe. But despite the cool tile beneath her bare feet, her cheeks still burned, and her gut twisted as though it held a den of snakes.

From now on, she needed to be wary of Farros.

2

"That went beautifully," Titus said, his blue eyes twinkling as they stepped down from the Deizian chariot that had magically carried them through the streets without the aid of horses or wheels. "The people seemed very pleased with my future bride."

"So you think," she replied. He may have only seen the smiling faces of the Elymanians and the Alpirions and heard nothing but shouts of joy, but her trained eyes saw more than that. The scoffs of the blond Deizian women from their perches high above the crowds. The sneers that twisted the mouths of their husbands and fathers. The constant reminder that she wasn't one of them, that she was a usurper. The fresh tattoo of the Legion itched along her right wrist under her bracelet, reminding her of the vow she had made to protect the emperor in exchange for being pardoned of her past crimes. "Thankfully, no one made an attempt on your life today."

"And why should they? After all, I am marrying the Rabbit." He pulled her into his arms and kissed her in a way that made her forget about everything but him.

The scent of sandalwood filled her nose, and desire hummed through her veins. She threaded her fingers through his golden hair and kissed him back, opening her mouth to him and savoring the sensation of his tongue teasing hers. Only a week had passed since she'd almost lost Titus to the man who'd originally hired her to kill him, since she'd almost died in his arms after rescuing him, since she'd confessed how much she loved him. But since then, she'd learned never to waste a precious second in his company. Fate had a fickle side and could take it all away in a blink of an eye.

A man cleared his throat behind them. "Save it for the bedroom, Your Imperial Majesty," Marcus teased.

As the emperor's best friend, he was the only person who dared say such a thing and not live in fear of losing his head. His blue eyes proclaimed his Deizian blood, but his dark brown hair and beard were more typical of his Elymanian ancestry.

Titus broke away, the heat in his eyes letting her know he'd gladly pick up where he left off as soon as they were alone. Her sex tightened in anticipation, for when Titus made love to her, she was always left sated and exhausted.

"Leave him alone, Marcus," Titus's mother, Empress Horatia, scolded. Not a single strand of her golden hair had fallen out of place during the procession, yet she still patted it into place around her tiara. "He's just proclaimed his formal engagement to Azurha and has been on his best behavior all day. Let him enjoy one simple kiss."

"That was not a simple kiss. That was an 'I can't wait to get you out of your clothes and bury—"

"We get the idea, Marcus." Titus released her and straightened his toga before leaning over to whisper low enough so only she could hear, "He's right, though."

She ran her tongue over her lips, still tasting him there. "Then maybe we should have a very short dinner."

"Agreed." He winked and turned back to address at least a hundred guests who'd followed them into the palace. "We thank you all for coming to celebrate my engagement to Azurha. Please join us in the banquet hall as we continue the festivities."

Dozens of Deizian blue eyes locked in on her, picking her apart with their icy glares. Azurha had been born an Alpirion slave, had killed her master to gain her freedom, and had earned

6

a reputation for covering her hands in the blood of those she'd been hired to kill. She threatened the Deizians' power, both from her rise to the throne and from the dirty secrets she could expose if she revealed the details of her past jobs. They loathed her. They feared her. But would they ever accept her as their empress?

Horatia gave her a gentle smile and lifted her chin, reminding Azurha to do the same. It didn't matter what the Deizian nobles thought. It only mattered that Titus loved her, that he had chosen her to be his wife.

And if they dared to threaten them, she wouldn't hesitate to utilize the skills that had made her legend long before she met Titus.

Titus squeezed her hand before placing it in the crook of his arm and leading the procession into the palace's throne room. They took their seats on the raised dais at one end of the room and accepted the tight-lipped congratulations from the line of Deizians who followed. Azurha nodded to each of them, her smile as cool as the dagger strapped to her thigh under her stola. From the earliest days of her life, she'd been instructed to keep her eyes downcast, both because she was a slave and because her unusually colored teal eyes brought her unwanted attention. But now she was staring members of the ruling race dead in the eye, challenging them with the reversal in power.

Once they'd received the last guest in line, a series of three short claps came from the steward in the opposite corner. A wave of slaves entered the room with cushions for their guests to recline on during the meal. Then a second wave of slaves appeared from the kitchen, carrying trays of food and pitchers of chilled wine, all perfectly orchestrated under the direction of Varro.

Once the meal started and Titus had fallen into conversation with Marcus, Horatia crossed the dais and sat beside Azurha. "You did very well today, my dear. I almost passed out during my engagement ceremony."

"I find that difficult to believe, Your Majesty. You are

the epitome of calm grace."

"I've had years to master my emotions. Deizian women are brought up to never reveal what their hearts feel. It is considered a sign of weakness."

Azurha scanned the room for the one Deizian woman who'd made the mistake of showing too much emotion. "I haven't seen Claudia since she left the harem."

"And you probably won't," Horatia replied, her eyes sorrowful as she accepted a glass from one of the slaves. "Hostilius sent her back to Tivola and hasn't mentioned her name since then. I worry about the poor child."

Azurha almost choked on her wine. The poor child the empress referred to was nothing more than a spoiled, spiteful brat who had tried to steal Titus from her, and more than once insulted Azurha by treating her like a slave. "I have a hard time feeling any pity for Claudia."

"Yes, I've heard the abbreviated version of what passed between you two from Varro. But you only see things from your eyes, from your experiences. I've known Claudia since she was a child, and I can assure you she is caught in her father's ambitious web. She's been forced to marry three men she's cared nothing for to please him, and now that she's failed him, I worry she'll suffer the same fate as those who displease him."

The empress didn't need to continue. All of the empire knew the governor of Lucrilla didn't keep many enemies for long. Most of them either disappeared or were found dead at the bottom of a cliff. He'd even hired Azurha to dispose of a rival at one point. "Surely he wouldn't kill his own daughter."

"You know as well as I do what Hostilius is capable of doing." Horatia took a sip of her wine. "I just pray to the gods that his temper will cool before he returns home, and I'm thankful you and Titus agreed to a quick wedding so the nobles will be forced to stay in Emona a bit longer."

"Ah, yes, the wedding." Her heart stuttered, and her stomach flopped. She'd rather face the challenge of killing a hundred men in the space of a night than the pomp of the next three weeks. "If I had a choice, we would've been married the day I accepted his proposal."

The empress chuckled. "I'm sure Titus would agree with you there, but alas, that is not the way things are done in the imperial family."

"I have so much to learn." She closed her eyes, her crown heavier on her head than before. "I want to be a good wife, a good empress, but I fear my past will always haunt me."

"We cannot control our pasts, only our futures."

Wise words from a woman whose black palla proclaimed she was still mourning the loss of her husband. Azurha glanced at Titus, remembering the conversation she'd had with him the night before over the sudden loss of his father, Emperor Gaius Decius Flavus. Perhaps she might not be able to change the past, but she might be able to offer some answers. "May I have a word in private with you, Empress Horatia?"

A line appeared between the older woman's brows, but she nodded and followed Azurha into the empty courtyard reserved exclusively for the imperial family. The gurgling fountains cooled the air around them and added a layer of discretion to their conversation.

Azurha dipped her fingers into the water, picking her words carefully. "I wanted to talk to you about my wedding gift to Titus."

"Are you asking for suggestions?" Horatia's eyes brightened. "I know he's received so many gifts for his coronation last week, but I'm sure we can think of something unique and meaningful."

"I've already thought of something." She drew in a deep breath and prayed her choice would not open wounds that were still healing. "I want to solve the mystery of Emperor Decius's death."

Just as she'd expected, color drained from the empress's face. She sank onto the edge of the fountain, staring past Azurha. Her bottom lip trembled. "That's very kind of you, my dear, but—"

"It has nothing to do with kindness, Your Majesty. It has to do with justice, with the peace that will come with answers." Azurha dared to reach out and cover the empress's hand with her own, a gesture most Deizian women would never think of doing without permission, but she felt a kinship with Horatia over their shared love for Titus. "Everything I've heard so far indicates he died before his time, and I was hoping, with my background…"

She didn't need to continue. Once again, her past as the Rabbit had entered the picture. She knew dozens of ways to kill a man, including first-hand knowledge of poisons and the assassins that preferred to use particular ones. If she could identify a poison, she might be able to find out who killed the former emperor and why.

Horatia's eyes focused on Azurha's face. "Are you suggesting someone murdered him?"

She hesitated for a second before nodding.

A sob choked the empress's throat. She covered her mouth and stood, her back to Azurha. Her shoulders silently shook with grief. But in less than a moment, she regained her composure and turned back to Azurha. Unshed tears glittered in the corners of her eyes. "I had suspected as much, but hearing it from someone else, I…" Her voice cracked.

"I apologize if this news has caused you distress."

"No need to apologize, Azurha," Horatia replied with a wave of her hand. "Forgive me for losing control like this."

"Why do you think I asked you to step into the courtyard first?" She offered a sympathetic smile to the empress. "When you feel ready, I'd like to ask you what you observed in the days leading up to his death."

"I'm ready now." She swiped the back of her hand over her cheeks and adjusted her palla over her shoulders. "Gaius was in excellent health up until the last two weeks of his life. The illness struck him suddenly, robbing him of his strength. At first, he brushed it off as fatigue from the stress of his imperial duties. But as it worsened, he had trouble walking, standing, even drawing a breath."

She paused, rubbing the band of gold on her finger. "We sought the help of every healer in the empire, but none of them were able to cure him."

Azurha nodded, pulling important bits of information from the description the empress had given her. The first was that it was a poison she was not familiar with. In her career as an assassin, she only got paid when her targets were found dead. The poisons she'd always relied on tended to kill within seconds to hours.

The second important bit was that this poison could withstand Deizian magic. She was alive today because Titus had used his magic to remove the poison that pumped through her veins after her fight with Cassius. How was it he and every other skilled healer couldn't do the same for the emperor?

She chewed her bottom lip as she searched for answers, but none of them came readily. "I appreciate your information, Your Majesty. It has helped me get started on the path to answers."

"And do you have some available already?" Horatia asked, her breath catching.

Azurha shook her head. "But I have an idea on where to look."

Starting with a former Captain of the Legion.

***

Azurha caught Varro later that evening as he entered their chambers and pulled him aside. "May I ask you a few questions?"

The steward raised one brow, shifting the lines carved into his forehead from his years as a soldier. An Elymanian, he'd risen to the position of Captain of the Legion, the head of the emperor's bodyguards, because of his keen eye and brave loyalty. A battle wound that snaked around his leg and left him with a permanent limp had ended his military career, but he'd settled into the position of the palace steward to continue serving the emperor. "Yes, Lady Azurha?"

"I was wondering if you could share with me what you

observed during the last two weeks of Emperor Decius's life."

Now both brows shot up. He cleared his throat and gave a similar story as the empress's. Rapidly worsening weakness. Wasting of the muscles. Death when he no longer had the strength to breathe. And when Varro finished, he asked, "Is there anything else you wish to know?"

"Yes—did you notice anything out of the ordinary in the days preceding the emperor's illness? Any new foods? Guests? Anyone else with a similar illness?"

Varro shook his head, his mouth forming a thin line. "Only a few people had access to the emperor, and they all went through me or Captain Galerius. All the emperor's meals are tested for poison before they leave the kitchen by one of the slaves, and I have no knowledge of anyone ever contracting the same illness."

No wonder Pontus had made sure she entered the palace as a courtesan. He'd been familiar with the levels of protection already in place around the emperor. And yet, she'd managed to slip through with concealed tools of death.

Varro continued to regard her with a mixture of puzzlement in his brown eyes, so she said, "I have reason to believe Emperor Decius was poisoned, and I want to know the how and why."

He nodded. "As do I."

Some of the tension eased from her shoulders. "Do you have any other information that might be helpful?"

"No, but I might know someone who can assist you. My son, Modius, has developed a rather, um, interesting obsession with medicine. Perhaps he has stumbled upon something in his studies that might shed some light on this mystery."

She vaguely remembered meeting his son at the palace in Madrena and wondered how far Modius's "interesting" obsession went. "Please send for him, and please, not a word of this to the emperor. I do not want to revive any unpleasant memories unless I'm ready to give him answers."

"Understood, Lady Azurha." The steward bowed and

exited the chambers.

Azurha crossed the room, shedding the layers of jewels and clothes on her way to the baths. There, she found Titus soaking in the caldarium, his golden hair slicked back against his scalp, highlighting his perfectly carved features and deep blue eyes.

"Coming to join me?" he asked, his gaze traveling up and down her naked body.

She removed the last pin holding her hair back, letting it fall in a dark cascade to her hips. "If you don't mind," she murmured, her voice low and gravelly with desire.

She slid into the warm water, her sex already tightening in anticipation. After suffering years of abuse by her former master, she never dreamed she would ever crave a man's touch. And yet, from the moment she met Titus, she knew he was different. Her body responded to his kisses and caresses the same way her heart jumped from his murmured words when they made love. She'd found a man who loved her, and whom she loved with every fiber of her being.

He pulled her to him, the coarse hair on his chest brushing against her sensitive nipples and sending shivers of delight through her. "Ah, yes, I vaguely remember a promise to finish what I started before dinner."

His mouth covered her own, his arm tightening around her until they were pressed together from head to toe. The hard planes of his body contrasted with her soft curves, steadying her, teasing her, heating her blood. She threaded her fingers through his hair, deepening the kiss. Traces of sweet wine lingered on his lips. Her hips rolled in time with the flicks of his tongue, and her leg hooked around his thigh, opening herself up to the part of him that could soothe the raging need inside her.

Titus wasted no time accepting her invitation. He slid into her with one powerful thrust that made her cry out in delight. He moved inside her, slowly at first, each successive pump becoming stronger and faster. Their bodies moved as one, their kisses hungry. Her heart raced. Her breath hitched as her muscles coiled tighter and tighter, each thrust pushing her closer and closer to the edge. She dug her nails into his shoulders and held on for dear life, shouting his name as she came. His own roar of satisfaction quickly followed, and he slumped against her, completely spent.

Azurha ran her fingers over his shoulders, finding all the knots that still lingered from the stress of the day. "You feel like you could use a massage."

"How about you just joining me in bed?"

"We can do that, too, but first, let me tend to this." She unwrapped her legs from him and climbed out of the pool. "Where does Varro keep your oils?"

A look of defeat crossed his too-perfect face, followed by resignation. "There should be a drawer on the end of the table."

She found it and pulled a bottle out. "The sooner I work those knots out of your shoulders, the sooner we can go to bed."

He climbed out, his cock already half-erect as he approached her. "Do you have any idea how uncomfortable I'll be lying on my stomach while you stand there naked, rubbing oil all over my body?"

"Should I put my dress back on?"

"No." He pulled her against him, his hands resting on her hips. He placed a playful peck on her cheek. "I like you this way. If I had my way, you'd wear nothing as long as you were in my chambers."

"I think poor Varro would have some issue with that." She pulled away. "Now on the table."

Titus laughed as he lay down. "You do realize you're the only person who could get away with ordering the emperor around?"

She leaned over, her lips inches from his ear. "And I like having that power over you."

It was such a far cry from her life as a slave. Then, she'd been powerless. Now, she was two weeks away from becoming the second-most-powerful person in the empire. But she no

longer cared about having power, about having control of her
life. She'd gladly give up the title of empress so long as she had
Titus.

He winced as she poured the cold oil on his skin, the
muscles between his shoulder blades drawing closer together. A
minute later, he started to relax from the steady stroke of her
hands along his back and shoulders. A sigh escaped his lips.
"You were right, Azurha. I needed a good massage."

"Of course I was right." She pressed her thumbs into the
more stubborn knots, wiggling them back and forth in a tight
circular motion until the muscles surrendered. "When was the
last time you had a massage?"

"It was before my coronation."

"I need to speak to Varro about that. You need to take
better care of yourself, Emperor."

He rolled over, grabbing her hand and pulling her onto
the table with him. "I know how you can take care of me."

The hard ridge of his erection told her exactly where this
conversation was going, but she decided to tease him. "How?"

"You can start by letting me return the favor." He
poured a stream of oil along her side, coating her until her body
was as slick as his. Then he pulled her on top of him so her legs
straddled his waist and her hands pressed against his chest.
"Where shall I massage you first? Your thighs? Your back? Your
breasts?"

He touched each part of her body as he listed them,
mimicking the same steady strokes she'd used on his shoulders.
Then a mischievous glint appeared in his eyes, and his finger
trailed to the place between her thighs. "Or should I massage you
here?"

Her breath caught when he pressed against the sensitive
nub inside, releasing with a moan. Her hips tilted forward to give
him better access, to allow his fingers to delve into her sex while
his thumb continued to massage her clit. The orgasm ambushed
her before she could catch it, and his name spilled from her lips
as she cried out in release.

She fell forward, melting against him while her body still trembled with the aftershocks.

Titus ran his fingers up and down her spine, saying nothing in the moments that followed.

A chill of unease washed over her, and she lifted her head. His gaze was distant, his mind someplace other than the present. "What's wrong?"

He focused back on her and gave her a smile that didn't reach his eyes. "What makes you think something's wrong?"

"I know you."

His smile softened, but it was genuine this time. "Where did you find this oil?"

"It was in the drawer. Why?"

"It was the one my father favored for as long as I can remember." Melancholy cracked his voice, and her heart ached for him. Barely two moons had passed since his father's death, and yet the wounds were still fresh. "I never thought a scent could evoke such memories, but…"

"Should we crawl back into the bath and wash it away?"

He shook his head. "No, it's rather fitting, I think. I'm the emperor now, and like my father, I've been blessed to have the woman I love more than anything to rule by my side."

A dozen replies sat on the tip of her tongue. She could've told him she loved him. She could've told him she wasn't worthy of him. She could've told him she would give anything to wipe away his grief. But in every instance, words failed her.

Instead, she leaned forward and kissed him until desire replaced all other emotions.

3

Modius stepped off the airship and found his father waiting for him at the end of the gangplank. His shoulders tensed, followed by his hamstrings, slowing his steps. Three years had passed since he'd been caught dissecting the corpses of fallen gladiators and shocked the city of Emona. Three years had passed since he was sent to Madrena. Three years had passed since he'd last seen his father.

He stopped a few feet away from Varro, studying the man who was an older version of himself. His father's face revealed nothing. No joy at seeing him again. No traces of disappointment that he hadn't followed his father's footsteps and joined the Legion. Nothing other than the perfunctory acknowledgement Varro gave everyone who stayed here. "Welcome to the imperial palace, Modius."

"Thank you, Father." The last word came out sharp and bitter, much like his relationship with the man who bore that title. "I understand I am here at the empress's request?"

"Soon-to-be empress, and yes, Lady Azurha asked for your assistance. Come this way."

He followed his father into the palace, noting how Varro's limp had grown more pronounced over the years. Modius's earliest memories of his father had been of the warrior, the soldier who'd risen to become the Captain of the Legion.

17

Then, when Modius was barely old enough to wield a sword, his father had been struck down in battle. The injury had destroyed his father's military career, but it had awakened a new passion in Modius, a fascination with the human body and its workings. Even now, he foolishly clung to the hope that if he learned enough, he could restore the function in his father's leg.

Unfortunately, his dreams had been swept away with the public outcry when he was discovered with half a dozen bodies in various stages of dissection.

His prior encounter with Lady Azurha had been brief. She'd been sent to the imperial palace in Madrena in secret, but she had stayed less than a week. The emperor had come a few days later, and they rarely left their quarters. "Care to share why she sent for me?"

"That is for her to discuss, not me." Which, of course, meant that his father knew exactly why he'd been summoned, but refused to say.

"I find it odd that you hardly say anything to me over the last three years, and yet in the last month, you've written to me twice concerning her."

Varro's steps hitched, his bad leg dragging to a stop before he glanced over his shoulder. "Lady Azurha has done much to earn my respect."

"So I've noticed. Too bad I haven't."

His father's Adam's apple bobbed. "I've never indicated that."

"No, not with words, but you've made it very clear with your actions that you're not pleased with my interests." He braced for a few harsh words from his father, the usual lecture on how he should've focused more on his military career than his studies, but it never came.

"You are your own person." Varro resumed a brisk pace that exaggerated his limp even more. "Come along. I don't wish to keep Lady Azurha waiting."

Modius trailed behind, replaying the longest conversation he'd had with his father since he'd left for Madrena. It carried the same distant, vague vibe as his last conversation. His father admitted nothing, revealed nothing, which was probably one of the reasons the former emperor had trusted him.

Varro led him through the empty throne room and past the slowly rotating globe that depicted the barrier around the empire. As a child, Modius had witnessed the morning ritual of the emperor reinforcing the barrier that protected them from alien Barbarians. Today, it seemed brighter than he remembered, pulsating with a different energy that calmed any fears he had about the barrier falling.

His father pressed his palm against a bronze keypad. The click of locks echoed through the room. He opened the door to reveal a small antechamber. "Wait here," he ordered before he passed through another set of locked doors leading to a corridor.

Modius dropped his bag by a chair and poured a glass of wine. After years of isolation in Madrena, it was strange being back in the bustling city of Emona again. In Madrena, there would be some days where he'd hardly speak to anyone, save for a few orders to the slaves who maintained the palace. Now, he would have to remember all his courtly manners in front of the future empress. He stretched his back, and hoped he could bow low enough without it catching after the long flight from the coast.

The locks clicked again and his father returned, holding the door open for Lady Azurha. She was even more striking than Modius remembered. She had the inky-black curls and coppery skin typical of the Alpirion slaves, but he'd never seen eyes that color on a member of her race. Diamonds sparkled from the combs in her hair, from the earrings dangling from her ears, and from the necklace around her throat. The last time he'd seen her, she'd just been elevated to consort. Now, she was every inch an empress.

His father bowed as she passed, signaling Modius should do the same. "Lady Azurha, this is my son, Modius."

His gut twisted as his father introduced him. Varro almost seemed proud to call him his son. Too bad that wasn't the truth.

Lady Azurha nodded. "Yes, we've met before."

Varro gave a sharp nod and surveyed the room, checking the decanter on the table to make sure it was full. "Will you need anything else?"

"No, thank you," she replied.

"Very good. I'll make sure Modius's room is ready for him." Varro bent down and picked up the heavy pack containing his clothes and medical supplies.

Modius started toward his father, his mouth open to tell him not to bother with it, but a sharp glare from Varro stopped him. Despite his injury, Varro had never asked for assistance, never sought special treatment. Instead, he stubbornly insisted on trying to do all the things he had done before his leg had been weakened. This was just another example. Modius winced as his father took the first few steps carrying the weight of the pack, adjusting it so it balanced out on his good leg. He left the room with the sound of his sandaled foot dragging across the tiled floor.

"Stubborn old man," Modius muttered under his breath as the door closed behind his father.

"But you have to admire his determination," Azurha replied, sitting in one of the chairs by a small table that was laden with food. "Please, have a seat. You must be hungry after your journey."

He took the opposite chair and picked a few grapes off the stems. "I was quite surprised when you summoned me, Lady Azurha."

Her dark brows pinched together. "Did your father not tell you why?"

"No." He popped a grape in his mouth before he said too much.

She laughed, relaxing into her chair. "I've shared your frustration with him before. He guards a great many secrets, which makes him so invaluable to the emperor."

She poured a glass of wine and continued, "I brought

you here because your father thinks you may be able to help with a certain problem."

"My father suggested I help you?" This was a change. Usually his father liked to pretend he didn't exist.

"Yes. He said you were quite knowledgeable in the field of medicine."

Modius peered out the window to make sure there was no danger of lightning striking, for surely, hearing that his father had praised his "interests" in front of the future empress had to count as a similarly rare occurrence. "Was that all he said?"

She nodded. "And the matter I am asking you to investigate needs to be kept under complete secrecy, as it involves the former emperor. Do you agree to that?"

"Yes, Lady Azurha." Now his interest was piqued. Something secret involving the imperial family that required his knowledge of the human body? It was worth the three years of exile in Madrena to have a chance at this.

"I have reason to believe Emperor Decius was poisoned, but it was not by any poison I'm familiar with."

Unease slithered up his spine. "And what would a lady like you know of poisons?"

Her grin highlighted the cold, worldly glow in her eyes. She was a woman who'd seen death and had taken delight in it. "Did you not hear who I am?"

"No, my lady. We rarely hear anything in Madrena."

She rested her chin in her hand and stared at him as though she were trying to decide if he was telling the truth. "Perhaps it doesn't matter, then. All that matters is that I find out who killed Emperor Decius and why. It will be my wedding gift to Emperor Sergius."

From the merciless tone in her voice, he suspected that the culprit's head in a box would be the actual gift. He swallowed past the lump in his throat. "And how might I assist you with this?"

"Have you heard of a long-acting poison that wastes a man's muscles, slowly killing him over the span of a fortnight?"

He leaned back, letting the gravity of her question sink in first before plowing through his knowledge of poisons. All of them killed within a matter of hours, not days. And yet, somewhere in the deepest recess of his mind, he knew he'd stumbled across something that sounded like this before. "I can't recall of any, but I will gladly research this matter in the Imperial Library."

"The library is vast. Do you know where to begin?"

"Yes," he replied, his confidence returning. The Imperial Library rivaled the palace in sheer size, its rooms lined with rows of shelves containing neat stacks of scrolls. One room was entirely devoted to medicine. He'd lost count on how many days he'd hidden inside it, poring over the knowledge it held. "I've spent a great many hours there over the years, and I know which section to start in."

"Do you think you might be able to identify the poison before the wedding?"

"I will try my best."

She set her glass down. "If you need any assistance, don't hesitate to ask. I may not be an empress yet, but I have the power to accommodate most of your requests."

"Thank you, my lady." He stood and bowed, recognizing her dismissal. "I'll settle into my room and begin my search in earnest in the morning."

The locks clicked again, and he headed toward the door, fully expecting to see his father on the other side with an impatient expression. However, the person who rushed through the door was small and dark, with a stack of brightly colored gowns nearly concealing her face. She collided with him, her bundle falling from her hands like flower petals knocked loose by a storm. Modius reached out to steady her before she followed. "Careful."

"I'm so sorry, I—" Her words choked off as she met his gaze.

Her speechlessness was contagious because, for the life of him, Modius couldn't form a coherent word, either. She was an Alpirion, a palace slave perhaps, but there was something about her that drew him to her like a wave to the shore. Perhaps it was her full lips, ripe and rosy like fresh berries. Perhaps it was her eyes, large and dark, and framed by the thickest lashes he'd ever seen on a woman. Perhaps it was the exotic scent of saffron and honey that rose from her warm, sun-bronzed skin. Perhaps it was the lush curves she rubbed against him, reminding him how long it had been since he enjoyed the company of a woman. It didn't matter. He wasn't in any hurry to let her go, and based on the way her hips swayed against him, she wasn't in any hurry to leave.

She licked her lips before lifting the corners in an inviting smile.

The blood rushed from his head to his groin. A small voice in the back of his mind shouted for him to let go before he lost all control and embarrassed himself in front of the future empress, but his hand refused to move from the small of the woman's back. Instead, it drew her closer to him.

Her eyes widened, followed by her smile.

A bolt of lust shot through him. By the gods, if he wasn't careful...

A man cleared his voice behind the woman. "Izana, Lady Azurha needs to get ready for dinner."

At the sound of his father's voice, Modius backed away so quickly, Izana wobbled on her feet. A flush rose into her cheeks, and she dropped to her knees to retrieve the scattered dresses.

Modius knelt beside her, helping her gather the pile of gossamer silks. "I'm terribly sorry for almost knocking you down."

She shook her head, loosening several curls with her vigor, her eyes downcast. "No, I'm the one who should be apologizing. I need to learn to watch where I'm going."

She took the gown he offered, her hand grazing his. Another bolt of desire coursed through him. A groan rose in his chest. He fought to contain it, jerking his hand away before she

23

reduced him to some sex-crazed lunatic. He stood, adding a couple of steps between them. Perhaps he needed a trip to a local *lupanar* to satisfy this newly awakened infirmity before it distracted him from his duty.

Izana rose to her feet, watching him through her lashes as she passed on her way to the inner halls. Lady Azurha followed, a trace of a grin forming on her mouth as though she'd enjoyed watching him embarrass himself over a slave.

His father cleared his throat again.

Modius snapped his head around, his hands reflexively clasping in front of his groin as though he were some overly eager youth.

His father raised a brow but said nothing about the exchange between him and Izana. Instead, he beckoned for Modius to follow him. "This way. I've prepared a room for you in the guest wing of the palace."

Modius cast one more glance over his shoulder to the door Izana had disappeared behind and hoped the next time he saw her, he'd have the opportunity to explore their seemingly mutual attraction.

***

Izana draped the palla over Azurha's head and shoulders, arranging the folds of the pale blue silk before fastening it with a comb. Her cheeks still burned from her collision with the strange man an hour ago. Usually, she'd notice an attractive man and forget about him a few minutes later. Not this man. The feeling of his hard body awakened all kinds of delicious sensations in her. And based on the evidence of his arousal, he was affected the same way.

She hesitated bringing it up in front of her mistress. For all she knew, the man could be an old acquaintance, another assassin, perhaps even a former lover. But finally, her curiosity got the better of her. "Who was that man I ran into this evening?"

Azurha met her gaze in the mirror. "His name is Modius. He's Varro's son."

The mild tingle of desire morphed into the sting of embarrassment. An Alpirion curse slipped from her lips before she could stop it. Of course she'd made a fool of herself in front of the steward's son. She could almost hear the reprimand that awaited her once she finished dressing her mistress for dinner.

But she saw no censure in her mistress's expression. Instead, Azurha seemed more intent on watching her reaction. "Why do you ask?"

Because I want to crawl into his bed and do all kinds of naughty things to him. She didn't need to glance at her reflection to know her cheeks were fully red. That still didn't keep her mind from imagining what it would be like to lie under him as he slid into her. "Um, just curious, that's all," she lied.

Azurha turned around on her stool and studied Izana with pursed lips. "Why do I have the sneaking suspicion there's more than just curiosity involved?"

She lowered her eyes and wiped her palms on the coarse linen of her chiton. Did she dare confess her reaction to Modius? "I'd just never seen him before, that's all."

"Did his behavior make you uncomfortable?" Azurha's question had a steely edge to it as though she were ready to mark Modius as her next target.

"Oh, no," she said, the words tumbling out as quickly as her tongue would allow. "Not at all."

"Then what effect did he have on you?"

Izana bit her bottom lip, weighing her options. How much did Azurha know about her former mistress, about her past before she was sold to the palace? "I found him very... likable."

"Likable?" Azurha repeated, the tone of her voice making it very clear she'd noticed what had passed between Izana and Modius.

Izana sighed. Time to be honest and pray it worked in her favor. "Very well, I admit I'm attracted to him."

Azurha nodded, giving her permission to continue.

"I mean, he's handsome." The image of his face

appeared in her mind. She slowly took account of his pleasing features, from his strong jaw to his straight nose to the flecks of green and gold in his warm brown eyes.

"And well proportioned," she continued. *Very well proportioned*, she added, remembering the sensation of him pressing against her.

"And more importantly, he was polite and respectful," she finished, hoping that would appease her mistress.

"And is that why you found him attractive?" Azurha asked.

She nodded. "I've found that most men who treat a woman with respect outside the bedroom will treat her with respect inside the bedroom."

The smile faded from Azurha's face, and a splinter of fear lodged in Izana's chest. Had she said too much? Overstepped her bounds? Become too casual with her mistress?

"Izana, please understand that I will never force you into a man's bed, and if anyone here in the palace tries to do so, let me know immediately. Such behavior will not be tolerated."

"Yes, my lady, but—" She paused, wondering if this bordered on saying too much again.

"But what?" Azurha's expression darkened, leaving Izana no other choice but to confess.

Her heart quickened as she said, "But I wouldn't mind joining him in his bed."

Her mistress inhaled sharply and held her breath for several wild beats of Izana's heart before exhaling slowly. "You don't find it demeaning to be forced to sleep with a man?"

"Who said anything about forcing me to sleep with him?" She turned and pretended to peruse Azurha's jewels, even though she knew exactly what necklace she'd pair with her mistress's ensemble. "I said I wouldn't mind joining him, and I meant that. He seems like he'd be a satisfying lover."

"You can enjoy being with a man after what your former owner forced you to do?"

Izana's gut twisted, her hand reflexively covering the scar

on her neck. Even though she'd asked to be branded with the imperial family's mark when she'd arrived at the palace two years ago, she still saw traces of the wolf's outline under the burn. "Because despite the fact I was a *lupa*, I still retained some control over my clients. Those whose company I enjoyed, I encouraged, and they would pay generously to have me for the night."

Azurha's brows drew together as though this was a foreign concept to her. And maybe it was. After all, she doubted her mistress had many lovers during her years as the Rabbit. Not many men—save the emperor—would feel comfortable sleeping with a woman who could kill them in a matter of seconds.

"And those men whose company you didn't enjoy?"

"Then I just closed my eyes and prayed they'd come quickly." Izana decided it was time to change the subject and held up the necklace she'd picked out earlier that evening. "I think this would go nicely with your gown tonight, my lady."

Azurha nodded and turned back to the mirror. "Modius is here on official business. I've given him a task to complete before the wedding."

Izana nodded as she fastened the necklace around her mistress's neck, trying to appear disinterested even though her tongue itched to ask more questions.

"If I needed you to deliver a message to him, would you be willing to do so?"

Her breath hitched. She'd jump at any opportunity to see Modius again. But she forced her voice to stay calm as she replied, "Yes, my lady."

"Thank you, Izana." Azurha went to her desk and scribbled a note on a piece of paper before sealing it. "Modius is staying in one of the guest rooms. Please deliver this to him tonight and wait for his response."

She took the letter, her hands only trembling with a fraction of what her insides were doing. Desire and anticipation raced through her veins. She'd be in his room, hopefully alone with him. And hopefully, she'd find out if he truly was the lover she imagined him to be. "Is the matter urgent?"

Azurha shook her head, one corner of her mouth rising into a conspiratorial grin. "Just make sure he gets it before he falls asleep."

Perfect! It would give her enough time to wash away the sweat and grime of the day, to change into a clean chiton and perhaps even outline her eyes with kohl before seeing him again.

"Yes, my lady, and thank you." She dropped into a quick curtsy before racing back to the slave quarters to prepare for her next meeting with Modius. If all went according to plan, she would be humming with contentment in a matter of hours.

4

Azurha's lips twitched as Izana scampered off, the letter to Modius clutched in her hand. She'd never played matchmaker before, but judging by the way the two of them had acted around each other earlier today, they wouldn't mind her interference.

"What's so funny?" Titus asked, emerging from the baths, the ends of his hair still damp.

"Izana," she replied as she placed a quick kiss on his cheek. "I find her highly amusing at times."

"And now you know why my mother snatched her up when her former mistress offered to sell her."

A heaviness dropped into her stomach like a stone, and Azurha's grin faded. As much as she enjoyed Izana's company, she was still a slave. She could be bought and sold at her owner's whim, much like every other slave in the empire. And now, she'd become the one person who controlled her fate.

She rubbed the golden cuff bracelets that covered the scars on her wrist. Despite Izana's flippant remarks, had life as a *lupa* left any scars on her body or soul?

"I've said something that upset you, haven't I?" Titus pressed his forehead against her temple as though he were trying to extract her thoughts from the contact.

"No, it wasn't so much what you said, just what it triggered in my mind." She cupped his smooth, freshly shaved cheeks in her hands and inhaled the rich scent of sandalwood that rose from his skin. "Once the wedding is behind us, we must work on a way to free the slaves."

"Without throwing the empire into chaos," he added, his voice grim. "I welcome any ideas you have, for I want to prevent anyone from suffering what you did at the hands of your master."

He brought her palms to his lips. Despite the chasteness of his act, her blood stirred with desire, a sentiment she saw reflected in his eyes as they darkened into the color of the night sky.

"If you continue along this course, we'll be late for dinner with your mother," she teased.

"Then perhaps I should plant a few wicked thoughts in your mind to ruminate on until we return." He pulled her to him, his hand traveling down her back, over her buttocks, along her thighs until he came to the golden dagger strapped against her thigh.

He unsheathed it and stepped back with a frown, all lust gone from his eyes as he dangled it in front of her. "Expecting any trouble tonight?"

The engraved rabbit on the blade flashed in the light. A chill grew between them. "I expect trouble every minute of every day."

"And you don't trust me or my men enough to protect you?" His jaw hardened, and she was left trying to find the right words to soothe him.

"I'd rather be prepared in case we ever are separated." When her explanation didn't move him, she added, "We've both seen how danger can stand right in front of us without our knowledge. It's not that I wish to insult you or the Legion. It's just that I have certain skills that I can use, if needed. I'd rather be part of the solution rather than another liability."

The tense line of his mouth softened, but his eyes still simmered with displeasure. "Azurha, I want you to be my wife, not my bodyguard. I need you to be an empress who will help me shape the empire into something greater, not an assassin who is ready to slit a throat at my command."

"I'm ready and willing to do that, but old habits die hard." She took the dagger back and slid it back into the sheath under her dress before unfastening her bracelet to show him the mark of the Legion tattooed on the inside of her right wrist. It was the result of an ancient law that pardoned criminals who pledged to protect the emperor with their lives, and provided Titus with a way to spare hers after her crimes became known. "Besides, I am a member of the Legion, remember?"

He stared her down a moment longer before exhaling in resignation. "Just promise me you that you won't go off killing someone and dropping their bodies into a ravine during dinner tonight."

"That depends on who's there." She offered him a sly smile as she inched closer to him. "After all, if I recognize another assassin—"

"Then you will alert Captain Galerius and let the rest of the Legion deal with it. Understood?"

Now it was her turn to clench her jaw and glare. How dare he suggest she sit back and let others deal with things they knew nothing about? After all, she knew the dark shadows of the underworld far better than anyone in the palace. The few seconds it took to alert the Legion about a potential threat would be more than enough time for a skilled assassin to strike.

Titus closed the gap between them and stroked her cheek with his fingers, turning from the absolute ruler who never had his orders questioned into the man she'd come to love over the last month. "Please, Azurha, I almost lost you once because you kept the truth hidden from me."

Her voice quivered as she replied, "Because I wanted to protect you, just like I do now."

"I know. But can't you see I can better protect you if we don't have any secrets between us?"

She nodded, surrendering to his embrace. For briefest of moments, she let her guard down and enjoyed the simple pleasure of resting her head on his shoulder. For a few seconds, she forgot about the threats of the outside world and relished in the safety of his strong arms around her. And for the next few beats of her heart, she knew peace.

"Now let's go," he said at last, tilting her chin up. "We don't want to keep my mother waiting too long. Besides, I want to try something different tonight."

She chuckled to herself, recalling the one night she'd seduced him inside the enclosed carriage on the way to a dinner party. She wondered if he wanted to repeat that. Her suspicions changed when he led her to the waiting chariot surrounded by members of the Legion. "This should prove interesting."

"And perhaps safer than the airship." He helped into the chariot before standing behind her. "Why don't you drive tonight?"

"You know I can't," she said with a sigh. The last time he'd attempted to prove she was of Deizian blood, she'd almost crashed an entire airship.

"And I think you can. A chariot is much easier to control than an airship." He covered her hands with his own and led them to the controls. "Just please, try for me."

"Titus—"

"Remember what you did when you blew the doors off the hinges to save me? It's that same magic." He pressed her palms against the cold ore. "Call on it, gather it up inside you, and direct it into the chariot."

She closed her eyes and tried to recreate what had happened inside her the night Pontus had attacked Titus. It had started off like a fire raging in her chest, spreading like a wildfire through her blood until she could no longer contain it. That night, it had been wild, chaotic, destructive.

But tonight, she felt none of it, not even a flame.

She gritted her teeth, channeling her frustration trying to make the chariot move, but it didn't budge. Sweat beaded along her brow, but still, nothing. Her shoulders slumped in defeat, and she leaned back against Titus. "It's no use. I can't do it."

"Of course, you can. You're of Deizian blood."

"And what makes you so certain I am?"

"Because you have light colored eyes," he said as though she were an idiot for asking. "Only Deizians have eyes like that."

"Or perhaps I'm just a simple of Alpirion who was cursed with them, a deviant from the norm, a *wa'ai.*"

As soon as the word slipped from her mouth, the pain inside her chest doubled, squeezing the air from it. Her people had been forbidden to speak the Alpirion language from the moment Titus's grandfather had conquered them, and she'd just repeated the word she'd been called for as long as she could remember. The other slaves would stare at her in fear, point to her and whisper that word under their breath as she passed, all because she was different from them. In all her journeys, she'd never come across another Alpirion with eyes her color.

"I disagree. I've seen what you're capable of doing when you focus, and I'll prove to you and the rest of the empire that Deizian blood flows through your veins." He dragged her hands away from the console and took over.

The chariot rose into the air under his control as through it weighed no more than a feather, and glided effortlessly into the streets of Emona.

Azurha's heart, however, remained heavy with doubt. Titus seemed desperate to prove she was of Deizian blood, and she understood why. Deizian blood would justify her place as empress, legitimatize her children as heirs to the throne, and quiet all the nobles who dared to challenge Titus's choice for a bride. As much as she loved him, she knew their marriage would only cause him more trouble and become another hurdle he'd have to overcome to make changes to the empire.

They rode through the busy street in silence with Titus's arms on either side of her like a prison. When they were almost to his mother's villa across town, she finally said, "I can't change what I am, Titus, and I understand if you wish to choose a more suitable bride."

He stiffened behind her, and the chariot slowed. "You

are a suitable bride, Azurha," he said tenderly, "the only woman I'd ever want for my wife."

"Even if I'm not of Deizian blood?"

He tightened his arms around her, pressing his body against hers until she had no idea where she ended and he began. "Yes, my love."

5

Modius dipped his pen into the ink and, after mentally reviewing a list of what to he needed to research, scribbled a few notes of what texts to pull from the shelves of the Imperial Library tomorrow. Anatomy. Poisons. Diseases. All subjects that fascinated him. All subjects he'd become well-versed in after poring over the available scrolls in Madrena's small library.

The small seaside town was the place where healers from around the empire came to hone their craft with medicinal herbs. The gardens contained specimens of every useful plant, so the healers could learn to recognize them both in their fresh and dried states. For a few weeks every fall, classes were held on brewing potions and mixing poultices. And as steward of the castle, he oversaw it all, from making sure the garden was tended to making sure the students were accommodated during their brief visits.

Unfortunately, his duties also meant he wasn't able to play the part of a student and actively participate in the lessons. Still, over the last three years, he'd managed to glean enough from the masters to feel confident in his abilities to extract the healing qualities from the plants.

On the flip side, he also knew enough about the plants to recognize their dangers, to know which ones were used to make poisons, and the effects they had on their victims. And he'd never seen anything like the poison Lady Azurha described.

He sat back in his chair and let his mind drift from the task at hand to Izana. Emperor Decius had been kind enough to offer him the position at Madrena after the scandal he'd caused, knowing the classes there would feed his interest in medicine and keep him from pursuing knowledge elsewhere. But the remote location resulted in relative isolation, especially with the additional barrier which surrounded the palace, and prevented him from leaving without the emperor's permission. The few slaves assigned to it were brought over as families. Any woman he came in contact with over there was either already married or a child. And none of the healers who came for instruction stayed long enough to capture his interest, which made his brief encounter with Izana all the more puzzling. He'd maybe spent a minute in her company, and yet he couldn't stop thinking about her.

It's just because you haven't enjoyed a woman's company in over three years, he scolded himself. Yes, she had a pretty face. Yes, she had a body that tempted him more than he cared to admit. Yes, she had made it quite clear she'd welcome his advances if he made them. But then what? Was she so receptive because she was a slave? And seeing that he would only be here a couple of weeks at the most, would it even be worth dallying in a brief affair with her?

The image of her licking those full lips flashed before him, and his cock stiffened.

Yes, it would totally be worth it.

Now he was left with the tricky situation of finding her again without his father knowing about it, for surely, such behavior with a slave would be frowned upon.

Before he could come up with a discreet way of pursuing her, a knock interrupted his plans. He opened his door and froze, wondering if the gods themselves had eavesdropped on his thoughts.

There, standing in the hallway with an inviting smile, was Izana.

She appeared to have come straight from the baths, with

damp curls framing her face and a fresh glow to her skin. The scents saffron and honey were stronger than he remembered, creating an intoxicating perfume that wafted past him as she came into his room. And the clean tunic she wore clung to her curves in all the right places before stopping at her knees and exposing her shapely brown calves.

"My lady asked that I deliver this message to you and wait for your reply," she said, her hips swaying ever so slightly as she held out the folded piece of paper.

He closed the door behind him and wondered how quickly he needed to give his answer. If he was lucky, he'd have a few moments to enjoy her company. "Is it urgent?"

She shook her head, her dark eyes dancing with mischief. "She told me to make sure I delivered it before you fell asleep."

He took the note and stifled a laugh when he read the contents.

Modius,

Please feel free to use Izana as an assistant during your stay, if you are in need of one. She is quite clever and may be able shed some light on our mystery. She has earned my trust, and I hope she will earn yours.

Azurha

"Did you know about this?" he asked, holding out the paper for her to read.

She scanned the paper before looking back up to him, her expression guarded. "I don't know what it says."

"Read it." He offered the letter to her again, but she didn't take it.

"Slaves aren't allowed to read," she said, her words clipped. Her kohl-lined eyes hardened like obsidian.

"Pity." He folded the note in half and laid it on his desk, perplexed by the sudden change in her demeanor. "It seems your mistress has offered your services as an assistant to me."

Her face softened, the hostile edge fading from it. "And are you in need of an assistant?" Her voice regained the seductive purr she'd arrived with, but instead of reviving his desire, it set off warning bells.

Something wasn't right with her. She was either hiding something, or was crazy. Maybe both.

He sat back in his chair, studying her. She'd done more than just have a bath before coming to his room. The heavy kohl lines around her eyes accentuated her already thick lashes, adding a smoky layer of mystery to her eyes. When she blinked, he got a glimpse of sparking gold on her lids. Combined with lips that were the perfectly kissable shade of deep pink, it was quite obvious that she'd spent time on her makeup this evening. More than she had this morning, which made him wonder why she went through the effort if she was just delivering a message.

Then she gave him a come-hither look that shot straight to his groin, and he knew why. She was on the prowl, and he was her prey.

Normally, he wouldn't have any objections to a woman freely inviting him to join her in bed, but that wasn't the case with Izana. She had been quick to remind him that she was a slave and wasn't free.

He cleared his throat. "Izana, I'm here to help your mistress solve a problem, and if you wish to assist me, then I welcome your help. However, if you were sent here solely to warm my bed, then please know that I don't feel comfortable with that arrangement."

Her eyes widened before blinking rapidly. She straightened and took several stumbling steps back. A flush stole into her cheeks, one he mistakenly interpreted as embarrassment until he heard the anger in her voice. "You think Lady Azurha sent me here to ensure you had a comfortable stay at the palace?"

"I, er—" Now he'd done it. He'd somehow managed to insult both Izana and her mistress. He ran his fingers through his hair, stumbling over his words as he pieced together an apology. "I'm not sure what to think, and I apologize if I misinterpreted this situation."

Her lips curled up into an amused smile, and a note of laughter broke free from her throat. "You don't know my mistress very well. If you did, you'd realize she would rather slit a dozen throats than force a woman to lie under a man when she didn't want to."

He was so hung up on the "slit a dozen throats" that he almost missed the invitation at the end of her reply. Everything about her suggested that she was open to satisfying the ever-growing need churning inside him, but he still wasn't ready to abandon all precautions.

Work. Focus on work and get your mind off how much you want to taste her lips and feel her warm flesh writhing underneath you.

He dug his fingers into his palm, squeezed his eyes shut to block her enticing beauty from his mind, and turned back to his desk. When he opened his eyes, his gaze fell to his notes and pulled him from the brink of giving into his base desires. "Do you know why Lady Azurha asked me to come here?"

"No."

Her scent grew stronger. He didn't dare risk looking over his shoulder to see how much closer she'd come to him. "How long have you been at the palace?"

"Almost two years."

Which explained why he'd never seen her before. He'd practically grown up here in the palace and knew most of the slaves who tended the imperial family. "Who did you serve before Lady Azurha?"

"Empress Horatia. I wasn't her primary maid, but I assisted with hair and clothes." She dragged a stool over to his desk and sat beside him, close enough that he could feel the heat coming off her skin.

Almost too close for comfort. He shifted in his chair, painfully aware of the effect she was having on him. He glanced at Azurha's letter and wondered if Izana might truly be able to shed some light on this mystery. "And were you there during Emperor Decius's final days?"

The wariness crept back into her actions, slowing them as though she were weighing the risk of each movement. She nodded her head once. "Why do you ask?"

His blood cooled. Izana was definitely a woman who

guarded secrets. The question was, how much did she know about the former emperor's death? "Lady Azurha has asked me here to determine the cause of his death."

Her shoulders relaxed, and her breathing resumed its normal depth. Whatever secrets she held, none of them seemed linked to the emperor's death. "What do you wish to know about it?"

"What do you remember?"

She chewed her bottom lip, her eyes focused on something in the distance. "He seemed to waste away before my very eyes."

It was the same answer his father had given him, but it did little to answer his question. "What do you mean by waste away?"

"Just that." She looked at him as though he were a simpleton before she sucked in a breath. "Perhaps I can show you. Do you have a charcoal pencil and some paper I can use?"

"I think so." He rummaged through his bag, intrigued by her novel approach to helping him, and retrieved a pencil.

She snatched it from his hand and started sketching on a blank piece of paper on the desk. "You remember what Emperor Decius looked like in good health, right?"

"Very clearly."

"This is what he looked like a few days into his illness." She handed him a sketch and started working on the next one without looking up from her work.

The face in front of him was of a man who'd seemed to have aged twenty years from the emperor he remembered. The cheekbones seemed more prominent, with deep, heavy wrinkles weighing down the skin in what had been a relatively young-looking face. Whatever poison had caused this transformation was strong.

And unfortunately, foreign to him.

"Here's what he looked like on his deathbed." Izana handed him a new sketch, and his breath caught.

Her drawing of the former emperor resembled more of a

40

skeleton than the strong and virile man he'd known his entire
life. The eyes had sunken deep into their sockets, staring back at
him with a haunted light. The lips had withered around his
mouth. The skin hung loosely over the skull, a mocking image of
living death.

He let the paper flutter to the desk and rubbed his chin.
Azurha had given him quite a puzzle to solve, one that both
intrigued and terrified him now that he saw the impact. What
must his father have felt, watching the man he'd served and
protected for decades, stricken with this mysterious illness? How
did the emperor handle his ever-weakening body being stripped
of its strength until death became inevitable?

"Is something wrong, Modius?"

Hearing his name from Izana's lips pulled him from his
macabre musings. He glanced at the drawings, then at her. Worry
tugged her bottom lip.

"I'm finally seeing what everyone meant about Emperor
Decius wasting away."

"Did you know him well?"

"Not as well as I would've liked. My father served him
for years, as you know. But as for me personally…" His gaze
wandered to the last image, and a wave of grief washed over him.
Emperor Decius had stood by him when the rest of the city was
calling for his head, offering him a place to hide until the scandal
was forgotten, a place where he could continue his studies out of
the public eye. "I owe him a debt."

Another woman might have prodded him to continue,
but Izana merely squeezed his hand in understanding. "Now I
know why my mistress asked you to help her."

He stared at her small brown hand around his,
wondering if she would be willing to touch him if she knew the
whole story behind his exile. Was she was one of the outraged
citizens who'd gathered in the streets when he was dragged from
his laboratory to the palace? Did she remember his name from
the scandal? Would she run screaming away from him if he told
her everything?

And yet, when his gaze traveled up to her face, he found the same uncomplicated acceptance there as he'd felt in her touch. She may have harbored secrets. He did, too. And perhaps she was looking for a way to leave her past behind just like he was. Warmth filled his stomach, but instead of heading south along the path of desire, it rose into his chest, creating an uncomfortable tightness that made him break the contact between them before it became unbearable.

He rose from his chair, pacing beside his desk as he focused on the drawings and not the woman who'd produced them. "You're a talented artist. Does Lady Azurha know of you skill?"

She shook her head. "I'm afraid my drawing skills have suffered since I came to the palace."

Based on the accuracy of the sketches in the short time it took her to draw them, he'd have to disagree. "I might have use of your artistic skills. What other hidden talents do you have?"

"I have a few more skills you might be interested in." She stood in one languid motion, blocking his path. Her body brushed against his, teasing him, tempting him. The wicked heat in her unwavering eyes revived his earlier desire threefold. "Would you like to discover them?"

His mouth went dry as all the blood rushed from his head to his cock. By the gods, she was making it hard to say no. In fact, she was making everything hard. He inched closer to her. "Depends on what you're offering."

"Depends on what you want." She snaked her arm around his neck, threaded her fingers through his hair, tilted his head down until he couldn't see anything else by her lips.

"I have no desire to offend you, but…" His voice cracked from the overwhelming lust she'd awoken inside him.

Which was a blessing because he'd been about to say that he wanted to bury himself inside her over and over again until they both collapsed in exhaustion.

Her lips were now a breath away from his. The throaty whisper of her voice proved his undoing as she asked, "But what?"

He licked his lips, cursing himself for being too weak to play the part of a gentleman in these circumstances. "I want you."

"Good, because I want you, too."

And then she covered his mouth with her own.

6

Kissing Modius was even better than Izana had anticipated.

Correction. It proved to be almost more than she could handle. She needed to taste him, to feel his hands all over her body, to satisfy the ache building deep within her. After spending years in the arms of men who'd paid for her company, she'd been celibate since arriving to the palace, focusing on being her own person instead of who her clients wanted her to be for the evening. But tonight, after two years of going without, she needed the mind-blowing release that came at the hands of man who knew what she wanted. And she wasn't above giving directions, if necessary.

Thankfully, Modius knew how to please a woman, despite his noble pretenses. The solid thickness of his erection made her wonder why he'd been holding out on her, why he'd been trying to hide how much he wanted her. In a way, it was sweet. Slightly endearing even, him not wanting to take advantage of her. But it didn't matter now. She made it quite clear she wouldn't say no.

She'd started off as the aggressor by kissing him, by bolding sweeping her tongue into his mouth when he opened it. In a matter of seconds, he'd turned the tables on her. Now, he was the one making her moan with each swirl of his tongue.

Now he was the one holding her close, lacing his fingers in her hair, rocking his hips in a teasing rhythm that promised so much more.

He spun her around on her heels, backing her up against his desk. Papers scattered across the floor, but it didn't deter him as his hungry kisses consumed her. He trailed his lips along her cheek, nibbling at her ear and eliciting another moan from her. By the gods, if he had her nearly coming from just doing that, she could only imagine what he was capable of doing once he'd set his tongue and teeth on her breasts, on her navel, on the sensitive nub between her legs.

"Izana, please." The two words came out as a growl through gritted teeth.

She understood all too clearly what he was begging for. Her sex was already slick with desire, clenching in readiness for him. She broke his kisses long enough to yank his tunic over his head. "Stop talking and get inside me now."

He had the gall to chuckle at her order. "As you wish."

Her tunic flew over her head and across the room, landing in a heap against the far wall. The coarse hairs on his chest grazed her nipples, sending little shocks of pleasure to her sex. His hands were everywhere–cupping her breasts and buttocks, lifting her up onto his desk, spreading her thighs apart. His mouth had returned to plunder hers, the sweet taste of figs mingling with his undiluted lust. His masculine scent enveloped her, heightening her arousal.

But it was his cock that took her breath away. Firm, thick, and strong, it teased her. He brushed between her thighs, against the opening of her sex until she wrapped her legs around his waist and dug her heels into his ass, letting him know in no uncertain terms to stop playing around.

He slid into her with one confident stroke.

Her breath caught. Her inner walls stretched to accommodate him, the slow burn bringing far more pleasure than pain. He'd merely whetted her appetite instead of satisfying it, and it wasn't long before her hips grew impatient and demanded more.

"Patience," he rasped, wincing until she stilled. "I want to make sure you enjoy this as much I do."

She froze. In all her years as a *lupa*, only a handful of men ever expressed any concern for her satisfaction, and even then, it was only after she'd trained them to know what she liked after hours of teasing. Her gut tightened. She'd been right about her assumption that Modius would be a considerate lover. Now, she had to wait for him to follow through.

He opened his eyes and gazed down at her, his face full of wonder as though she were some radiant goddess. His stubble prickled her cheeks as he placed a trail of feather-light kisses along her jaw. Inch by inch, he pulled out of her with agonizing slowness.

She whimpered, already missing the sensation of him filling her completely.

He silenced her with one of his breath-stealing kisses. The tip of his cock remained barely sheathed at the opening of her sex, lingering there while his tongue demanded surrender. She fought, tensed, tried to pull him deeper into her, but his will proved stronger. At last, she gave into him, submitting to the rhythm he'd set. Once she did that, he rammed his full length into her.

The force of it made her gasp, followed by a sigh. He started with a leisurely tempo at first, giving her time to explore the chiseled planes of his body, to trace the corded muscles that stretched and flexed with the movements of his hips. She let her head fall back, exposing the side of her neck without the brand and guiding his lips there. He eagerly devoured it with the series of alternating nips and kisses as he made his way down to her breasts.

When he caught her nipple with his teeth, she almost came right there. She hissed in a breath through her teeth as her sex clenched. Her response only encouraged him. He grew bolder, sucking on the tender peak until she cried out his name. His hips picked speed, his thrusts coming sharper and faster. She rolled her own, grinding against him to maximize the pleasure of each stroke. A quiver formed deep within the pit of her stomach, growing stronger and stronger until it threatened to explode.

His movements became more desperate, more erratic, more like her own. She gripped the edge of the desk, her legs still wrapped tightly around his waist, and held on as the first waves of ecstasy slammed into her. Stars danced in front of her eyes. The first syllable of his name broke free from her mouth before he smothered the rest, never breaking his stride as he continued to drive her over the brink. Her whole body now trembled from the force of her orgasm, while her pulse fluttered in her ears.

Modius tightened his arms around her and plunged into her one final time with a roar. His cock twitched inside her as he came, his body stiff as though she'd run him through with a gladius. Then he slumped against her with a satisfied groan.

Izana held on to him to keep him from sliding onto the floor, leaning back on the desk until her shoulders rested against the refreshingly cool plaster wall. Her fingers swirled in his hair while her body hummed in satisfaction. Several minutes passed before their breathing returned to normal. Once she knew he'd recovered enough to stand on his own two legs, she teased, "Now I'm offended."

He lifted his head from where it had rested on her chest, his brown eyes filled with worry. "What do you mean?"

"You only made me come once," she replied with a grin.

The corners of his mouth rose into a smile. Then he kissed her in a way that made her toes curl and left her wanting more. "Perhaps I'll have to try better next time."

"Yes, you should. Starting now."

He chuckled, pressing his forehead against hers. "Are you always this bossy in the bedroom?"

Now it was her turn to laugh. As a slave, she'd always been forced to take orders, never give them. But with Modius, she was finally free to be in charge. She squeezed her thighs around his waist, her ankles still locked. "Only if you let me."

"And if I don't?"

"Then you'll have to prove to me that I won't have to tell you want to do."

"Yes, my lady." He hoisted her off the desk and carried her to his bed. "Let's try this again."

He unhooked her legs and brought her ankle to his lips. Despite the chasteness of the kiss he left there, the wicked gleam in his eyes promised more.

Much, much more.

Her breath quickened as he moved up her leg, his kisses growing bolder the closer he got to the junction of her thighs. She dug her fingers into the mattress when his tongue discovered the tiny nub there. He drew it into his mouth, sucking, nibbling, swirling around it.

Within minutes, she was writhing under him, lost in a world of bliss. The first orgasm had barely ebbed when he entered her again, sending her back over the edge and into a sated state of exhaustion.

As she closed her eyes, she murmured, "Point proven."

The rumble of his chuckle vibrating through his chest was the last thing she remembered before drifting off to sleep in his arms.

***

Modius awoke with a start when he realized he wasn't alone in bed. A soft, warm body curled up against him, the curve of her inviting ass pressing against his cock and making all the blood rush to that area. Sunlight beamed through the window and fell on the tangled mess of dark hair that fanned across the pillow.

All and all, not a bad way to wake up.

He shifted on the mattress to stretch his tired muscles. He couldn't remember the last time he'd slept so well, and he suspected it had something to do with the Alpirion woman nestled in his arms.

Izana murmured something in her sleep, the shift of her hips increasing his arousal. It was all too tempting to pull her from her dreams by making her purr with pleasure again. And

48

then, once she was both fully awake and fully aroused, he could find some relief for his morning erection.

He leaned forward and pressed his lips against the silky skin of her shoulder.

She stiffened.

Then she bolted from the bed with a curse.

Had the circumstances been different, he would've enjoyed the view of her naked body, but the panic in her eyes dulled any lustful thoughts. His mouth went dry. Did she find his advances offensive? Did she regret last night? He longed to ask her what was wrong, but his tongue seemed to double in size, making coherent words impossible.

"Where's my dress?" she asked, her dark eyes frantically searching the room.

He pointed to the corner where he'd thrown it last night.

She scooped it up and pulled it over her head. "I'm going to be in so much trouble. I overslept."

He didn't realize he'd been holding his breath until it flowed out of his lungs in one long whoosh. She wasn't upset about waking up next him, just at the late hour. "I'm sure everything will be all right."

"Easy for you to say—you're not the one risking ten lashes for not being where you need to be." She hopped on one foot as she fastened her sandal.

"I doubt you're going to be punished for oversleeping."

"You of all people should know what a stickler for rules and regulations your father is." She fastened her other sandal and started raking her fingers through her snarled curls.

Modius stayed in bed, trying to bite back his laughter as he watched her rush around the room. "Just tell him you were with me."

She rolled her eyes. "Like that's going to go over well. Please forgive me for being late this morning, Varro, but your son fucked me so well last night, I overslept."

"So you're saying you enjoyed last night," he teased.

Izana paused long enough to given him a straight look,

both brows raised. "I thought that much was obvious." She gave up on combing out her knots and snatched the leather tie from one of his scrolls, using to pull her hair up and out of her face.

"Wait," he said, jumping out of bed to catch her before she ran out of the room.

"I'm already late as it is. What—"

He silenced her with a kiss. At first, she pressed her palms against his chest, trying to push him away. A few seconds later, those same hands were circling his neck, holding his head down so he couldn't end the kiss.

Not that he wanted to. If he had his way, he'd be dragging her back to bed to finish what he had woke up wanting to do. But he also didn't want her to suffer because of his selfish wants. He pulled himself away from her, his chest shaking from the effort. "You'd better go before you get in trouble, but I wanted to make sure you knew how much I appreciated your assistance last night."

Her gaze flickered to the rumpled sheets.

He steered her chin back to him. "I was talking about your sketches, but that was an added bonus. I'd love to have you come with me to the library later this morning."

"You want to have sex in a library?" She gave him a naughty smile that said she was more than open to the suggestion, but he shook his head.

"I said come *with* me, not on me."

"If I remember correctly, I was coming with you last night—several times, in fact."

He closed his eyes and tried to purge his mind of all the wicked thoughts that she was invoking. As much as he wanted to continue to indulge in them with her, he had to focus on his mission. "I meant I would appreciate your help in solving the mystery of Emperor Decius's death."

She stepped back, her full lips pressed into a thin line. "I don't know how much help I would be, nor if my mistress will allow me to forgo my normal duties to go."

"Her note said she was willing to offer you to be my

assistant, and I would like to have someone who was there in the emperor's final days to let me know if I'm on the right path with my research."

Her brows drew together, forming a crease above her nose. Worry, hesitancy, and a hint of fear all flickered across her face. His stomach tightened, and that suspicion that she knew more than she let on snuck up on him.

At last, she said, "Let me speak with Lady Azurha. If she is not angry with me for being late, I'll meet you at the front gate in an hour."

She left the room, her movements as guarded as her emotions.

Modius picked up the note from Azurha and read it one more time before staring at his closed door. Izana was proving to be as clever as her mistress deemed her to be. More importantly, she seemed to be hiding something.

Something that perhaps could shed some light on this mystery.

7

Izana sprinted through the kitchens. It was the shortest route from Modius's room to the imperial apartments, but it also meant she fell under the scrutiny of every other slave in the palace. She kept her eyes down, not wanting to see the accusations on their faces.

That Izana—once a whore, always a whore.

It didn't matter that she hadn't been with a man since she came to the palace, that she'd tried to make a fresh start in her life. They all knew she'd been a *lupa* before coming here, and they all thought she'd landed the prime position as maid to the empress because she'd slept with someone to get it. She'd heard their whispers as they passed. Some suspected she'd slept with Varro, others Emperor Decius himself. None of them knew the true story of how she'd ended up here.

She'd almost reached the end of the kitchens when she collided with a wall of muscle. A head reached out steady her. "Careful, Izana," Farros said.

She waited a second to let her pulse quiet before she dared to look up at him. "Sorry."

He cocked one brow, his hand still on her elbow. "Have an interesting evening?"

Heat flooded her cheeks. She jerked her arm free. "That's none of your business."

The way his gaze traveled up and down her body said he'd like to make it his business. "You might want to wash your face before appearing before the future empress." Then he walked away, still wearing a smirk.

She backpedalled, wondering why he'd said that. Then she changed her course for the cistern that held the water for the kitchen. Horror filled her when she got a glimpse of her reflection in the rippling surface. The neat kohl lines that had she'd drawn last night now smeared her eyes and cheeks. Her lips were red and swollen, a sure sign of a woman who'd been kissed often and thoroughly. And a tell-tale bruise was forming on the side of her neck opposite from her brand.

She cursed and scattered the image by diving her hands into the water. The icy temperature made her breath catch as she splashed it onto her face, but the scrubbing that followed helped the blood return to her cheeks. She pulled a lock of hair out from the messy pile she'd made with the leather tie to cover the bruise. When she checked her reflection again, she looked a bit more presentable, even though she was now even later than she'd started out being.

Varro was standing by the door to the imperial apartments when she arrived. He didn't say a word. He didn't need to. The censure from his hooded eyes spoke volumes.

"I overslept," she said in a rush as she approached.

"Be thankful Lady Azurha did, too." He pressed his palm against the keypad and let her inside. "I hope this is not the start of a new behavior."

She could've told him exactly where she'd been and what she'd done with his son, but instead, she bit her tongue and shook her head. As much as she had enjoyed her evening with Modius and looked forward to repeating it while he was here, she refused to allow herself to fall asleep in his arms again. It carried far more risks than just getting ten lashes for being late.

The door closed behind her, and she continued on to Azurha's dressing room. Her mistress was sitting in front of the mirror, brushing her hair. She took the brush and took over the task. "I'm sorry I'm late, my lady. It won't happen again."

"Do you mind telling me where you were?"

She met Azurha's gaze in the mirror. "I, um, was assisting Modius late into the evening."

"So my letter was helpful?" Her mistress grinned, and Izana ears burned. She'd been set up.

"Yes, my lady, very helpful." She turned her attention to styling Azurha's hair. "So helpful that he's asked me to accompany him to the library today."

"Then you should join him."

"I would, my lady, but my first priority is to serve you." She coiled a curl around her finger and pinned it in place. "If I'm assisting him, who will take care of you?"

"You can serve me best by assisting him." She paused, adding, "Within reason, of course."

Izana looked back in the mirror to find her mistress staring at the fresh bruise. She pulled the lock of hair back into place, mentally making a note to find a more permanent way to cover it until it faded.

"Izana, did he—"

"No," she blurted out before remembering to whom she was talking. "I mean, no, my lady, he did not force himself on me. We just got a little carried away last night."

In fact, the place between her legs was still humming with pleasure from last night, but she kept that information to herself.

Azurha gave one slow nod before continuing. "Even though I noticed the attraction between you two, I had another reason for sending you to him last night. I meant what I wrote about you possibly being able to help solve this mystery. I also need someone I can trust to make sure he doesn't withhold any information from me."

Izana froze. "You're sending me to spy on him?"

"More like keep me updated on his progress."

She failed to see the difference between the two, but she nodded. "But who will take care of you in my absence?"

"I'm sure Varro can assign someone in the interim."

A wave of anger rolled in her stomach. She'd worked too hard to achieve this position, and she didn't relish the idea of surrendering it to someone else. "Are you certain?"

"Yes, Izana. If Emperor Decius was poisoned, then it was probably by someone here in the palace." Her teal eyes took on a hard edge, the one that marked her as a woman who let nothing stand in her way. "I need to find out what happened to ensure Titus doesn't suffer the same fate."

The implications of Azurha's words sank in Izana's stomach like a stone. If Emperor Decius was poisoned, it was by someone she knew. Someone she'd seen come and go from the imperial quarters during the past two years. Someone who had access to the imperial family and could strike again.

"I promised to do my best to help you, my lady."

***

"Are you ready to go?" Izana asked Modius from behind. He'd been so engrossed in what he was reading that he didn't see her approach.

Not that it mattered. When he looked up, his grin spoke volumes and made her heart lurch. He seemed actually happy to see her. "Yes. I have a lot of reading to do the next few days, and I'm hoping you can help me wade through it all."

Her insides knotted, a warning from her gut that she might be walking into a trap. "You do realize that slaves are not allowed to read and write?"

Even though she'd secretly learned to do both years ago. Her former mistress thought it was important for her *lupas* to be able to read. She always claimed that one never knew where she'd find something that would serve as blackmail. And based on the clientele she served, her former mistress had plenty of secrets she'd unearthed over the years.

The corners of his mouth turned down. "I'm sure I can find something for you to do, then, even if it's just fetching me scrolls."

"If you think I'm going to be more a nuisance—"

"No, I don't think that all. I think you're an astute observer, someone I'll need to answer my questions as they come along." He closed the space between them. "And I'll add that I enjoy your company very much."

She gave him a wry grin. "Where did you come from, exactly?"

"Madrena." He rolled his scroll back up and tucked it into the leather sack slung over his shoulder. "I'm the steward of the palace there."

That explained so much. Why he seemed so confident and gave orders so easily. Why Azurha had sent for him. Why he was so starved for company that he seemed to enjoy hers. Her heart dropped when she realized that, but she kept her disappointment buried.

They ventured out into the city streets. Izana made sure she stayed the required two feet behind him, befitting her station as a slave. It wasn't until they hit a crowded intersection that Modius reached behind him for her hand.

The act caught her so off guard, she stumbled. Her pulse pounded in her ears. Did he even understand the consequences of his act? She wrestled free of him and added another foot between them.

Modius whirled around and quickly jumped out of the way of a Deizian chariot that zoomed through the streets without regard for whom it knocked down. He came toward her, nostrils flared, backing her up against the side of a building. "Why did you do that?"

"I could ask you the same thing."

"I didn't want to lose you in the crowd."

"And you won't. I can keep up with you." She rubbed her arm with the hand he'd held a second before, trying to erase the memory of his touch. As much as she liked the sensation of his hand around hers, convention dictated that wasn't allowed.

"I'd feel better if you'd walk beside me, then, so I can keep an eye on you."

She closed her eyes and leaned her head against the wall.

It was only mid-morning, and already, the sunbaked bricks were hot enough to cause sweat to trickle along her spine.

At least, she wanted to blame the warm bricks for it.

Her voice sounded hard and cold as she explained, "If I were an Elymanian like you—or even a freed Alpirion—I could walk down the street beside you, holding your hand without fear. But I'm not, and there are consequences for slaves who appear to be acting above their stations."

His jaw tightened as though he wanted to challenge what she'd said. After taking a moment to digest this information, though, he stepped back, giving her more space. "I understand what you're saying, even though I don't agree with it."

"I didn't make the laws. I'm just forced to adhere to them."

His eyes darkened, but she couldn't tell if it was from anger or sorrow. He turned around, stretching his arm out to shield her from one of the six-legged horses pulling a cart through the street. "Stay close to me."

"I will." And even if they got separated, she knew the way to the library. She could always find him there. His concern for her safety, however, unnerved her far more than the possible threat of punishment. Her owners, even her prior one, had always treated her well for a slave. She'd never been beaten, never felt the sting of the whip, never been forced to dirty her hands or work until her body gave out on her. She'd been cultured, taught to read and write, been given special treatment most slaves only dreamed about.

But no one had ever treated her like an equal until now.

With one simple, instinctual act, Modius had done just that. On one hand, it made her insides turn soft and her heart thump a bit harder than normal. On the other, though, it further increased her apprehension about spending too much time with him. She feared she'd only get hurt in the end, especially if she ended up trusting him with her heart.

When they reached the library, Modius's pace quickened. He didn't bother to read the inscriptions above the doors that listed the information held inside. Instead, he moved through the library like a man who knew this place inside and out. He led her through room after room until he stopped in front of a shelf full of scrolls. His finger traced his path as he read the titles carved on the wooden knobs until he found the one he was looking for. He pulled it from the shelf and went to one of the tables, unrolling the parchment and leaning over it. His lips moved as he silently read.

Izana peered over his shoulder at the contents. It was a medical text about poisons, listing information about their qualities—what they smelled like, tasted like, what they did to their victims. None of them matched what she had witnessed. She kept her tone innocent as she asked, "What are you looking for?"

"To see if there's a poison that does this." He pulled out her sketches from his bag, his eyes never leaving the words in front of him.

"You do realize that all the imperial family's food is tasted before it's placed before them, and that no one else has come down with the same illness?"

He nodded. "Which means there's a chance someone could've added the poison after it was tasted."

She sat down on the chair across from him and rested her chin on her palm, studying him. He seemed so intent on going along this path that he failed to see any other possible explanations. "What if one of the Deizians used their magic to curse him?"

"Don't be ridiculous. Their magic doesn't work that way."

"Fine, but there are plenty of Alpirion tales about magical curses." As soon as she said it, she wished she hadn't.

Modius looked up from the scroll and stared at her, his eyes narrowing. "What did you say?"

"Nothing." Yet another thing she was forbidden to know. If word got out that she could read and write, it would probably end with her being taken to the pillory, perhaps even being sold. However, knowledge of the Alpirion ways carried a much higher punishment.

Death.

"Repeat what you just said."

"I just mentioned there were stories, legends, I heard as a child," she stammered. Her feet itched to run away, but her legs didn't feel like they'd be able to support her if she stood. "They're nothing more than tales meant to frighten children to sleep."

His features relaxed, and his gaze traveled past her. "There's always some truth to legends," he murmured.

Then he jumped from his chair and disappeared into another room.

Izana grabbed his bag and followed him. "What are you looking for now?"

"Historical accounts." He stopped in front of the doorway to another room, reading the inscription, before moving on to the next one. "I asked my father once why the Deizians decided to conquer the Alpirions after centuries of living on the same planet with them."

"Greed, power, boredom. Take your pick."

"You'd think that, especially with the ore deposits in Alpiria, but I remember him saying the peace between the two kingdoms was broken by an Alpirion curse."

Her heart rose into her throat. It sounded oddly similar to the story she'd been told as a girl, although she couldn't remember the details, and she was too busy trying to keep up with Modius to recall them. "It's probably just something the Deizians made up to justify their conquest."

"Maybe, maybe not." He paused to read the inscription above the entrance to a large room and nodded before ducking into it. "Help me find some texts about the Alpirion War."

Her eyes bugged. "The war lasted over thirty years. It would take days to read all the accounts of it. Not to mention, I can't help you read through them, remember?"

He finally halted in the middle of the room, his back to

her. His shoulders sagged. "Fine, but if I write down what words to look for, you can pull the scrolls from the shelves."

He took the bag from her, tore off a piece of paper, and scribbled a few words on it. "Look for scrolls that have those words on them and bring them to me."

She glanced down at the paper as she took it from him. *Cause, Alpirion, and Ovidius Avitus.*

"I'll go this way," he said, pointing to his left, "you go that way."

Izana spent the next hour searching the shelves for scrolls with those words. She almost felt like dancing for joy when she found one to bring to Modius. But when she brought it to him, she found him reading at a table, surrounded by stacks of scrolls. "It seems you went in the right direction."

"What?" He looked up, a streak of ink along his forehead.

She stifled a laugh and set the scroll on the table. "Find anything useful?"

"Lots of information about the war itself, but still nothing about the cause." He rolled up the scroll he was reading and opened a new one. A separate sheet of parchment fell out of it and to the floor. Modius bent down to pick it up. "What's this?"

Izana's chest tightened when she saw the Alpirion glyphs. She lowered her eyes, afraid she would give away too much. "I have no idea," she lied.

"Seems to be something written in the Alpirion language." He studied it for a few minutes before setting it aside. "Too bad there's no one here to translate it for me."

I could translate it for you, if only it didn't mean I'd be executed for doing so.

She waited until he was completely absorbed in his own scroll before taking the Alpirion one. It was torn at the bottom, hardly longer than her forearm, but she started reading at the top. The glyphs were organized into blocks, running horizontally from left to right until they came to the end of the page. Then

60

they picked up on the next block down.

She gasped when she realized it was an Alpirion account of the first time a Deizian emperor had visited Alpiria. Almost a century had passed since the day Emperor Atorius had come to meet with King Sutkumon. The purpose of the visit was to discuss the veins of ore buried beneath the blue sands. The Deizians needed it to conduct their magic and power their airships. The Alpirions feared it would be used against them and were hesitant to mine the ore and sell it to the "People from the Sun," as the Deizians were called. Not even the proposal of marrying Atorius's son to Sutkumon's daughter could ease their hesitations.

But what had started out as a diplomatic envoy took a deadly turn when Emperor Atorius and his son fell ill. The historian wrote that the flesh seemed to shrivel from their bones, and their life force was unraveled like stray threads from a cloth.

Izana's hands shook when she read that description. It sounded all too familiar to what she'd witnessed a couple of months ago.

She kept reading, hoping to find an explanation for the illness. Instead, the page ended at the point where the Deizians accused the Alpirions of poisoning them. She cursed under breath and looked up to find Modius watching her.

"Find anything interesting?" he asked, his voice carrying a suspicious edge.

The tremor in her hands worked its way up her arms, moving in time to the rapid beat of her heart. She dropped the paper with the Alpirion glyphs. "I was just wishing I could read it."

He reached across the table and grabbed her wrist. He gaze bore into hers, never wavering. "I need you to be honest with me."

Sweat broke out along her hairline. She swallowed hard. "And I need to know I can trust you."

"We're both working together to help your mistress."

She nodded. "But some things are forbidden." She

lowered her voice and added, "Some things can become deadly."

Finger by finger, he loosened his grip on her and let go, still staring at her. He pointed to the scroll he'd been reading. "This is an account of how King Sutkumon killed Emperor Atorius, thus ending the uneasy peace between the two kingdoms."

"Oh?" She risked taking a glance at it to see if it was a translation of what she'd read or another account told through the Deizian perspective.

"It goes on to say that King Sutkumon declared that he was innocent of such a thing. The emperor died, but his son somehow managed to survive and kill the Alpirion king to avenge his father's death. The Alpirion forces rallied around Sutkumon's children and drove the Deizians back behind the border, but the seeds of war had been planted."

Definitely not was she was reading. Of course, her version of the story ended before she saw the outcome.

She wiped her palms on her skirt. "Did they give a description of the poison's effects?"

"My account never mentioned anything about a poison."

Izana forgot how to breathe. A million curses exploded through her mind, but her body refused to move. She'd just given herself away to Modius, revealed a secret that could lead to her execution, and now her fate hung on the whims of a man she'd known less than a day.

He stood, his eyes never leaving hers and circled the table to stand beside her. Gone was the man who seemed content to pour over scrolls and get lost in his studies. In his place was a man as dangerous as any member of the Legion. He crouched next to her, his hand on the back of her chair, and whispered in her ear, "No more games, Izana. Tell me what your scroll says."

"These are Alpirion glyphs. Like you said, there's no one to translate them."

"Except you." He dragged the torn parchment along the table toward her. "If you want me to keep this between us, then tell me what you've read."

She glanced around the room, making sure they were alone. Then, in a rapid whisper, she summarized the contents, including the description of the emperor wasting away.

"Did they name the poison?"

She shook her head, her gaze fixed on her lap. "The rest of the scroll is missing."

Modius rocked back on his heels. Now it was his turn to curse. "So Lady Azurha was right—we are dealing with a poison here."

"Did your scroll mention how the emperor died?"

He shook his head. "It was just referred to as the Alpirion curse."

Her pulse was beginning to slow enough to where she could analyze the story again. She reread her scroll, catching one detail she'd overlooked before. "Your account said the emperor's son survived?"

"Yes. He went on to become Emperor Salvius. Why?"

She pointed to the column of glyphs describing the illness. "Because this account says he was struck by the same illness. I watched as every healer in the empire tried to save Emperor Decius, but none of them could. How is it that Emperor Salvius suffered the same illness, and yet survived?"

A fire lit up in Modius's eyes. "By the gods, I think you're on to something." He raced back to his scroll and read through it again. "There's no mention of him being affected by the curse—only that he avenged his father's death."

"Funny how history is always shaped by those in power. He probably didn't want people to know he'd been weakened by the poison."

"Damn it!" He banged his fist against the table, shaking his hand out afterward. "What I wouldn't give to be able to go back in time and find out what really happened."

"To Emperor Decius or Emperor Atorius?"

"Either one." He ran his fingers through his hair. "The further we dig into this matter, the more complicated it becomes."

She drummed her fingers on the table, wishing she at least had the rest of the scroll. Something about the son's name bothered her. She could've sworn she remembered hearing something about him before. "What was Emperor Salvius's praenomen?"

"Tiberius."

Her head swam as the words of an old bedtime story came rushing back to her. A story of two lovers torn apart by war.

The story of Tiberius and Ausetsut.

8

Modius looked up in time to see Izana's face turned a sickly shade of grey. Her warning, that these things could be deadly, rang in his mind. He searched for a poisoned dart protruding from her body or some other sign of foul play. After finding none, he focused on her face, trying to decipher what new secret she withheld from him. "What is it?"

Fear burned in her dark eyes, intensifying the contrast with her already pale face. She clutched his arm. "Please, I have to know I can trust you."

She didn't have to tell him why. Her translation of the scroll already revealed that she knew things which were forbidden by the law and could lead to her execution. But the knot in his stomach warned him that was just a hint of what she might know, what she was trying so desperately to hide from him. "I promise that I won't betray you, especially if what you know can help solve this mystery."

The fear eased into wariness, but never reached the level of trust he desired. She pushed him away and stood, straightening her simple tunic. "It's not me I'm worried about."

"Who is it, then?"

She chewed on her bottom lip. "Does your promise extend to others who might help you with my mistress's task?"

The pool deepened, and he weighed the consequences of

his response. What if she was somehow connected with the emperor's death? "It depends on what information they can provide."

Now it was her turn to assess him. He tried to keep his face open and honest while he offered a silent prayer to the gods that he hadn't silenced the one person who might answer his questions.

After a few seconds, she nodded. "We'll have to stop by the market first for bread, figs, and some good wine."

Her response intrigued him, but he knew better than to ask questions. At this point, he'd comply with her plan if it meant uncovering more information about the poison that killed Emperor Decius.

When Lady Azurha had offered Izana's assistance, did she know some of the secrets the slave held?

***

Izana pressed her palm into Modius's back, pushing him forward through the crowded streets while she juggled with the basket of food and wine on her other arm. "Keep going for about two blocks and then make a left."

"I still don't see why you can't walk in front of me and lead me there."

"I told you this morning—I am required to walk two feet behind you."

"True, but you can always walk ahead and let them think I'm following you discreetly."

She snorted out a half laugh. They were just beginning to enter the twisted maze of streets that formed the oldest part of Emona. The aristocratic Deizians preferred the hills over-looking the city where the cool breezes flowed through their homes. The middle-class Elymanians spread out along the surrounding foothills.

But this part of the city belonged to the poorest of the poor, most of them freed Alpirions. The air here was hot and muggy, filled with the stench of rotting waste and human excrement. Flies buzzed in her face as she continued to push him forward. A distant call of an older *lupa* echoed down the alley, her advertised price for a quick encounter barely enough for half a loaf of bread.

Dozens of pairs of dark eyes watched Modius as they passed, followed by a hushed murmur of Alpirion words. They were in her part of the city now, and her chest tightened when their gazes changed from curious to hostile. He was an intruder, and the locals didn't welcome his presence.

Izana moved forward to walk beside him. "Stay close to me."

He grinned. "Finally decided to say the hell with the law?"

"No, more like let those men over there know you're with me." She nodded toward the three youths with gold flashing from their ears, proclaiming their freed status as much as the way they cracked their knuckles while staring down Modius.

He wrapped his arm around her waist. "I don't like the way they're looking at you."

"I could say the same thing about the way they're looking at you. When we arrive at Hapsa's, you'd be wise to let me do all the talking."

His arm tightened around her, and his lips came closer to her ear. "Why do I feel like we're about to break a dozen laws and end up in trouble?"

"A dozen laws is a low estimate." Her pulse quickened, and her steps slowed. Perhaps she'd been wrong to trust him. Perhaps this would lead not only to her death, but the death of Hapsa and her family.

She drew to a stop, wavering on her decision once again. "Modius, please, I beg you, do not share anything you're about to learn this afternoon."

His jaw tightened, and his stance stiffened. "Except for what pertains to the poison."

She drew in a shaky breath and nodded. "Except for that."

He waited for her to move forward, lingering a few steps

behind her as she wove deeper into the Alpirion quarter. A few blocks later, she spied the familiar blue door of the home where she'd spent most of her childhood. It opened less than a minute after she knocked.

Baza's eyes hardened with suspicion when she saw Modius behind her. "What do you want, Izana?"

"My mistress has sent me to speak with Hapsa."

Baza's dark gaze flickered to Modius again, the door not opening more than a crack. A beam of sunlight fell on the thin gold chain around her neck. "And the Elymanian?"

"He is with me."

Baza's lips thinned, and the door started to close.

Izana thrust her foot into the gap and pushed back, slipping into the dimly lit house. "Why aren't you letting us speak with your great-grandmother?" she asked in Alpirion.

"Because he's not one of us," Baza hissed, pointing to where Modius stood on the other side of the doorway.

"He's been hired by Lady Azurha, who is one of us."

Baza crossed her arms and shook her head. "I don't trust him. You place us all in danger by bringing him here."

"Please, I need to speak to Hapsa. It's urgent, and you do not want to face the wrath of my mistress when I tell her that you refused to help her servants on this matter." Izana lifted her chin, daring the other woman to deny them access.

"Let them in," a deep voice said in the common language from the shadows. Baza's brother, Djer, entered the room from the courtyard and filled the room with his commanding presence. He was the only Alpirion she knew who could battle Farros in size and was the complete opposite of his thin, nervous sister. "If our future empress asks something of the lorekeeper, who are we to deny it?"

Modius rolled his shoulders back, his attention fixed on the well-muscled Alpirion. "Thank you."

Djer smiled, losing some of his intimidating presence as he did so, reminding Izana of the boy she'd grown up with. "You are most welcome. I know Izana would not risk bringing you here unless it was important."

"You two know each other?" he asked.

Izana almost laughed when she caught a glimpse of jealousy flaring in Modius's eyes. "Djer and I used to belong to the same mistress."

Instead of easing his worry, it only added to the heat of his glare.

Djer cocked one brow, silently asking her about Modius's behavior.

She shook her head. How could she explain things when she had no idea what they were. Yes, she had enjoyed last night, but after revealing too many of her secrets to him today, she feared allowing him any closer. "Is Hapsa in her room?"

Baza opened her mouth to object, but Djer took his sister by the shoulder and steered her into the next room. "She just awoke from her nap."

Alone now, Izana beckoned for Modius to follow her to the back rooms of the home. "Keep quiet and let me do all the talking," she whispered.

"Yes, I got the impression I wasn't welcome."

"They have their reasons for being protective of Hapsa."

"And I suppose none of it has anything to do with the conversation you had with the woman in Alpirion?"

She silently cursed. One more crime he could bring against her. At this rate, she'd be lucky to live past sundown. "I hope to the gods I'm not making a mistake bringing you here."

He took her hand. The warm strength of his touch steadied her, calmed her worries, and strengthened her convictions. "Remember, we're both here for Lady Azurha."

And her mistress struck her as a person who didn't mind breaking several laws to achieve her goal. That still made her uncomfortable with confessing her part in revealing the information they'd gathered so far.

She withdrew her hand and carried the basket of food and wine into Hapsa's room. The pungent scent of incense burned her nostrils when she first crossed the threshold, then swirled around her like a familiar blanket on a cold night. She'd lost track of the number of hours she'd spent at Hapsa's side as a child, hearing the stories she was forbidden to know, learning the language that was fatal to speak. Now she was back again, a grown woman, but the old crone seated on the cushions hadn't changed.

She knelt in front of Hapsa, noting how the lorekeeper's clouded eyes seemed to shine out from the dark brown wrinkles like two moons. Hapsa was the oldest Alpirion in Emona—perhaps in the whole empire—and one of the few people living who remembered when Alpiria was a free kingdom. If anyone knew the information Izana sought, it was her.

Modius crouched beside her like a scout hiding in a bush, still and silent. Very unusual for a man who claimed to be a scholar and steward.

She took a deep breath and said in Alpirion, "Good afternoon, Hapsa."

A smile appeared from the folds of the old woman's face. "I was wondering when you'd come to visit me, Izana."

"Yes, I have been away too long." She opened the bottle of wine and poured a cup for Hapsa. "My duties do not allow me to stray from the palace often."

"And yet you come not only bearing gifts, but a friend," she said in the common language and sniffed the air. "An Elymanian at that."

Modius's mouth fell open, but Hapsa silenced him with a cackle before he could say anything.

"Young man, I may be blind, but I still have the use of my other senses. Elymanians have a distinct smell, although yours carries a hint of something more." She sniffed again. "I smell the sea on your clothes."

He quirked his lips into a half smile. "I don't know if I should be impressed or suspicious."

"I'd go with the first one." Izana gave Hapsa the cup and began placing the figs and bread on her plate.

The old woman took a sip. "Oh, you must be in

desperate need of a story to bring me such a fine wine."

"Or I could be making up for my long absence."

Hapsa laughed again, this time with a softer edge. "You always were too clever for you own good, Izana. Which story would you like?"

She smoothed her hands on her dress. "I would like to hear the story of Tiberius and Ausetsut."

Hapsa's brows rose, sending ripples along the loose skin that hung from her face. "Are you certain? It does not have a happy ending."

"Yes, please. I have a feeling it might aid my current mistress."

"Ah, I see now." Hapsa took another sip of wine. "Your mistress is not the first Alpirion chosen to become the wife of a Deizian emperor. Many years ago, there was an Alpirion princess named Ausetsut. She was much beloved of her people, a guardian chosen by the gods who took her duties seriously, a *wa'ai* who had the power of the moon flowing through her veins.

"One day, the emperor of the People from the Sun came to visit her father. He brought his son and heir, Tiberius, with him. Ausetsut took one look at the young prince and fell in love. The emperor of the People from the Sun saw the budding romance between the two and decided to use it to his advantage. He approached the king of the People from the Moon to ask for Ausetsut's hand in marriage to his son.

"The king of the People from the Moon regarded this offer with suspicion, for he'd seen how the People of the Sun consumed the land with their wars and conquests. He also knew the emperor desired the thick veins of bronze metal hidden beneath the blue sands of the desert. But most importantly of all, he knew his beloved daughter would be forced to leave the lands and people she was bound to protect."

Izana slid a glance to Modius to make sure he was following the story. His face was blank, but his gaze remained fixed on Hapsa.

"After much debate, the king finally consented to the

match because he saw how much his daughter loved Tiberius. Celebrations were ordered to announce the royal engagement, and a treaty between the two lands was drafted. But before the wedding could take place, tragedy struck the young lovers."

Ignoring her earlier request to let her do the talking, Modius interrupted, "Yes, we've found several accounts that mentioned King Sutkumon poisoned the emperor and his son."

"Poisoned?" the old woman spat. "A Person from the Moon would never resort to such a cowardly way to kill his enemies. That is the way of the People from the Sun."

"Then why did the emperor and his son fall ill?"

Hapsa took her time chewing the fig in her mouth. "Izana, have you ever heard of the Royal Flower of Alpiria?"

"Yes." Her voice shook from the strain of searching her memories. "It blooms under the light of the moon, and it is so precious that only members of the royal family could possess it. They used it everywhere, from their perfume to the flowers that adorned their hair. They even mixed it with the olive oil on their food and muddled the petals in their wine."

"As a gesture of respect to the emperor and his son, King Sutkumon allowed both of them the same access to the flower."

Modius stiffened beside her. "Do you think the oil or the flowers were poisoned?"

Hapsa shook her head. "They were from the king's personal supply. He was bestowing a great honor on them, but it was a gift that turned into a curse, for that flower caused their life threads to unravel."

Izana sucked in a breath through her teeth. It was the same description she'd read in the account. "But why would the flower affect them that way and not the Alpirion royal family?"

"Magic?" Modius suggested.

Izana shook her head. "Alpirions don't have magic."

"Ah, there you are wrong, Izana," Hapsa chimed in, "for we are the People of the Moon, and its light shines in the dark of night. But only a few of us may harness the power of the moon, the land, and use it. Even then, that power may only be used to heal or protect."

The lorekeeper turned to Modius. "But this was not the workings of our magic, Elymanian. Your people are from the earth, and you are part of this land. Our plants and flowers will affect you the same way they do us. But the Deizians are from the sun and are not part of this land. Does that help answer your question?"

His eyes lit up, and he nodded. "Yes, Hapsa, it does. Thank you."

"Then I am glad my story helped you." The old woman shifted on her cushions and pulled her palla tighter around her withered body. "I think the wine has gone to my head."

"Then we will leave you to rest." Modius cupped Izana's elbow and stood, pulling her up with him. "Thank you for sharing your knowledge with us."

"You are most welcome to return if you seek more."

Izana raised both brows. Hapsa usually preferred to share the Alpirion lore among her own people. The invitation intrigued her as much as Modius's response to the story.

She leaned forward and placed a hand on Hapsa's cheek, speaking softly in Alpirion the same farewell she'd used as a child, "Thank you for welcoming us and telling us a story."

The old woman covered her hand. "I trust you will remember it and let it live even after I am gone."

"I will." She followed Modius, pausing at the doorway to cast one final glance at Hapsa. The old woman shivered, despite the heat of the day. How many more stories would she be able to tell before death claimed her?

Djer met them in the front room. "I trust you found what you were looking for?"

She nodded toward Modius, who was already out on the street. If she let him get too far ahead of her, he might run into trouble from the local youths. "He seems to have found the answer he sought."

"But not you?"

Disappointment weighed on her chest, slowing her breaths. "I had hoped to hear the end of the tale, but it's more important I return him to the palace."

"Then you should return another day and ask Hapsa to finish it."

"Perhaps I will." And maybe next time, she'd bring a scroll and a pen to record the tales before they were lost to her people.

9

Modius stalked blindly through the streets, his mind churning. *Why didn't I see it before?* During his time in Madrena, he'd learned that different tinctures had different effects on Deizians. Why would this moon lily be any different? If only he could find a sample to test his theory. Perhaps Izana would know where to find it.

Izana. He'd been so lost in thought, he'd completely forgotten about her. He paused and turned around, searching for her.

She was right behind him, keeping the required distance between them. "Is something wrong?"

He shook his head. "Just making sure I hadn't lost you."

"You'd have to be much quicker for that."

His mind eased on that account, he continued back to the palace. Every time he glanced over his shoulder, she was behind him. But when they passed the palace gates, she caught up to him and murmured, "Please, whatever you do, don't tell my mistress about Hapsa."

Then she darted off and disappeared into a side building.

He took a step to follow her, to see what other secrets he held, but froze when he heard his father's voice.

"Back already?"

Some other time, Izana.

He changed his route and followed his father into the palace. "Yes, and I think I might have found something that will interest Lady Azurha."

"I'm sure she will be pleased to hear it." A hint of praise laced Varro's words and chased away some of the weariness that ached in his muscles. "I will take you to her after you've cleaned up."

Modius shook the dust from his tunic. A bath would feel wonderful right now. The only thing that would make it better was if a certain Alpirion would join him.

But would the pleasure be worth the risk? He may have found information for Lady Azurha, but in the process, he'd opened up at least a dozen questions about the woman who shared his bed last night. "What can you tell me about Izana?"

His father drew to a stop. "Why are you asking?"

"I'm curious why Lady Azurha sent her to assist me. Perhaps you can shed some light on her past, where she came from, what her skills are."

His father's face hardened. "A slave's past is none of your concern. If Lady Azurha sent her to assist you, then there was a good reason why, and you should keep your interest in her limited to that."

In other words, he shouldn't be dallying with a slave when there was work to be done. He waited for his father to lecture him about last night, but it never came. Instead, the palace steward resumed the brisk pace that accentuated his limp. "Meet me outside the throne room in an hour."

***

With the grime of the day washed from his skin and a fresh tunic on, Modius hurried through the halls.

His father stood by the throne room doors, the corners of his mouth tilted downward in disapproval. "You're late."

"I needed more time to get clean." Not to mention, the caldarium felt exceptionally wonderful after the long day. The steaming water helped clear his mind so he could process the information he'd gathered.

"Lady Azurha is waiting."

Once again, Varro led him to the room just off the main throne room, where the future empress waited.

Modius bowed as the doors closed behind him. "Thank you for seeing me, my lady, and I apologize for keeping you waiting."

She swept over him with those cold, calculating eyes before gesturing to the chair on the other side of the table. "Varro tells me you discovered something that might explain the former emperor's death."

He sat, not touching the food or wine that had been laid out on the table. He was too busy trying to find a way to present his findings without incriminating Izana. "I found a historical account where a prior emperor and his son were stricken by a similar illness while visiting the Alpirion court. After further investigation, I think I may have found the source of the illness."

"Which was?"

"The royal flower of Alpiria."

Azurha propped her elbow on the arm of her chair, leaning over to rest her chin in her palm. "Very interesting. But how would that poison the emperor and his son when it has been used by the Alpirion kings for generations without harm?"

"I asked myself the same question, but then I was reminded that the Deizians are not from this planet. They are very different from us when it comes to the healing arts, requiring different medicines and treatments. From there, I extrapolated that perhaps this flower acted like a poison to their system when they ingested it. It would explain how the poison could have gotten past the food tasters without harming them."

"And do you have any proof to support this claim?"

He shook his head. "I don't even know what this flower looks like, much less where to find it to test my hypothesis."

But I have feeling Izana does. Unease prickled along his back. He was tempted to tell the future empress what else he'd learned about her maid, but he curled his hand into a fist in the hope it would keep his lips sealed as tightly. Until he learned the whole truth about her, he was willing to guard her secrets.

Azurha's lips twitched. "And was Izana helpful today?"

He licked his lips. "Very much so." *Not to mention, last night.*

"Good. Then I will release her of her normal duties while you are here so she may continue to assist you."

Something about the future empress's relaxed demeanor made him wonder if she already knew Izana's skill with the Alpirion language and lore. Why else would she have volunteered her services? He uncurled his fingers, letting the blood flow back into the numb tips.

"Thank you, my lady. I plan on returning to the library in the morning to discover all I can about this moon lily."

"And I'll make sure Izana meets you at the gates when you leave." She stood, prompting him to rise from his chair as well. "If you are correct in your theory, then the next question would be how did the flower come in contact with Emperor Decius?"

"Perhaps my father will be able to assist you there. No one knows more about what happens within these walls than him."

"Very true. In the meantime, I need you to find that flower."

"Yes, my lady." He bowed as she left the room, his mind once again racing with ideas. The only thing constant among them was that he needed to speak to Izana—alone.

***

Azurha returned to the private quarters she shared with Titus and searched the shadows, her nerves on edge. Somewhere in this palace lurked a murderer.

She pressed her dagger's sheath against her thigh, letting the cold metal soothe her anger so she could think more clearly. Her thoughts turned to the day Pontus had hired her to kill Titus. He'd known about the emperor's illness. He'd even mentioned that he doubted Decius would live past a fortnight. But did he know the person who'd poisoned the emperor? Had he been the one who'd planted the poison?

She stared at the place where she'd killed Pontus days ago. The slaves may have scrubbed away the blood stains, but they could never erase the images from her mind. All her life, she'd been taught to kill. Now, she wished she'd saved Pontus's life, if only to extract answers from him. The only other person who might have been privy to Pontus's plans was Cassius, and he'd met the same fate as Pontus.

Too bad dead men didn't talk. Otherwise, she'd have a grand conversation with the heads displayed just outside the palace walls.

The locks clicked, and Titus entered the room, rubbing the back of his neck.

"Long day?" she asked before placing a kiss on his cheek.

"Insufferable Senate. I swear, I'm this close to disbanding them."

"But if you did, they'd label you as a tyrant and work even harder to depose you."

"I know," he sighed. "That's the only reason I sit through their tedious sessions and break up their bickering. At least I get to spend a restful evening with you."

He drew her into his arms and kissed her in a way that hinted their evening would be anything but restful. Fire churned through her veins, mixing with desire and stealing her breath away.

Titus broke away, grinning. "Why don't we discuss this over a nice, leisurely bath?"

"You make it hard to say no." she teased, already unfastening her gown.

She pulled his tunic over his head, admiring the stiff length of his erection. She trailed her fingers over it, noting the way he hissed through his teeth. "I'm just good at making you hard."

"Yes, but you knew that already." He pointed to her dagger and frowned. "I thought I'd convinced you that you don't need that anymore."

"Old habits die hard."

"Perhaps, but we don't need it tonight." He unstrapped the dagger and led her into the caldarium, ignoring the usual order of the bathing ritual. "I've waited all day to make love to you."

He kissed her again, softly this time, while his hands explored the curves of her body. Every touch, every caress, heightened her arousal. Teased her. Left her wanting more.

Impatience finally got the better of her, and she led him to the wall of the pool. "Please."

She didn't have to tell him what she wanted, what she needed. Their hearts and bodies knew each other well by now.

The blue in his eyes thinned into a bright rim around his pupils as he lifted her up against the wall, positioning her to where the tip of his cock pressed against the entrance of her sex.

The need inside her multiplied until her mind was clouded with lust. She wrapped her legs around his waist and pulled him deeper until he filled her completely.

"By the gods, you feel wonderful," Titus whispered. "I'd sit through the Senate day after day if it meant I got to come home to you like this."

Emotion swelled in her throat from the love shining in his face, strangling her words. She cupped his cheeks in her hands and thanked the gods her path had crossed his. "I love you, too."

"I know." He began to move inside her, his hips pumping in a leisurely pace while his lips traced a path down her neck and shoulders toward her breasts. The rough stubble of his cheeks heightened the exquisite pleasure-pain of his mouth, scratching the sensitive skin left behind after the combination of nips and kiss.

She laced her fingers through his golden hair, inhaling the scent of sandalwood from his wet skin, urging him to move faster as the tension coiled deep within her. A moan rose from her throat. "More. Faster."

He covered her mouth with his before she shouted out more orders. The tempo of his hips quickened, bringing her closer and closer the brink until she finally shattered against him. He followed a few strokes later, his breath hitching a second before his body shuddered from his release.

She waited until their pulses slowed to say, "I don't think I'll ever tire of coming in your arms."

"Good, because I see many more nights like this in our future."

Azurha brushed his hair out of his face and covered his cheeks with whisper-light kisses, offering a prayer of thanks to the gods who'd seen fit to bless her with Titus. "I love you," she murmured.

"I love you, too," he replied, his voice husky with emotion. "And I look forward to spending the rest of my life with you."

Her heart squeezed so tightly, she feared it would burst from the overwhelming flux of emotions churning inside. "And I, you."

They climbed out of the pool and paused only long enough to towel off before falling into bed together, their bodies entwined as Titus drifted off to sleep. Azurha lay beside him, watching his chest rise and fall, and knew peace. She'd once told him she belonged to no man, but now, it was very clear to see that all of her belonged to him—body, heart, and soul.

10

Izana knocked on Modius's door. The sky was dark tonight with the exception of the ever-present purple glow from a distant supernova, but the flickering light pouring out from under his door told her he was still awake.

When he opened it, she had to cover her laugh. His hair stuck up at odd angles, and a smear of ink ran along his jaw. "Yes?"

"May I come in?"

He stepped aside and closed the door behind her. "What brings you here at this late hour?"

Had it been the prior night, she would've replied by helping him out of his clothes and dragging him to bed. But after today, caution now dictated her movements. She kept her eyes on the floor and wrapped her arms around her waist. "I wanted to thank you for not telling Lady Azurha about Hapsa and me."

He stayed by the door, keeping his distance from her. Perhaps she wasn't the only one feeling wary tonight. "How do you know what I told her?"

"I was listening on the other side of the door."

"So you're a sneak, too?" His words contained no malice, but they weren't teasing, either.

"I had to make sure Hapsa was safe."

He took a step toward her, his shoulders as firm as his

voice. "And what if I had told her about Hapsa?"

She bit her bottom lip, her eyes still lowered to conceal the thoughts racing through her mind. "I would've sent a message to Djer and Baza to move her someplace safe."

"I see." He went to his desk and sat down, running his fingers through his hair and adding a new smudge of ink to his temple. "Izana, if we're to work together, we need to be honest with each other—understand?"

She nodded.

"So, let's start with a few basic things. Can you read and write?"

She kept her voice flat as she repeated the same answer she'd given him earlier. "Slaves aren't allowed to read and write."

"I didn't ask you that." His dark eyes glittered with danger. "I asked if you could read and write."

She edged toward the door, but he jumped up from his chair in one fluid motion and blocked her route.

"Izana."

The way he said her name carried a hint of a threat and sent a shiver down her spine. He was going to force an answer out of her, one way or another. She nodded again.

"How well?"

"Well enough," she replied, hoping her vague answer would satisfy him without further incriminating her.

"Who taught you?"

Her mind raced to find an answer. "Taught me what?"

He closed the space between them, his hand wrapping around her wrist. "No more games, Izana. I need to know what you're capable of doing if we're going to be solving this mystery together, not constantly being surprised to find out you knew the answer all along."

Then his jaw fell slack, and his grip on her wrist tightened. "Or perhaps you do know all the answers."

Her pulse jumped. She tried to pull free, but he subdued her in a matter of seconds by pinning her arm behind her back. "Don't be ridiculous."

"What am I supposed to think? You've already admitted to spying on me. For all I know, you could've been the one who poisoned the emperor."

Her mouth went dry, and a surge of betrayal siphoned the air from her lungs. "How dare you accuse me of such a thing!"

"I'd be a fool if I didn't keep you on my list of suspects. After all, you did have access to the imperial quarters. You do have knowledge of the Alpirion lore."

She kicked him in the shins, punched him in the ribs, but his hold on her remained firm. "You're an ass, and I can't believe I came here tonight to thank you for protecting me."

"Then answer me honestly."

"Let me go, and maybe I will."

They stared at each for several breaths, a wordless battle of will raging between them until Modius finally released her. "Who taught you to read and write?"

She rubbed the red marks on her arm from his hand. Everything about him tonight went against what she'd originally thought of him. Stewards and scholars didn't move like that. "Who taught you how to subdue a person like that?"

"You first."

"I'll answer your question if you answer mine."

His gaze flickered to the marks he'd left, and a shimmer of guilt washed over his face. "I was trained as a soldier, like my father before me."

"And yet unlike him, an injury didn't end your career. What happened that turned you into a steward?"

His nostrils flared, and his expression hardened. Whatever the reason, he didn't want to talk about it. "It's your turn to answer a question."

She stepped back, running into the bed. "My former mistress taught me to read and write the common language."

"Why?"

"It's your turn." She lifted her chin, daring him to reveal the part of his past he wanted to keep hidden.

But instead of answering her, turned away and paced the length of the room.

She sat down on the edge of the bed. "It seems I'm not the only one with secrets."

He stopped and glared at her. "My past is none of your concern."

"I would say the same is true for mine."

"No, your past is the key to unraveling this whole mystery." He went back to his desk and scribbled something on a piece of parchment. "I already know you can speak and read the Alpirion language, which is a blessing if I ever hope to find anything on this moon lily."

"So you're not going to turn me over to the emperor for violating the laws his grandfather enacted?"

He stopped and flung his pen onto his papers. "No, not likely. You've already proven that your knowledge is useful, and I'll need it if we're to succeed."

"So what you're saying is that you're willing to turn a blind eye as long as I'm useful to you?"

He banged his fist on the desk. "Damn it, Izana, everything points to the fact the emperor was poisoned. It wasn't some mysterious illness or a blight of old age. It was murder. And if it was poison, then it was given to him by someone here in the palace, someone he trusted."

Frustration rolled off of him in heated blasts like a furnace's bellows. This was more than just a task given to him by her mistress. This was personal for him, and she couldn't help but wonder if his secretive past had something to do with it.

She stood and placed a hand on his shoulder. "And like you, I want to find out the truth. I respected Emperor Decius. I grieved with his family when he died, and I'm willing to do whatever it takes to get to the bottom of this." She drew in a shaky breath and added, "Even if it means risking my own life."

There. She'd placed it all on the line for him.

He took her hand and pulled her into his lap, tucking a loose curl behind her ear. "I know that, and rest assured, you can

85

trust me. We're in this together, all the way to end."

A spark of trust bloomed into a flame, spreading its warmth through her. She'd promised herself that she was only here to thank him, not to end up in his bed, but her body had a different plan. The tiny circles his thumb massaged into her palm, combined with his intoxicating scent, overruled her better judgment, and she leaned closer until her lips connected with his.

Modius was secretive, dangerous, but he could also kiss her in a way that made her forget about that. Gone was the hunger than that had dominated their actions last night. Their sexual needs had been well sated. In its place was something slow and sensual, warm and welcoming, passionate and pleading. Tonight's kiss was like drinking a fine wine, starting with a slow burn through her insides that ended up leaving her dizzy by the time she ended it.

The oil lamp caught the flecks of green in his eyes, highlighting the thinly veiled desire. He murmured her name and leaned in to kiss her again.

She slid from his lap before he seduced her back into his bed. "I should go."

"You don't kiss a man that way and then leave."

"I know, and I'm sorry, but I think since we will be working together, we should minimize distractions like this." She missed the heat of his body, but her mind cleared with each step she took away from him.

His lips thinned, but he nodded. "I suppose you're right."

She'd made it to the door without him stopping her. "So, I'll meet you at the gates tomorrow morning?"

He nodded again, the desire cooling from his eyes.

"In the meantime, I'll check a few sources I know about the moon lily. If we can find it and if we can prove that the emperor was poisoned—"

"You're talking about a lot of ifs there. One step at a time." He turned back to his papers, his back to her.

She slipped out of his room, her heart more confused

than her mind, and whispered, "Yes, one step at a time."

***

The next morning, Izana splashed the cold water from the cistern outside the slave quarters on her face, scrubbing away the last traces of sleep. After she left Modius's room, she had hunted down some of the slaves who'd been at the palace the longest, searching for clues about the moon lily and finding a small tidbit that might lead them to more information about it. She had no idea what time it was when she finally crawled into her bed, but the hour had been late enough to mark the quiet stillness of the palace.

"Need a towel?" Farros asked.

Her spine locked, but she took the cloth he offered. Ever since the day of the engagement procession, warning bells tolled whenever he was near her, and her body refused to relax. "Thank you," she said and dried her face.

A smirk played on his lips. "Another late night with the Elymanian?"

"And what business of yours is that?"

He raised his brows and backed away. "More concern, actually. After all, he's just visiting, and you're merely a slave. I wouldn't want you suffering from a broken heart when he's gone."

"I'm quite aware of my circumstances." She tried to leave, but he stepped in front of her.

"Be careful, Izana," he warned, sliding his finger along her neck and resting it where her pulse throbbed. "I'd hate to see you get hurt in all this."

"Is that a threat?"

He shook his head. "Just expressing my concern for you. We Alpirions need to look out for each other."

The tremble that started her stomach thankfully didn't make its way to the surface until after he'd left, but her heart didn't cease fluttering until she reached the gates and saw Modius waiting for her.

His brows knitted together. "Why are you pale?"

87

"Am I?"

He nodded and dropped his voice so only she could hear him. "What upset you?"

She forced a laugh and waved his concern away. "It's nothing. Just an unpleasant encounter with another slave."

"You should tell your mistress about it."

"It's nothing, really." She only wished she could believe her words. But until she knew the motives behind Farros's "concerns", she would keep this morning's exchange to herself. "Ready to spend a few more hours in the library?"

His lips curled down into a frown, but he nodded. "Stay close."

He led the way, the streets partially empty at this early hour. Izana had no trouble keeping up with him, even though he glanced over his shoulder at nearly every intersection to make sure she was still behind him. Unlike yesterday, he paused at the entrance of the library instead of plowing through to the section he wanted.

She scanned the map with the different sections. "What are you looking for?"

"Botany." He pointed to the room on the map. "This way."

Izana followed him to the section and waited until he set his bag on a table to say, "Do you mind if I do a little research on my own?"

"What about the whole slaves aren't allowed to read thing?"

A grin appeared before she could smother it. "This is different."

"Meaning?"

She hesitated. After all, what good would it be to get his hopes up if her snooping from last night proved incorrect? "I think I might have a lead on what we're searching for."

He crossed his arms, the frustration from last night simmering in his eyes. "Why won't you share it with me, then? We're a team—remember?"

"I will, but first I need to find the information on my own. It's difficult to explain, but you'll have to trust me." She closed the space between them. "You can do that, right?"

He exhaled, his shoulders falling in the process. "I suppose I'll have to, but if you're correct, I'd like to know why you needed this secrecy."

"Because there are some things only slaves know." She spun around on her heel and went off to find one of the slaves who manned the library.

Three rooms later, she found one. An older man, perhaps the age her father might have been. He was climbing down from a ladder to the top shelves when she approached him. "Do you think you can help me find something?"

Suspicion tightened his features. "Depends on what you are looking for. After all, I'm not allowed to read the scrolls."

But something in his voice told her that he could read them.

She pulled him into a corner, lowered her voice. "I've heard there's some artwork hidden here."

The slight uplift of one brow answered her question. "This is the greatest library in the empire. There are many things here."

It would be a gamble, but it might be worth it. She took a breath and whispered in Alpirion, "I'm looking for art from the homeland."

His eyes widened, and he checked behind her to make sure no one overheard their conversation. He took her arm and pulled her into an empty room, his voice a harsh whisper. "Where did you hear about that?"

"From others like us." Thankfully, the older slaves in the palace loved to talk. "I heard Emperor Decius wasn't as fond of it as his father had been, so he had it stored here."

"And why does it concern you?"

She turned her head to the side, revealing the brand on her neck that marked her as slave from the royal household. "It concerns my mistress, the imperial consort and future empress."

He let go of her arm and chuckled. "Very interesting, indeed."

"I take it you've been here long enough to remember the transfer."

"I've been here since before Emperor Sergius was born."

"Then can you show me where the art is?"

"You know we are forbidden to look upon things like that."

"I know, but this is a special exception." She batted her eyes and gave him a smile that she hoped would win him over.

His mouth twisted into a half-smile, half-frown. "I suppose I could if you promise to guard that information."

"I will only use it for my mistress's task."

"Then follow me."

Her heart skipped, and a huge weight lifted off her mind. If her assumptions were correct, they'd be able to find more information on the moon lily from the artwork than they'd ever find in the scrolls.

11

Modius scanned another scroll, searching for any
mention of a moon lily or the royal flower of Alpiria. So far, he
had found information about just about every flower north of
the Alpirion desert, but the native flora of that region might as
well have been from another planet. Not one scholar had taken
the time to catalog it.

Adding to his exasperation was the fact he hadn't seen
Izana in over an hour. Something about the way she looked this
morning left an uneasy knot in his stomach. Someone had scared
her. She'd risked a great deal taking him to Hapsa. Hopefully,
none of the other slaves would seek retaliation against her for
exposing their secrets.

But then, everything about this mystery was shrouded in
secrets. With every bit of information he gleaned, he uncovered a
dozen more secrets, all of them somehow connected to the
Alpirions. And the nagging suspicion in the back of his mind
kept telling him this was part of a much larger scheme.

A hiss interrupted his thoughts. Izana lingered by the
doorway, beckoning him to join her while glancing over her
shoulder. "Bring some paper and a pen," she whispered.

He gathered the supplies, then followed her. "Found
something?"

She chuckled. "You could say that."

At the entrance to every room, she'd pause, search the room, and then dart across the open space like she was trying to avoid being caught.

Knowing her, it probably meant she was going to show him something that was just as illegal as the lorekeeper she'd introduced him to yesterday.

She finally stopped at a book case hidden in the very back of the astronomy section. "Can you help me move this?"

He eyed the ten foot case packed with scrolls and wondered if she'd lost her mind. But when he pushed, the shelves moved forward as easily as a solid wood door, revealing a hidden staircase on the other side. Orange light flickered along the walls in the distance, but the rest of the path was concealed in darkness.

Izana looked behind her once again before descending. "Make sure you pull the shelves back behind you."

By the time he'd done that, she'd retrieved the torch and waited for him below. "Watch your step—some of the stairs are a bit uneven."

"What is this place?"

"And here I thought you knew the library inside-out," she teased.

"I never dreamed this existed." He eased down the rough-hewn stairs that had been carved from the rock. "How did you find it?"

"I just asked another slave."

"And if I had asked?"

She paused and chewed her bottom lip. "You wouldn't have found it."

Yet another secret guarded by the Alpirions. How many more would he discover by the end of this? "I'm beginning to think you Alpirions know more than most people in the empire."

"That's because most people pretend we don't exist. We're slaves, part of the silent background that makes the empire run. We're ignored unless someone notices us long enough to give orders. But what people don't realize is that we see and hear everything."

The stairway turned, creating a switchback that took them deeper underground. "And how did those invisible eyes and ears lead you to this?"

"I'd heard a rumor that when Emperor Livinius conquered Alpiria, he displayed some of the artwork he'd stolen from the temples in his palace. I asked around last night, and I not only got verification that was true, but I also got a lead on what happened to it."

"Which lead you to this staircase?"

"In a roundabout way." She reached a door at the bottom of the stairs and handed him the torch. "The trick was getting this key."

The torchlight flashed on the piece of bronze metal as she inserted it into the lock. A click echoed through the staircase, followed by the groan of seldom-used hinges.

Izana grinned. "Behold—our own private gallery of Alpirion art."

Modius stepped forward, not knowing what to expect. A blast of cold, musty air hit his face. Shadows bathed the walls, elongated by the torch's fire before disappearing into the blackness beyond the light's reach. As best as he could tell, the underground chamber stretched the length of the entire library.

Izana found another torch and lit it from his, adding to the light and revealing more of the room's treasures.

His jaw dropped. The scene that appeared exceeded his expectations. Statues filled the center of the room like a crowded marketplace, and hundreds of paintings lined the walls. "I have no idea where to start."

"I suggest starting from the beginning and working our way down the room." She took a sheet of paper from him and drew a set of pictures. "These are the glyphs for the moon lily. If you find those, let me know."

In a strange role reversal, she was now the expert, and he was the assistant. He followed her down the aisle, holding the paper in his hand while scanning the columns of symbols surrounding portraits of ancient rulers. The paintings were on slabs of clay bricks, many of them broken along the edges as through they'd been ripped from the walls. Some of them depicted landscapes of the blue sand desert juxtaposed against the fertile fields along the river. Others showed battle scenes, sparing none of the blood and gore that accompanied it. All were exquisitely done with precise lines and bold colors, so very different from the muted art preferred by the Deizians.

"Can you come here?" Izana asked, already halfway down the aisle. "I need a little more light, please."

The hitch in her voice hinted to excitement, and he hurried down to her. The painting that captured her interest showed an Alpirion king sitting on a throne. He was clad in white, contrasting from the rich mahogany tone of his skin. His head was shaven, and black kohl lined intense eyes that managed to intimidate Modius as though he were a living breathing man. Beside him, a priest poured oil on his head from a jar with a lily painted on it.

Izana knelt on the ground, her finger running down the columns of glyphs while her lips silently moved.

He knelt beside her and held his torch near the painting. "What does it say?"

"It's describing the coronation of King Nemetsaf II." Her finger stilled over a picture of a flower. "See, here it mentions him being anointed with the oil of the moon lily."

His pulse quickened. The oil could be the means by which just the emperor was poisoned, either through ingestion or through contact with his skin. He leaned closer to Izana, catching a whiff of the sweet honey scent that rose from her hair. "Anything else?"

She reached the end of the glyphs and sighed. "No. Just what we already knew."

Her disappointment leeched into him, and he reached out to comfort her, drawing her into his arms. "Don't give up hope yet. We've only just started."

"I know. But I can't help but feel we're so close that

anything less that the answer feels unsatisfying."

From where he held her, his gaze fell from her profile to the mark on her neck. The scarred brand of the imperial family rose from her skin in a pale, twisted ridge, almost completely covering the tattoo hidden beneath it. He touched it with his finger.

Izana flinched, sucking in a breath through her teeth like he'd stung her, and pulled away.

He rose and followed her. "Does it still pain you?"

"What?"

"The burn."

She shook her head, refusing to look at him.

"Then why did you act like it did?"

"It just surprised me—that's all." But she pulled her hair over her shoulder, covering the mark.

He'd stumbled onto yet another of her secrets, and he wasn't about to let her go now. "Is there a reason why you asked to be branded in such a delicate place?"

She nodded, but didn't provide any other information.

He ground his teeth together. The woman was as stubborn and guarded as his father. She wouldn't tell him anything until she was ready to. He tried changing the subject. "Have you ever thought about asking your mistress for your freedom?"

She started, finally turning to him. "Why?"

"Why not? You're a talented woman, and your knowledge is being wasted on simply attending your mistress."

"There's nothing simple about my duties. I have a position in the household most slaves long for."

"Perhaps, but if you were free, you wouldn't have to worry about being punished for being able to read and write."

"No, I wouldn't, but I'd inherit a whole other set of problems." She resumed walking, holding her torch up as she read the glyphs.

"Such as?" He'd assumed most slaves would jump at a chance for freedom, but her elusive answers intrigued him. Did she fear punishment for saying she'd like to be free? Or was there more to her desire to remain a slave?

"As a slave of the imperial household, I'm offered a great deal of protection. Very few people would harm me once they saw my brand."

"Is that the reason you chose to put it on your neck?"

Her silence told him there more to it than that.

"Then what are some of the problems you think you'd face if you were free?"

"I'm surprised someone as intelligent as you would be asking that." She ran her hand over the lock of hair that covered her mark. "But then, you're a man. You probably have no idea how different things are for women."

"Enlighten me."

She twirled a curl around her finger, staring at the scene of two Alpirion lovers in front of her. "If I were a man, I could learn a trade, seek gainful employment. But as a woman, there are little opportunities for us. Either we marry," her voice caught, shaking as she added, "or we go into the one form of employment available to us."

She didn't have to elaborate. He'd seen the Alpirion women who lined the streets outside the *lupanars*, soliciting customers.

"I've known women who chose to be sold back into slavery rather than face that, hoping that their new masters wouldn't use them in that way," she continued, setting her torch into the holder beside the painting.

He tilted her chin so she faced him. The fear and longing shining from her dark eyes struck him squarely in the center of his chest, leaving behind an ache he couldn't identify. "And you assume it would be that way for you?"

"How can I not?"

"Maybe because you're different from the other slaves. You're clever, resourceful." But no matter how he tried to overlook it, he couldn't ignore the fact she was beautiful enough to attract her share of male attention. Even now, his blood warmed, and his body desired the press of her soft curves against him.

She gave him a wan smile as though she knew his thoughts. "I may be clever, but I'm still a fool when it comes to some things." She leaned in and brushed her lips against his.

The walls holding up his self-control crumbled. He dropped his torch to the stone floor, his hand finally free to pull her to him. She responded by deepening the kiss. Every slip of her tongue stripped him of his defenses. Every soft moan that rose from her throat intensified the need rising in his cock. Every sway of her hips left him wanting to rip his clothes off and make love to her, surrounded by the exotic remnants from her ancestors' homeland.

In his years as a man, he'd been surrounded by attractive women, but none of them awakened the same level of mind-numbing lust that Izana did. He didn't want to think when he was around her. He wanted to feel, to taste, to smell, to completely drown himself in her.

His lungs heaved before he finally ended the kiss. "Should I stop?"

Izana trembled in his arms, her fingers grazing his jaw as she looked at him. "No."

"Good, because I don't know if I could after you kissed me that way." He leaned in to taste the sweetness of her mouth again, only to have her stiffen.

She pressed her finger against his lips and stared past him at the door.

At first, the muffled sounds seemed like a hallucination from his lust-fogged mind, but after a few seconds, he heard voices.

Izana cursed and threw her torch from its holder onto the ground, stomping out the flames with her sandals. She pointed to where his lay a few feet away. "Put it out before they find us."

He followed her command, plunging the room back into darkness. He reached for her again, his desire doused as quickly as the flames of their torches, and pulled her into the crowd of statues.

The door creaked open, and a light flickered in the distance. Two silhouettes filled the doorway, their gruff voices breaking the silence.

Modius's pulse jumped, and he pushed Izana behind him, hiding her deeper into the shadows cast by the sandstone and granite gods who peered down at them. His muscles tensed. For the first time in years, he missed the calming weight of a gladius hanging from his belt. The short sword would've come in handy if the men decided to attack.

The men came closer, their words clearer now. Whatever language they were speaking, it wasn't the common language accepted by the empire.

The light from their torches came close enough to illuminate the spot where he hid. Sweat prickled his skin. He pulled Izana to the other side of a lyger-headed deity and shielded her with his body, his eyes never leaving the intruders. Her breath hitched, the only sound he'd heard from her since she'd ordered him to put out his torch.

The men were close enough now for him to see their features. They were free Alpirions, the firelight glinting off the gold jewelry they wore to proclaim their status. One of the men had a glyph tattooed on the inside of his bicep. They murmured back and forth to each other as they peered into the spaces between the paintings and statues, their words menacing even though he couldn't understand them.

As soon as they passed them, Modius took Izana's hand pulled her in the opposite direction. She yanked back and shook her head, her eyes wide with panic. Again, she pressed her finger to his lips and grew as still as the statues around them.

The Alpirions circled back along the other aisle, speaking less and moving quicker than before. The tension eased from his muscles as he watched them open the door and slam it shut behind them.

Then the click of a lock followed, and his gut clenched.

"Don't worry," Izana whispered. "I still have the key." She pressed it into his hand to prove her point.

"What were they saying?"

"They were looking for us."

"Why?"

She slipped away from him, taking the key with her. "Do you have flint handy so we can relight our torches?"

Changing the subject, as usual. "No, but I know another way to produce a flame."

He pulled the leather laces from one of his sandals and wrapped it around his pen. Then, after fumbling in the dark for one of the torches, he pressed the tip of the pen into the oiled clothes and pulled the leather from side to side. The pen twirled in a blur against the cloths, the heat from the resulting friction igniting a flame.

Izana crouched beside him, the fire highlighting the smile on her face. "And I thought I was the clever one."

"Now are you going to tell me why they were looking for us?"

The smile fell from her lips. "No one's supposed to know about this place."

"And we're trespassing?"

"In a way." She found her torch and lit it from his. "We need to hurry, though. They might return."

"Then why did you pull me back when I tried to get you out earlier?"

"Because there was a third man waiting on the other side of the door."

Was that what made her breath catch? Or was it something else? "If you knew they were Alpirion, why didn't you just speak to them in your language? Why hide from them?"

"Because they were specifically looking for me." Everything in her body was tight with fear, and her voice wobbled as she continued, "Apparently, I've been asking too many questions, and they weren't happy about it."

"What kind of questions have you been asking?"

"I've already told you." She continued down the row of paintings, her attention on the glyphs that surrounded the art. "I asked about this, I asked one of the library slaves about where the art was hidden."

"You think there was something here they didn't want you to know."

"Precisely, which is why we need to keep searching for information on the moon lily." After a few minutes of strolling down the aisles, she added, "I asked about you, too, you know, but that got me nowhere."

"Why were you asking about me?"

"You may have trouble trusting me because I have a few secrets, but you're just as much a mystery to me. What would prompt a soldier to become a steward, especially when he's still very fit for duty?"

His spit dried up. "And what did you hear from those gossiping slaves?"

"Nothing." She kicked a pebbled across the floor. "It seems the slaves are just as protective of your family as they are of the imperial family, maybe more."

He released the breath he'd been holding. So she hadn't learned of his downfall and the reason behind his exile. He fought to keep the relief from seeping into his voice as he asked, "Do you trust me, Izana?"

She turned and stared at him, the torch creating a mask of shadows across her face. "I suppose I'll have to." She took a step toward him, her words forming a hard edge, "But don't ask about my past unless you're willing to share your own."

12

Izana's stomach rumbled. The underground chamber hid the sun's passage across the sky from her, but it had to be well past midday. She hadn't eaten anything since last night, and now hunger and fatigue weighed upon her body.

She glanced through the statues at Modius. After he had agreed not to delve into her past, he wandered off to the other side of the chamber, saying they could move through the collection more quickly if they split up, and then adding under his breath something about him being unable to think clearly around her.

He wasn't the only one. She'd seen the flare of desire in enough men's eyes to recognize when it entered his. Despite his praise of her intellect, he still saw her as woman he wanted in his bed. And she was stupid enough to give into her own desires and kiss him again.

Perhaps old habits die hard. Her years as a *lupa* had taught her recognize those subtle signs of lust. The dilated pupils. The slight flare in the nostrils. The licking of the lips. The barely contained tremor in the hands. The more obvious rising bulge beneath the tunic. When she'd seen those signs in a prospective client, she knew he was ready to reel in. A few kisses later, and he'd be willing to pay whatever price she'd set.

But with Modius, it was different. She no longer was the

lupa who slept with a different man every night to keep her mistress happy. This wasn't about survival. It was about the confusing swirl of emotions that plagued her every time she got within arm's reach of him. And even though sex with him left her melting in a post-orgasmic glow, she feared her feelings for him went beyond purely physical.

A silly fantasy had danced through her mind when he asked about her freedom. For the briefest of moments, she'd wondered if he'd ask her to come with him if she were free. But the mark on her neck still stung from where he touched it as though he'd re-branded her all over again. He thought of her as some overly-educated lady's maid. Would he still hold her in the same high esteem if he knew what she'd been before she came to the palace?

She returned to the sections of the mural in front of her. She'd have time to sort out her feelings for him later. Right now, she needed to find out all she could about the moon lily.

"Izana," Modius called from the other side of the chamber, "come here."

She cut through the statues to where he stood. "Did you find the glyphs I showed you?"

"No, but this is interesting." He pointed to the painting of a woman who bore a chilling resemblance to Lady Azurha.

"A *wa'ai*." The Alpirion word for the cursed ones fell from her lips before she could catch herself.

Like her mistress, the lady in the painting had glowing blue-green eyes the color of the rivers that flowed through the desert. She was dressed in black and wore a silver crown with a crescent moon on her forehead. Her dark hair fanned about behind her as though blown by a gust of wind. Lightning flashed across the cloudless sky behind her, and the light of the full moon reflected in her pupils. She rose from the water, surrounded by pearly lilies, and seemed to be coming right toward them.

"At first, I thought it was Lady Azurha, but then I remembered you saying this chamber had been filled years ago."

She nodded and leaned closer to the painting, noting the fine cracks that covered the surface and the blanket of dust that dulled the bright colors. "The *wa'ai* are creatures of legend, the cursed ones."

"Why are they cursed?"

"I never asked why, even though I serve one."

"Why?"

"Because I was scared to know too much." She blew off some of the dust to take a closer look at the lilies. "I think these might be moon lilies, though."

He handed her his pen and sheet of paper. "Time to put those drawing skills to use."

She made a quick sketch of the flower before examining the glyphs around the painting. Part of them had been broken away, but she picked up where she could. They spoke of a princess who'd been spurned by her lover after she saved his life, a woman whose father was murdered by the same lover, a *wa'ai* who, in the end, killed her lover to save her people.

Modius closed the space between them. "I don't like that look on your face."

"I think this might be Princess Ausetsut." She pointed to the glyphs at the beginning of the story. "It says here she fell in love with a Prince of the Sun and saved him from a poison."

"How?"

"I don't know. The part with that information broke off here." A little voice in the back of her mind whispered that it not be a coincidence. Much like the scroll she'd found yesterday, the information she'd sought was missing. "But it says here the Sun Prince killed her father in battle, and after many years of war, she ended it by destroying the man she loved."

"I think I know why she was called cursed."

Izana crossed the painting to read the glyphs on the other side, finding the cartouche that named the woman in the painting. "I was right—this is Ausetsut."

"It makes me wonder if Lady Azurha is a descendant of hers."

She studied the ill-fated princess's face, noting the differences between it and her mistress's. The face was rounder, the eyes closer together, the mouth wider. The only thing they had in common was the eye color.

But then, that was the one defining feature of a *wa'ai*.

"I doubt it. I don't think Ausetsut ever had children." She cast one more glance at the woman in the painting, seeing the power radiating from her and understanding why the mention of the *wa'ai* had terrified her as a child. "Now we have an idea what the moon lilies look like. Maybe we can find some more information on their location if we keep looking."

She continued down the row, but Modius stood in front of the painting for what felt like another ten minutes before he turned and went in the opposite direction.

Her thoughts eventually returned to her mistress and the legend of the *wa'ai*. Would Lady Azurha suffer the same fate as Princess Ausetsut? She offered a silent prayer to the gods that her mistress would be spared the grief of losing her loved ones, and if she could help ensure that, she would gladly play her part.

Izana reached the end of the row but found nothing. Her stomach twisted in on itself from hunger, and her head swam from the hours of squinting at half-faded glyphs. Perhaps she'd been wrong to assume she'd find answers down here. All she'd managed to do was anger some freed Alpirions and reveal more forbidden information to Modius.

She leaned back against one of the statues to take some weight off of her aching feet, but instead of hitting solid stone, it slid out behind her. Her head connected with the granite elbow of some long-forgotten king, and cry of pain broke free from her lips. Jaw-clenching shocks reverberated through her body. The torch fell from her hand and died in a cloud of dust, adding the blackness that was already swimming in front of her eyes.

Then, just as her sense were coming around, a pair of strong hands wrapped around her and pulled her from the ground. "Izana, are you hurt?"

She waited until the ringing in her ears subsided before

shaking her head. "Just a bit surprised, that's all."

"Did you trip?"

"No, I could've sworn the statue moved." And yet, the king beside her looked as solid as he had before she tried reclining against him. "Maybe I did stumble."

"No, I think you're right about him moving. Look." Modius pointed to an opening in the statue's base and held his torch over it. "It looks like there's something in there."

"Help me open it a bit wider."

They both pressed their weight against the statue. The sound of stone scraping against stone filled the chamber, and the opening widened enough for her to reach in and feel around. Her hand grasped a roll of papyrus. "Scrolls."

"Let's see them." Modius wedged his torch between the chest and arm of another statue and took the scrolls she pulled from the compartment. He broke the seal on one and opened it up to reveal rows of glyphs. "You translate—I'll keep searching in there."

She held the scroll up to the light, taking care to keep the delicate papyrus from the heat of the flames. Her blood chilled as she read the first few columns. "These are spells reserved for the high priests."

"What do they say?"

She shook her head and rolled up the scroll. "I dare not read them aloud."

A look of exasperation crossed his face as though he were dealing with a child who was convinced there was a demon living under her bed. He handed her another scroll. "Then take a look at this one."

Both it and the next scroll were more spells and incantations reserved for the most holy of men. She rolled them back up with care and set them aside, eyeing them as though they were poisonous snakes poised to strike.

The third scroll he handed her was different. It wasn't sealed like the others, and the glyphs were more crudely drawn than the spell scrolls. Her pulse quickened when she spotted the glyphs for the moon lilies. "I think we found something."

Modius peered over her shoulder, the heat from his body making her heart race for a different reason. "What?"

She pointed to the glyphs. "It's a recipe for extracting the oil."

"Good. We're taking this with us." He reached around her and started to roll it up, but she wrenched it free from him.

"No, we can't take it or any of the other scrolls from here. There's a reason why they were hidden, and if this flower truly is poisonous to Deizians, we don't want this information falling into the wrong hands."

"But how am I to test that theory if I don't know how to make the oil?" He reached for the scroll, but she turned away before he could touch it.

"I'll make notes for you if you promise to burn them when you're done."

His jaw hardened, but after a few seconds, he nodded.

"Give me some paper." She copied the glyphs from the scroll, leaving room for her translations. As she continued to unroll the papyrus, her heart stumbled to a thudding stop before racing again. "I think I found the location of a grove of moon lilies—or at least, where the high priests found them when this was written."

"Where?"

She pointed to the glyphs as she translated them. "It speaks of an oasis two days east of the palace with a waterfall, a small grotto, and a grove of date palms planted in the shape of the glyphs for 'king' and 'blessing.'"

"I bet we'd be able to easily spot it from an airship." Modius grinned like a child about to embark on a treasure hunt.

"But you're forgetting that Emperor Livinius changed the desert when he conquered the Alpirions," she reminded him, referring to the way the emperor had called upon the ore buried beneath the sands and used it to swallow up the Alpirion army. "The grove may not be there anymore."

"We won't know unless we go there ourselves." He took

the paper from her hands. "Let's take this to Lady Azurha and see what she thinks."

Izana gave a slow nod, a heavy stone of apprehension sitting in the center of her stomach, and placed the spell scrolls back into the compartment. "Can you help me move the statue back into place?"

Modius rolled his eyes, but helped her shimmy the granite king back to the center of the base, closing the compartment. "I'll have to remember this statue in case we need to come back one day."

"You can try, but I'd advise against it."

"Are you letting a silly superstition control your actions?"

She pointed to the painting of Princess Ausetsut. "Does she look like a silly superstition? The magic of the Alpirions may not be as obvious as the Deizians, but it is old and it is powerful. It's not something to be toyed with."

"And what if there's no magic?"

"There has to be. How else would you explain how the Alpirions survived the Barbarians all those centuries without being under the protection of the barrier?"

He opened his mouth to answer, then shut it. "Point taken."

She folded up her paper notes and slid them into the bodice of her dress. "But I agree with you—let's take this to Lady Azurha and see what she has to say."

Modius grabbed his torch and led the way to the door. The key worked as well as it had before, and once they were in the stairwell, Izana took care to lock the chamber again. She'd promised the library slave that she would keep its secrets safe with the exception of what her mistress required, and she intended to keep that promise. They left the torch in the holder by the exit and pushed the panel concealed by the shelves open.

Izana stepped into the library first, only to be greeted by the sting of a cold blade against her throat.

13

Modius's heart jumped into his throat as Izana was yanked from the opening of the stairwell. A pair of hands reached in for him, but he stepped back far enough from their grasp, his mind racing to form a plan.

It had to be the Alpirions who'd been looking for them. No one else knew they were there. And he'd been stupid not to think that they would be up there waiting for them.

A tight yip of fear came from the other side of the bookcase, and a rush of anger replaced his fear. They had Izana, and based on what she'd shared with him, they were out to punish her.

He bolted up the stairs and threw all his weight against the panel. The shelves connected with a body, followed by a grunt of pain, but Modius kept moving forward. The late-afternoon sun filled the library with an amber glow, but his eyes still found it too bright after the darkness of the underground chamber.

The pause gave his attacker the time he needed to recover. A fist connected with the underside of Modius's ribs, driving the air from his lungs in a bone-jarring whoosh. He fell to his hands and knees, Izana's voice fading into the distance.

A swift kick to his gut lifted him off the ground and landed him flat on his back. The metallic taste of blood filled his mouth. His vision swam, clearing just in time to see the Alpirion with the tattoo on the inside of his arm coming toward him.

Instincts developed from his years as a solider kicked in. Modius rolled to the side. His attacker fell forward, carried from the momentum of his attempted blow, and smashed his fist into the marble tiles of the floor. Modius jumped to his feet, ignoring the sharp pain in his chest, and locked his arm under his attacker's chin. Ever so slowly, he increased pressure against the Alpirion's windpipe and spun him around to his comrade holding Izana. "What do you want with us?" he asked in a snarl.

The other Alpirion grinned, his blade still resting against Izana's throat. "You and your companion were someplace you don't belong."

Izana gasped, her eyes widening, and trickle of blood ran down her neck.

Modius responded by tightening his chokehold on his attacker. "What are hiding?"

"That's none of your business." His cold smile showed no hint of mercy. "Of course, that won't save her from the punishment she deserves."

"For what?" Modius asked, ignoring the wheezes coming from his prisoner and the bluish tinge of his lips.

"She knows what she's done." He bent over and murmured something in Alpirion to Izana.

She kept her face blank, her eyes pleaded with him for help.

A new wave of rage enveloped him, more intense than the one before. If that bastard laid one hand on her…

The man in his hold crumpled, and Modius threw him at the Alpirion holding Izana. Time slowed. He caught a glimpse of understanding in Izana's eyes as the unconscious man lurched forward. Her attacker loosened his grip and stepped back. She twisted to the side and out of his grasp a split second before the other man collided with them. Modius held out his hand for her, his fingertips catching the inside of her wrist. He wrapped his hand around her arm and pulled.

The next thing he knew, she was in his arms, and their attackers were in a heap on the floor. Scrolls rained down on them from the shelves above. Part of him wanted to demand more answers, but Izana was already sprinting toward the door, taking him with her. They raced through the rooms of the library, past the shocked scholars in the halls, and into the crowded streets of Emona.

Modius lasted another two blocks before the stabbing pain in his ribs forced him to stop. He pulled her into an alleyway and leaned forward, gulping in the humid air. "Why do I have the feeling these men are connected to the emperor's death?"

"As much as I hate to think an Alpirion was behind it, I have little choice but to agree with you." She wiped her hand along her neck, and her palm came away smeared with blood. "They would've readily killed us in the middle of the library."

"Which, of course, would mean their death. Too many witnesses." He straightened and twist to the side, discovering new sore spots. Tears stung his eyes. "Damn, that guy hit hard."

Izana pressed her hand against the bruised ribs and applied just enough pressure to ease the pain. "You should see a healer about this."

"I am a healer." He took a deep breath and exhaled slowly, focusing on something other than the protests from his battered body. "I'll wrap them when we get back to the palace."

Then he finally took the time to examine her. A thin red line marred the elegant planes of her throat, but the bleeding had stopped. "Any other injuries?"

She shook her head. "I just want to get back to the palace. Lady Azurha needs to know about this."

After a few minutes, he finally felt strong enough to venture back out into the streets. Unlike before, Izana stayed by his side, her arm around his waist as she steered him through the river of people. Her presence steadied him and allowed him to push past the pain, step by agonizing step.

When the palace gates came into view, she said, "I don't know the reason why you left the army, but today, I was thankful for your combat knowledge."

"You and me both." He paused before adding, "All I could think about was getting you away from that bastard."

She gave him a bitter laugh. "You should watch what you say, Modius. I'm beginning to think you might actually care about me."

He stopped and looked down at her, his chest throbbing from something other than pain. In just a few days, she'd gone from a stranger to someone he was willing to risk his life to save. He didn't know how or why. He just knew with every beat of his heart that he'd do it all over again, if necessary.

He laced his fingers through her other hand, noting how she'd supported him all the way back despite the laws that dictated she walk behind him. "I could say the same for you."

She smiled and looked away, a flush of pink rising into her cheeks. "We'd better keep walking before someone runs us over."

Twice as many members of the Legion stood guard at the palace gates. When they recognized him and Izana, they unlocked the gates and opened them just wide enough to let them squeeze through. They'd barely made it to the front door before his father appeared, worry adding to the wrinkles already creasing his face.

He came to his other side, supporting Modius the same way Izana did. "I heard of the attack in the library. I should've known it involved you."

"Glad to know you were worried about me, Father," Modius replied, not bothering to soften his sarcasm. "I take it that's the reason behind the increased security."

"Yes," his father paused and dropped his voice, "and no."

Izana leaned forward. "What else happened?"

"I'll let Lady Azurha explain. In the meantime, you two need to get cleaned up. You both look like you've been mauled by a group of common thugs."

Modius laughed and instantly regretted it. A new shock

of pain ripped through his chest, catching his breath and halting his stride.

Izana tightened her arm around his waist. "Please, Varro, I think he needs a healer."

Perhaps it was just a hallucination, but Modius could've sworn he saw a look of concern on his father's face. Varro nodded. "I'll send for one right away. You go to your room and clean up before meeting me outside the imperial chambers."

Izana released him, his weight now falling fully on his father, and took a hesitant step back. "Are you sure I can't help—"

"Do as you're told," his father ordered with the authority of a general.

Her face hardened, but she turned around and scurried off to one of the side buildings.

Modius straightened, not wanting to overwhelm his father's bad leg, and walked into the palace under his own strength. "You didn't have to be so rough with her."

"She's a slave, and she needs to remember her place."

"But you're missing one important detail—they were after her." He pushed his father aside, no longer wanting his assistance. "The Alpirions who attacked us wanted to punish her for helping me."

His father's lips thinned. "Then it seems this is far more complicated than I first assumed."

"Meaning?"

"I'll defer to Lady Azurha on that." He reached to support him again, but Modius avoided his outstretched arm. His father stiffened. "Very well, if you think you can make it back to your room on your own, I'll have a healer sent to you directly."

Varro turned on his good heel with military precision and limped down the hallway before disappearing around a corner.

***

Izana ran her finger along the fresh cut on her neck and frowned at her reflection in the cistern. There was no way to conceal that without looking like she was dressing above her station. She splashed the water, dissolving her image in a sea of ripples.

The hair on the back of her neck stood on end. A shadow moved along the colonnade, just on the edge of her peripheral vision. Someone was watching her, and the chill that ripped through her left no doubt in her mind as to who it was.

She stood and went directly toward Farros. "When you offered your warning this morning, did you run and tattle to your friends afterward?"

His face revealed nothing. "I have no idea what you're talking about, Izana."

"Then how do you explain this?" she said, pointing to the mark left behind by the knife.

He crossed his arms and cocked a brow. "I was merely trying to warn you to stay away from the Elymanian."

"Why?"

"Besides the fact I think you'd be better off with a member of your own race?" He didn't have to add "like me" for her to catch the meaning behind his explanation. "If I remember correctly, Varro's son left Emona under very unusual circumstances. You might want to inquire about them before something worse than this," he pressed a finger to her cut, "happens to you."

"Why don't you just tell me yourself?"

"If I did, would you believe me?" He chuckled and backed away. "Don't worry, little Izana, I'll be watching out for you."

She ran her hands over her arms, shivering despite the heat of the day. Once again, his words of concern unnerved her. She didn't dare look away from him. At last, he turned around and headed toward the stables.

The setting sun painted the clouds a fiery red, but she didn't have time to marvel at their beauty. The folded paper still hidden in her bodice scraped against her skin, reminding her of the information that had almost cost her and Modius their lives today. They had to be on the right path to attract this much attention.

Izana hurried through the corridors of the palace, her steps matching her pulse. Lady Azurha needed to know about this before someone else tried to silence the secrets of the past.

But when she reached the door leading to the imperial chambers, Varro prevented her from opening them. "This way, Izana. Lady Azurha prefers to meet with both you and Modius in the antechamber."

He steered her into the small room off the main throne room. Modius was already sitting in a chair, his face no longer tight with pain. He stood when she entered. "Do you still have our notes?"

She pulled the paper out of her bodice.

Varro's gaze flickered to it, disapproval glowing from his brown eyes. "I'll let Lady Azurha know you're here."

Izana lingered by the door after Varro left, Farros's warning still fresh in her mind.

Modius watched her from his chair, his brows drawing together in an unspoken question. When she didn't come closer, he crossed the room, his movements guarded. "How is your neck?"

Her hand flew to her cut. "Fine."

"Let me take a look at it."

"No, really—"

He cut her off by taking her hand and pulling it aside. His keen eyes assessed the wound for a moment before he nodded. "It shouldn't leave a scar so long as it doesn't get infected. If you cover it with honey, that should help."

She didn't miss the way he winced when he turned around. Her caution gave way to concern, and she stopped him by resting her hand on his shoulder. "Did you have a healer look at you?"

He nodded with a wry smile. "He didn't tell me anything I didn't already know. I've wrapped the ribs for now. Maybe tonight, I'll be able to drown the pain with some good wine."

"You mentioned earlier that you were a healer yourself. Is that why you left the army?"

He was in the process of sitting when he asked her question and froze, his bottom hovering inches above the seat of the chair. "I thought we had an agreement not to delve into each other's pasts."

She rubbed her brand before covering it up with her hair. "Yes, I suppose we do."

That did little to ease her mind after Farros's warning.

Modius eased into the chair and poured a glass of wine. "Would you care for some?"

She shook her head. After today, she'd be seeing enemies out of every shadow. She couldn't afford to have her senses dulled by wine. "I'm sorry I couldn't warn you in time about those men."

"You gave me enough warning. I just wish I hadn't let that first one get the first punch on me." He took a long drink from his cup. "What has me more worried is the fact the Legion is on edge. Something else must have happened."

"Something else did happen," Azurha said behind her. She brushed past Izana and went straight for her chair, waving off Modius when he tried to stand. "You father told me of your injuries. I'll have one of the Deizian healers tend to you when we're done."

He blinked several times. "You mean you'd have one of them use their magic on someone as insignificant as me, my lady?"

"I need you both in good health." She sat, her sharp teal eyes going from Modius to her. "Tell me what happened in the library today."

"Do you mean with the attack?" Izana asked.

"I mean from the beginning. The report I got was that two freed Alpirions attacked you. By the time the city guard cornered them, however, they'd both decided to take their lives. Do either of you know why?"

"'There is freedom in death, even for traitors.'" The

words fell from her lips as she remembered what the Alpirion had whispered in her ear during the standoff.

Azurha pressed her index fingers to her lips, her hands folded together, and stared past them. A moment later, she straightened and said, "Start from when you left this morning."

Between her and Modius, they described the discovery of the hidden chamber and the different artifacts it contained. Neither one of them mentioned the painting of the *wa'ai* to Azurha, even though they both exchanged glances when they came to that point in their stories. When Modius was telling her about the two Alpirion men who came down into the chamber looking for them, he noted one of them had a tattoo of a glyph along his arm.

A prickle of sweat formed at the base of Izana's spine. "Can you describe the mark to me?"

Her mistress raised a brow, and Izana cursed her own stupidity. But then, as their story continued, she would eventually have to admit that she could read the glyphs. She just hoped her mistress would be understanding and shield her from the law.

Modius held out his hand. "Let me draw it for you."

She handed him the paper with her notes and peered over his shoulder as he drew a feather. "That's the glyph for 'freedom'."

Azurha's expression darkened, and Izana's throat tightened. But instead of being irate at learning about her forbidden knowledge, her mistress seemed more focused on the attack. "Then I was correct in assuming this was connected to the news we received this afternoon. A small patrol of the Imperial Army was attacked in southern Alpiria by a group of freed slaves. One man lived long enough to pass on the message the group had for the emperor."

Modius stilled, his attention fixed on the future empress. "Which was?"

"There is freedom in death."

Izana's breath caught. "My lady, do you think this is a start of a slave rebellion?"

"I pray to the gods it's not. The emperor has plans for freeing the slaves, but if these Alpirions rise up and trigger a revolt, he'll have a hard finding support from the nobility."

A deep voice came from the door leading to the imperial chambers. "I'm more curious about what the collection of Alpirion art has to do with the massacre."

Emperor Sergius came into the room and crossed his arms, his stance demanding answers.

Izana's feet itched to flee, but the rest of her body was held prisoner by the emperor's hard glare. She looked to Modius, hoping he'd offer an explanation that wouldn't reveal her crimes, but he was too occupied with trying to bow without causing more injury to his ribs.

Instead, it was her mistress who spoke first. "I think Modius and Izana have stumbled across something they didn't want anyone to know about."

The emperor's expression hardened. "Which is?"

"I'll explain more in private." Azurha lifted her chin, every inch an empress even though her wedding and coronation were over a week away. "In the meantime, I'd like a Deizian healer to tend to Modius, and I think it best that Modius and Izana complete their research in Alpiria as soon as possible."

The emperor nodded. "I've already sent for Marcus. They can go with him."

Her mistress stood and dropped into a brief curtsy. "Thank you, Your Imperial Majesty."

Then she turned to them. "Modius, I'll send a proper healer to you. Go and collect your things in the meantime. Izana, I'd like to speak to you in my chambers when I'm done with the emperor." She took Emperor Sergius's arm and returned to the imperial quarters.

Izana's stomach added an extra knot to the painful twists already present in her gut, and she wrapped her arms around her midsection. Her mistress knew she could read glyphs, and she only assumed the discussion would revolve around that.

A warm hand caressed her shoulder. "Don't worry,

Izana," Modius said low by her ear. "She wouldn't be sending you with me to Alpiria if she wanted to punish you."

"How is it that you know my thoughts?"

A half-smile played on his lips as he stroked her cheek. "You're pretty easy to read at times. Remember, it's your knowledge that's opened this mystery up. Without you, we'd all be lost."

His words eased the tension mounting inside, and she allowed herself a moment to lean into him. "And now it's more important than ever that we see this through."

14

Azurha waited until they were alone before she spoke. "I'm sure you've heard the expression that no good ever came from eavesdropping."

"I have, but I was a bit concerned when I learned a member of my household was attacked in the library." Titus unwound her arm from his and turned to face her. "Why were they down there?"

"They were researching something for me."

"What are you trying to hide from me, Azurha?" The tone of his voice left no room for arguments.

She sighed and reclined back on the sofa. "It was supposed to be my wedding gift to you."

He arched a brow. "The art?"

She shook her head, debating on whether or not this was the right time to tell him the truth.

"Azurha, I thought I made it clear that I don't want any secrets between us." He crossed the space between them and stood over her. "What are they researching that almost got them killed today?"

"I've long suspected that your father was poisoned, although it was not by any poison I am familiar with. I asked Modius and Izana to look into the matter, and it seems they've discovered an Alpirion plant that produced the same type of illness in one of your ancestors."

His face paled with disbelief, and he sank on the edge of the sofa. "Are you certain?"

"No, but the attack today only strengthens my suspicions."

He rubbed his cheeks, but the color didn't return to them. "But how? How could someone poison my father?"

"I've already proven to you how easy it was for an assassin to slip into the imperial quarters."

"Yes, but my father fell ill before you came to Emona. Furthermore, why would anyone want him dead?"

Azurha replayed the initial conversation she'd had with Pontus when he'd hired her for the job. "I remember Pontus mentioning that your father was ill and wouldn't last a fortnight, but he never revealed if he knew about the poison or who was behind it. The why is also a mystery."

Titus sat in stunned silence, his elbows on his knees and his hands clasped in front of him. When he finally spoke, his voice cracked with grief. "Tell me everything you know."

She shared how Modius and Izana had stumbled across the story of how the emperor and his son were struck with the same illness while visiting Alpiria. "They seem to think it was due to a plant called the moon lily, which only sickens Deizians. Today, they were looking for information about it in the artwork."

"And did they find anything?"

"They now have an idea what it looks like and where a grove might be in Alpiria."

He straightened, his face still too pale for her liking. "Then I agree with your plan to send them there right away. If they can find a specimen and test their theory…" His voice trailed off as though he wasn't quite ready to acknowledge that his father had been murdered.

Azurha reached out for him, pulling his head against her breasts. "Once we know the how, we can figure out the who and why. And then, I promise, I'll make them pay."

As the vow fell from her lips, a strange sensation formed in her chest, surging through her body like a rushing river overflowing its banks after the spring thaw. She'd do anything for Titus, even exact revenge on his enemies, one by one. Violence was nothing new to her. The blood stains on her hands were more familiar and comforting than the jewels that hung from her neck. He wanted her to be his empress, but inside, she would always be a killer.

The locks on the door clicked, and Marcus entered the room, followed by the Captain of the Legion, Galerius. Titus rose from the couch, leaving behind a brief warm spot where his head had rested so close to her heart.

"You sent for us," Marcus asked, his mirth at odds with the news they'd received today.

Titus crossed the room to his desk, where a map of the empire lay stretched over the entire surface. "A group of soldiers was attacked here, just east of Silbus, by a group of freed slaves."

Galerius's eyes flickered to her, hostility glowing from their grey depths. "I've posted more men on the perimeter with instructions to pay close attention to any Alpirion that approaches the palace."

"The enemy may already be within our walls," she said, joining the men at the desk. She drew the symbol Modius had shown her. "One of the men who attacked my maid at the library bore this mark. It's the Alpirion glyph for freedom. Any person bearing that mark should raise our suspicion."

Galerius took the paper, mistrust still guarding his movements even though she'd joined his brotherhood of imperial guardians. "I'll pass this around to the men and tell them to be on the lookout for it. I'll also order a search of all the slaves."

"And I suppose you want me to sniff out any information I can find on this group of rebellious Alpirions." Marcus rubbed his beard. "Of course, if I had access to your ship, I could get there in half the time."

"You can take it, but on one condition. Azurha has some

121

guests she'd like you to take down there with you."

"Oh?" A quirk of curiosity rose in Marcus's voice.

"My maid, Izana, and Modius Varro. They are looking for a particular plant that is native to Alpiria."

"Looking for something for your wedding bouquet?" he asked, grinning.

She exchanged a glance with Titus, who nodded, giving her permission to share her knowledge with them. "No, I think this plant was used to poison Emperor Decius."

Galerius's jaw clenched, and a low rumble of anger laced his words. "Are you saying that an emperor was murdered under my watch?"

She met his gaze, never flinching. "I am."

His hands curled into fists, but he didn't reach for the sword that hung from his belt. "On what grounds?"

"On the grounds that there was a similar incident nearly a century ago, and if Modius proves his theory is correct, then we need to be looking for a traitor in our midst."

Marcus broke the tension with a low whistle. "That's a pretty heavy accusation, Azurha."

"But if anyone would know poisons and murder, it's her." Galerius continued to stare her down. "I'll check with Varro and review any and everyone who's had access to the emperor in the last year, starting with your maid."

"You think Izana had something to do with this?"

"You don't?" He took a step toward her. "Don't you think it's odd that she just happened to stumble upon where the Alpirion art was hidden in the library, only to be attacked when she was leaving? And without sustaining any injuries?"

Marcus grabbed the captain's arm and pulled him back. "I can vouch for Izana. After all, I was the one who recommended her to Empress Horatia."

But a seed of doubt had already taken root in the corner of Azurha's mind. Was Izana somehow involved with this? A wave of guilt washed over her for thinking that. Her maid had been nothing but loyal, even after her command to assist Modius had nearly cost Izana her life.

She steeled her voice, not wanting Galerius to pick up on her uncertainty. "If Izana was somehow involved in either of these events, then why would she be the one assisting Modius in finding the answers?"

"A double-cross?"

"Enough!" Titus's voice boomed through the chamber, and Galerius finally lowered his eyes. "Right now, we have so many unanswered questions, we can't begin to start pointing fingers. Galerius, meet with Varro like you suggested to see if you can come up with any suspects, and let your men know about the glyph. You have my permission to search any slave who might have had access to my father's food and drink. Marcus, my ship just completed repairs from that last attack, so please try to avoid any trouble on the way down to Alpiria. Find out all you can on that band of renegade Alpirions. I can't afford to have a slave rebellion days before my wedding."

Then he turned to her. "Azurha, I know are fond of Izana, but I need you to explore Galerius's accusations. If she's hiding something, we need to know about it.

"Now, everyone, please leave," he finished with a wave of his hand. "I need some time alone to digest all this."

Marcus and Galerius both bowed and retreated, but Azurha stayed where she was. Worry squeezed her heart. Titus's color still hadn't returned to normal, and his breath seemed too quick for her liking. She touched his cheek, expecting it to be feverish, but his skin was cool and clammy.

Titus took her hand and lowered it. "I'm fine."

"Are you?" The worry in her heart doubled. What if Titus had been poisoned? She searched for any signs of the wasting the others had described, but saw none, much to her relief. Perhaps he was still dealing with the shock of learning his father had been murdered.

He shook his head, his shoulders slumping. "No, but I can't afford to appear weak now. I meant what I said, though, about needing to be alone."

His rejection stung, but she gave him some space. "I'm sorry I upset you, Titus. I was just trying to give closure."

"I know, but..." He wiped the back of his hand against his brow. "Maybe a warm bath will clear my head. We'll talk more about this later."

He disappeared into his private baths, leaving her alone with the sea of thoughts churning in her mind. She might not be able to solve the mystery of the poison right now, but she could answer the questions surrounding Izana.

Her maid was waiting in her dressing chambers, her movements skittish as Azurha entered. "You wished to speak to me, my lady?"

"Sit." She pointed to the chair across from her own and waited until they were both sitting before beginning her interrogation. "How much did you overhear?"

Izana looked away, her eyes fixed on the floor. "Enough, my lady."

"Galerius brought up a good point—why weren't you injured?"

"A small blessing." She tilted her chin to the side to reveal the thin red line stretching across her throat. "I owe Modius a great deal of gratitude for rescuing me before my attacker's blade bit deeper."

At least that disproved one accusation. Unfortunately, there were still plenty of other questions which remained unanswered, starting with her maid's knowledge of what the tattoo meant. "I need you to be honest with me, Izana. Can you read Alpirion glyphs?"

The slave's breath stilled, confirming her suspicion.

"You do not have to worry about punishment from me," Azurha continued, hoping to gain her maid's trust. "But before I send you to Alpiria, I need to know what skills you possess. Can you read them, or are you just familiar with the glyph used by a rebel group?"

"I can read them," she said in a small voice.

"And can you understand the Alpirion language?"

Izana's fingers blanched where she gripped the arms of the chair, but she lifted her eyes and gave slow nod.

"Then you are at an advantage over me and every other member of the emperor's trusted circle. For this reason, I'll do my best to shield you from anyone who wishes to harm you for your knowledge."

"Even though it's forbidden?"

Now it was her turn to give the slow nod. Izana's honesty smothered the last of her fears about her possible involvement with the emperor's death. "So far, you've been the key to unlocking this mystery, and I will continue to require your familiarity of the Alpirion language if we are to get to this bottom of this. But I ask you to continue to guard you talents. You may learn more if our enemies underestimate you."

Izana's mouth opened, then shut. She squirmed in her chair. "I suspect you'll be requiring me to do more than just help Modius find the moon lily."

"I need you to be my eyes and ears in Alpiria. Unlike Marcus, you're an Alpirion. If there are rebels around you, they may be more likely to confide in you or perhaps speak their native tongue in front of you. Any information you can provide will be essential to stopping the rebellion before it turns into something that condemns all the slaves."

The color returned to her fingers, but she didn't let go of the chair. "I understand, my lady."

Azurha hesitated, hating the idea that she was putting her maid into danger. "If you wish to remain here—"

"No, my lady. You're right—I am one of the few people who can help stop this. The man who held me spoke in Alpirion to me. If he's part of the group that attacked the soldiers, then there's a good chance the rest of them will use the language to communicate with each other." She stood and came toward Azurha, dropping to her knees in front of her chair. "Please, my lady, I want to help in any way I can, and I appreciate your offer of protection."

"I can do more than just protect you from the laws."

Azurha reached under her skirt, her fingers sliding over the familiar blade pressed against her thigh, and unfastened the straps. She held out the golden blade to Izana. "Here, take this with you. That way, if you find another knife at your throat, you can answer with one of your own."

Her maid's eyes widened. "My lady, I can't take this. It's yours." She pointed to the rabbit engraved on it. "It even has your mark."

"Then perhaps you'll be mistaken for me, and men will think twice about attacking you."

"Or they'll look at me as a target. Who wouldn't want the bragging rights for killing the Rabbit?"

Azurha laughed in spite of the fear in Izana's voice. "Then keep it hidden until it's needed, just like your knowledge of the Alpirion language."

Izana hugged the dagger to her chest, her eyes still filled with unease. "Yes, my lady."

"I know I've asked you to aid Modius, but now I also ask you to aid Marcus. Do you think you can do that?"

"Yes, my lady," she repeated.

"Good. Then before I let you go to gather your things for your trip to Alpiria, I have one more question for you. Can you think of anyone who might have poisoned Emperor Decius?"

Izana chewed her bottom lip, her gaze fixed on the floor again.

"Who are you trying to protect?"

"I—" She stopped, her hand twisting around the dagger's hilt. "I do not want to falsely accuse this person because of my personal feelings."

Although Izana's hesitation frustrated her, Azurha also had to admit she admired the slave's restraint. Far too many people were willing to point fingers to gain the emperor's favor or to deflect suspicion from themselves. "I can respect your decision for now, but please know I may be forced to press you for an answer if things worsen."

"I understand, my lady. When I return, I'll look into the matter and see what I can find."

"I would appreciate that." She stood and offered her hand to Izana. "For now, I do not wish to keep you any longer. Marcus seemed anxious to take the helm of the emperor's ship, and I do not want him to leave you behind."

Izana let the tips of her fingers rest on Azurha's palm, but did not use it to help her up to her feet. "Thank you, my lady, for everything."

Just before she got to the door, Azurha stopped her by saying, "Oh, and one more thing."

Izana spun around, her eyes wide. "Yes, my lady?"

"When you return, I'll require lessons from you on the Alpirion language. It's about time we remembered our past."

A shaky smile spread on her maid's lips. "Yes, my lady."

15

Modius added the last of his things into his pack and tightened the strap, reviewing its contents one more time. He'd included several changes of clothes, extra paper and ink, a small medicine kit, and a gladius from the Imperial Armory.

"Is there anything else you think you'll need?" his father asked behind him.

Modius jumped. For a man with a pronounced limp, his father moved with surprising silence. "I think I have everything."

Varro perused the pack. "You might be better served wearing the sword instead of stowing it away."

"You make it sound like I'm looking for trouble." But he pulled the gladius out and looped the scabbard around his belt.

"It sounds to me like you've already found it." He took a step forward and cleared his throat. "When I recommend your help Lady Azurha, I never imagined you'd find yourself in a situation like you did today."

Modius slung the pack over his shoulder. "You actually sound like you're worried about me."

"I am." His father blocked the doorway. "Just because we haven't seen things eye to eye—"

"We've never seen things eye to eye."

His father's jaw trembled, but he straightened to his full height, not backing down. "Be that as it may, you are still my son. And although I never understood your fascination with medicine in the past, I now believe the gods might have blessed you with it for this very situation, and I was wrong to have judged you so harshly. If you can find out who killed Emperor Decius, you will have my gratitude."

His father's words hit him like a blow to the gut, making it hard to even breathe. All these years, he'd thought his father had been ashamed of him. He'd known since he was a youth that he'd make a pitiful soldier. His interest had always lain in saving lives, not taking them, a curiosity his father had always attributed to cowardice. The scandal surrounding the dissections had been the dividing blow between them.

Now, as his father stood before him, acknowledging how that once-berated fascination might be a useful blessing, Modius's chest tightened. He'd finally gained the acceptance he'd longed for years ago, and yet, his tongue refused to form the words of the speech he'd prepared long ago when he'd dreamed of the day he'd prove his father wrong. Instead, all he managed to say was, "Thank you."

"Be careful out there, Modius. If they're bold enough to murder an emperor, you know they won't hesitate to kill you." Varro stepped aside to let him pass, but Modius didn't move.

He held out his hand. "I won't let you down, Father."

His father took it gingerly at first, then tightened his grip into a firm handshake. The wrinkles around his eyes gathered as the corners of his mouth rose. "You never have."

Modius let go of his father's hand, his throat uncharacteristically constricted, and headed for the ship before the welling emotions from his newfound acceptance got the better of him and spilled forth from his eyes.

Outside, he found Izana standing a few feet from the gangplank, her wide eyes fixed on the ore-coated airship that gleamed in the setting sun.

"Waiting for me?" he asked.

She started and turned around. "No—I mean, yes—I mean…" Her gaze returned to the ship. "I've never been on one these before."

He resisted the urge to laugh. "Never?"

She shook her head. "I've never even left Emona."

"Did you pack your things?" The meager bundle in her hand seemed almost inadequate for their mission, but she held it up to him as evidence. "Is there anything I can help you procure?"

"We're just going to find a flower, right?" She focused her attention on his gladius. "Unless you're expecting more trouble?"

"I always expect trouble," Marcus said from the deck. "It seems to follow me wherever I go."

Izana cracked a smile and made her way onto the ship. "That I can attest to."

Her ease with the emperor's best friend awakened a primitive streak of jealousy inside him. During his years in the palace, he'd observed how Marcus always had a way with the ladies. Modius followed close behind her, making it as clear as he possibly could without physically touching her that she was his.

His temper cooled when Izana asked, "Still chasing after my old mistress?"

"Yes, and if you happen to know the secret to winning Sexta's heart..."

Izana bit her bottom lip and shook her head, her dark eyes lit with laughter. "If I knew the secret to gaining her favor, she wouldn't have sold me."

"Ah, but you landed in a much nicer situation." Marcus's gaze flickered to him. "I understand you're now assisting Modius."

"She is," he answered, voice sharp. "Lady Azurha was quite wise to pair her with me."

Now it was Marcus's turn to hold back a laugh, or so it appeared. "And I should never question Azurha's wisdom. Shall I show you to your rooms?"

"One room will be fine," Izana replied, and the last of his irrational jealousy faded. She still wanted to be with him.

Marcus arched a brow, amusement still glowing from his blue eyes, and said, "Follow me, then."

As they went below deck, Izana played with her hair, bringing it forward to cover the mark on her neck. She inched closer to him when they passed a group of sailors who made no effort to hide their leers.

Modius placed his hand on the small of her back and glared at them until they turned away. As long as he breathed, no one would harm one hair on her head.

Once they were alone in the room, however, he let his hand fall. "If you wish to have your own room—"

She silenced him with a shake of her head, still smoothing that lock of hair over her neck. "No, it's safer for me to be here with you."

Her answer left him deflated. "Oh, so it was just for safety."

She blinked several times, took a step toward him, then backed away. "Modius, I—"

"There's no need to explain, Izana. I saw how those men were looking at you." It wasn't too different from the way he'd looked at her on the previous nights. Even though his mind told him he shouldn't desire her, especially after witnessing what had just transpired, he couldn't ignore the way her sweet scent of honey and saffron heated his blood or the way her luscious curves almost beckoned him to hold her close. By the gods, even the way she'd leaned into him earlier this afternoon after he'd eased her fears had been a struggle. He'd touched her lips, craving the taste of them, and had resisted the urge to kiss her. He could do it again.

"Do you want to go up on the deck and see what it's like to fly?" he asked, hoping she'd accept his distraction.

Her faced turned a shade lighter, and she sank along the wall, pulling her knees up to her chest. "No, I don't think I will. I'm scared enough to know I'm on an airship. I don't need to see the ground hundreds of feet below me to add to my terror."

"There's nothing to be afraid of. This is the emperor's

ship, after all, and Marcus is a fine captain."

"My head tells me that, but it does little to calm the fluttering in my stomach. But don't let that keep you down here if you'd like to go above. I'll be fine. You made it very clear to the men that I was with you."

She was dismissing him. And in truth, he appreciated it. He needed a moment to form a plan for when they landed in Alpiria without being distracted by her. He climbed up to the deck and found himself on the bridge a few minutes later.

Night had fallen, and the stars sparkled across the sky like the sun on the waves. The purple glow from the distant supernova dominated the view as they flew west, the warm wind ruffling his hair. Marcus stood at the helm, guiding the ship's movements with an ease that defied the speed at which they traveled.

Modius edged closer to him. "You knew Izana before she came to the palace?"

Marcus nodded. "I'm the one who recommended her to Empress Horatia."

"What can you tell me about her?"

The captain's mouth quirked into a half-grin. "If you're thinking you can pry information from me, you're mistaken. If Izana wants you to know something, she'll tell you. If not, then I'm not going to betray any of her secrets."

"That's the problem." He raked his fingers through his hair. "She has too many secrets."

"All women have secrets, Modius. You just have to be patient until they decide to share them with you." He stared out into the night sky. "But to answer your question, I've known her since she was nothing more than a mischievous little girl, and I can I tell you that she must trust you a great deal."

"What makes you say that?"

"Because the old Izana I knew would never willingly share a room with a man unless it was under certain circumstances. She must either trust you completely, or there's more to your relationship than her just being your assistant." The tone of his voice said he'd put money on the latter.

"If only it were that simple."

"Nothing is simple when it comes to women." Marcus pulled the wheel to the left, and the ship turned away from the setting sun, toward the south. "Speaking of secrets, does she know about yours?"

Modius shifted his weight from his heels to the balls of his feet. "I don't know."

"Meaning you haven't told her."

"I just assumed she'd know, just like everyone in Emona did once I was exposed."

Marcus chuckled. "You underestimate how far Emperor Decius went to quiet the rumors."

The ache of grief mingled with the sharpness of regret. "I still wonder why he went so far to protect me."

"Perhaps he did it as a favor to your father. Perhaps he saw merit in your research. Who knows?" Marcus asked with a shrug.

"All the greater reason to find his killer."

"Agreed, but before you go prying into Izana's past, you might want to consider sharing your own."

"I will when the time calls for it." Time to change the subject. "By the way, I noticed some of the glances your men were giving her."

"I've already spoken to them about it. They're to keep their hands off of her or answer to Lady Azurha. It's amazing how just mentioning punishment from the Rabbit will keep a crew in line."

"The Rabbit?" He laughed at the idea at first, but the more he thought about it, the more he remembered the predatory gleam in the future empress's eyes. "Is she really the Rabbit?"

Marcus grinned. "Want to piss her off and find out?"

"Not really." The city lights of Emona faded from view, replaced by the rolling hills of farmland. "How long will it take to get to Alpiria?"

"With this ship, we should probably arrive in Silbus the day after tomorrow, early in the morning."

"Izana and I are searching for an oasis two days east of Silbus, per the Alpirion text we found. Do you think we could use the ship to drop us off there?"

"Depends."

"On what?"

"On whether you'd like to jump from the ship or let me land it at the closest landing dock."

A snort of laughter rose from his chest at the thought of Izana dangling from the ship while he convinced her to let go of the rope. He turned to go back to his cabin and check on her.

"One more thing, Modius," Marcus said, stopping him before he left the bridge.

"What?"

"I'm sure you've discovered what Izana knows about her people."

He tensed. "I'm beginning to think I've only scratched the surface."

Marcus met his gaze. "Now you know why I made sure she was placed under imperial protection instead of letting her former mistress set her free. It's not because I wanted to keep her trapped in slavery. It's because I wanted to make sure that knowledge would be protected with her." He went back to steering the ship, ending the conversation.

Modius pondered that bit of information on his way back to the cabin, weaving it in with his prior conversation with Izana over freedom. Nothing was ever as simple as it first seemed. When he was younger, he'd seen the world as black and white. Now that he was older, he'd come to appreciate the varying shades of grey. The forbidden knowledge that could get Izana killed was the one thing that might save the empire. But on the other hand, the very same thing—forbidden knowledge— that he'd chased after under the guise of the greater good, might forever haunt his past.

Izana was still in the same place he'd left her, sitting on

the floor with her knees drawn up to her chest. Her stare had turned blank, and she rocked back and forth, the knuckles of her clasped hands white.

"You should come up to the deck and see the stars."

She shook her head, revealing the wet streaks on her cheek.

He forgot about the ghosts of his past and knelt beside her. "What's wrong?"

"I'm terrified we're going to fall from the sky."

He fought the urge to laugh and pulled her into his arms. "Do you really think Marcus would let something like that happen to you?"

"No, but I saw what this ship looked like after it was attacked by pirates a few weeks ago." She turned her face up toward him. Tears glistened in her eyes. "Are you sure it's been repaired properly?"

"Do you think the emperor would allow us to fly on it if it wasn't?" He brushed his thumb along her cheeks, noting the red tip of her nose, and guilt squeezed his heart. She'd probably been crying since he left. "What can I do to put your fears at ease, Izana?"

She closed her eyes and drew in a deep breath. "I know I should remember why I'm here and what my mistress has asked of me, but I can't help but wish I was back on solid ground."

He squeezed his arms around her in a reassuring hug and placed a kiss on her temple. "We'll be there before you know it."

"Will we?"

He tilted her chin up and waited for her to open her eyes again before he nodded. "In the meantime, how shall we make you forget about being on a ship?"

A spark of desire flashed in her eyes and spread to him like a wildfire through a drought-plagued land. The next thing he knew, her lips were on his, her kiss seeking the desperate reprieve she needed. She straddled his lap so her hips ground against his rising cock. One of her hands sat at the base of his skull, her fingers threaded through his hair, while the other dug into the muscles of his back.

Then, as quickly as she initiated things, she backed away. "Your ribs," she whispered, concern tempering her desire.

"Fully healed." He drew her back to where she'd been moments before and continued to devour the sweetness of her mouth. When he'd taken enough, he moved to her ear. "Should I stop?"

"No." Her hands clawed at his tunic, yanking it up to expose his erection. "I need this. I need you."

Before he could argue, she'd raised her hips and impaled her sex on him. The tight heat felt so exquisite, all coherent thought fled his mind. All he could do was echo her sentiment. He needed this. He needed her.

She began to move up and down along his shaft, her movements shaky and hesitant at first until she found her rhythm. Once she had it, he tilted his hips to find that perfect angle of friction that made his breath hiss with every stroke. The deep moan that fell from her lips told him it affected her the same way.

He left one hand on her hip to steady her while he tugged her dress down with the other hand to expose one perfect breast. The brown nipple was pulled taut, revealing the pink fissures that laced the surface. He drew it into his mouth, delighted by the gasp she gave him as he nipped the sensitive flesh. When he finished with that one, he moved to the other breast and repeated the same dance with his tongue and teeth on it.

By the time he finished, Izana's nails dug into his back, and her movements turned frantic. Gone was the long, slow slide up and down his cock. Her hips now rocked with sharp jabs, centered over the area of her sex that made her breath quicken every time he hit it. Her lips captured his in a wordless confirmation that she was close to the edge.

His body responded to her demands. Sweat prickled the base of his spine, and his balls tightened. He was ready to come, but not until she went first. This was all about putting her fears to ease, keeping her mind focused on something other than the ground passing hundreds of feet beneath them. And he wasn't going to stop until she was left too exhausted and sated to care about the airship.

A burning formed at the base of his cock. By the gods, he would come any second now if she continued to ride him that way. He wedged a hand between them and found the tiny nub above the entrance of her sex.

His name came from her lips in strangled cry, and her inner walls clenched around him. He could no longer hold back, no longer resist the orgasm that rushed through him and left him blind and dizzy from the intensity. And yet he still wanted more, still needed to know she was beyond satisfied. He gripped her hips, moving them back and forth to draw out her release until the pleasure bordered on pain. And even then, he hated to stop.

Izana collapsed against him, her body shaking while her sex continued to squeeze around him in waves. He tucked her head under his chin and held her until they both came around. Minutes passed with only the sounds of their ragged breaths and the pounding of his pulse in his ears. Finally, he found enough air to ask, "Better?"

"Yes," she whispered, her voice hoarse. "Thank you."

He tightened his arms around her, remembering how wonderful she felt around him. "If anyone should be doing to the thanking, it's me. I love being inside you."

The words slipped out before he could catch himself. He offered a quick prayer to the gods she hadn't heard him, but she pushed back and stared at him.

"You do?"

He brushed a curl back from her forehead, deciding it was time to reveal some of his own secrets. "Yes. Sex with you— well, there are no words to describe it. All I know is that when I'm with you, nothing else seems to matter. And when we're apart, there's still part of me that longs to be with you again."

For a moment, her face remained blank. Then, ever so slowly, the corners of her mouth rose into a smile that made his heart jump and beat in a swift, unsteady rhythm. "You said it far more eloquently than I ever could."

She kissed him with a slow passion that told him it was the same way for her.

And in that moment, Modius realized it would be all too easy to fall headfirst in love with her.

16

Izana would've been content to spend the entire voyage in bed with Modius, but two things pulled her from the cabin to the bridge of the airship the next night.

The first was their arrival in Alpiria and their first chance to look for the oasis with the moon lilies.

The second was an urgent message from her mistress. When she arrived on the bridge, Marcus handed her a communication orb. The grim expression on his face warned her the news wasn't good.

He held on to the back, using his Deizian blood to activate it. The inside of the orb clouded with smoke, then cleared to reveal Azurha's face. The tense lines around her mouth matched Marcus's. "Izana, I need you to take a look at the emperor and tell me if you've seen something like this before."

Her mistress turned her orb around toward the bed where the emperor slept. Even though she'd seen him just yesterday, he seemed to have aged overnight. His skin was waxy and hung loosely on his face as though he'd lost weight.

Her stomach flopped, halting her breath. She had seen this before. "My lady," she started, unsure what to say next.

Azurha's face returned in the orb. "I thought as much. It seems the killer has struck again." An uncharacteristic wave of emotion broke in her mistress's voice as she added, "If this is the same poison, then the emperor won't live a day or two past our wedding day."

The grief and worry in her mistress's eyes traveled across the distance, striking her own heart. She imagined she'd feel the same way if the man she loved was afflicted by the same illness. Modius's face replaced the emperor's in her mind, intensifying the ache in her chest. "It won't come to that, my lady. There is a cure, and Modius and I won't rest until we find it."

"I pray to the gods you're right." The image faded from view, and the center of the orb cleared.

Izana looked up to find Marcus staring at her. "Do you have idea how this could've happened?"

She shook her head, retreating from the accusation in his tone until she ran into a man behind her. A comforting hand encircled her arm, followed by a familiar voice.

"I suspect the emperor came in contact with the same poisoned substance as his father," Modius said. "But as Izana said, until we can find the flower and confirm that it's the source of the poison on a Deizian, we have no hope of ever finding a cure."

"You'd better find one fast. I refuse to watch my best friend die." Marcus set the globe down and left the bridge.

Izana turned and buried her face against Modius's chest. "I can't believe it. I just can't."

He didn't hesitate to comfort her in his embrace. "Neither can I, but this only makes our mission more important."

"And if we fail?" A chill rattled through her as though she'd been dropped into the fridgidarium.

Modius tightened his arms around her. "We can't fail."

***

Azurha pressed a warm compress to Titus's face, hoping the heat would drive away the chill that clung to his flesh. Apprehension clawed at her insides as she counted his breaths, wondering how many more he had left to draw before the poison claimed him. She'd watched more men die than she cared to count, but this time, she prayed that the gods would spare this one.

The whispers from her fellow slaves came back to haunt her. They'd called her cursed. At that time, she'd thought it was because her unusual eyes had captured her master's attention and turned her into a victim for his pleasure. Now that she was free, she wondered if she was bound to be cursed the rest of her life. Why else would the gods take away the man she loved more than her own life?

If she could trade places with him, she would do it in a second. The empire needed him. They didn't need her. The only person who needed her was slowly dying.

His eyelids fluttered open, revealing the dull light in his normally piercing blue eyes. "What's wrong?"

She drew in a breath, wondering how much she should reveal to him. "I'm worried about you."

"Why?"

"You're not yourself."

He laughed and sat up with the slowness of a man twice his age. "I'm just tired—that's all. Perhaps it's because I've been up too many nights making love to you."

A sob choked her throat. If only it were that simple. "Then perhaps you should rest today."

"I wish it were that easy." He stood and wobbled on his feet until Azurha braced him. "I'm the emperor, and I rarely get a day's rest."

She stood beside him, her hand still on his shoulder. "You're right—you are the emperor, and your will is paramount to everything else."

"Yes, but I also have duties that I cannot ignore."

"Such as?"

"The barrier, for starters. If I don't reinforce it, the Barbarians could break through." He waved her off and stumbled out of the bedchamber like a man still half asleep.

"And what about when you were with me in Madrena? Who reinforced the barrier then?"

He stopped at his desk and leaned forward on it, his lungs bellowing. "It was different then. Before I met you, the barrier had always been a challenge to maintain. It took every ounce of magic I could muster to restore the lines." He paused, his voice growing softer. "But the morning it fell, you kissed me and told me you believed in me, and I felt this strange wild magic rush through me. That morning, I restored the barrier and made it stronger than it had ever been. I could go for days without restoring it."

He pushed off the desk and rubbed the back of his neck. "But yesterday, I noticed the struggle return. It was like my magic had been weakened, and I'm at a loss for why."

She took his hand. "Should I kiss you and tell you I believe in you again?"

He laughed. "I think there's more to it than that. I think the wild magic came from you."

"Titus, please, enough of this." She released his hand and turned away. "Haven't I proven to you time and time again that I have no Deizian blood, no magic?"

"And I know what I saw." He wrapped his arms around her waist and pressed his cool cheek against her warm one. "Until you can explain to me how you destroyed my doors, I will still hold on to the belief that magic runs through your veins."

It was an argument she'd never win. Instead, she lost herself in the scent of sandalwood and steady throb of his heart as it beat against her back. He was still so alive, but how much longer did she have? "May I come with you and watch?"

"I would like that." He placed a kiss on her cheek and released her.

"Then perhaps I can convince you to cancel the rest of your appointments and spend a lazy day with me."

He grinned as he pressed his hand against the lock plate. "My dear, there is nothing lazy I want to do when I'm with you."

"Then we should try keeping our clothes on for once."

"But you've already proven that you can make love to me in a crowded room, completely clothed."

A flush rose into her cheeks when she recalled her brazen actions that night. She'd wanted to distract him from her absence at the party and employed the only thing she could think of at the time. "Then maybe I should call on your mother while you rest." *And share with her my fears.*

"I think she'd enjoy your company."

The throne room was empty this early in the morning, but the globe into the center of the room still spun on its invisible axis, three rings dancing around it with the occasional wobble. Glowing red lines marked the borders of the empire. Titus stopped in front of the globe and frowned. "The red light means the barrier is weak, but thankfully, there are no areas that are flashing."

"And what does that mean?"

"It means it's about to fail." He pressed his finger along the glowing red line and squinted his eyes. "Every morning, I use my magic to reinforce it, to strengthen that invisible wall that keeps the Barbarians out."

She came closer in case she needed to steady him. Sweat beaded along his brow, but the glowing lines turned from red to orange before he stopped. Again, his breath came sharp and fast as though he'd run across the palace instead of merely standing next to the globe.

"There—that should be enough for today." He took a step back, his knees buckling under him.

Azurha dived to catch him. "Titus, this is a sure sign you need rest."

"I just slipped, that's all." He waved her away and took his time rising. "But yes, I think I might take you up on your offer to spend the day being lazy."

"I'll let Varro know to cancel your meetings." She watched him return to his chambers, her heart filling with dread. The poison was already taking its toll on him. At this rate, would he even live to see their wedding day?

143

17

"I see another grove of palms ahead."

Izana gulped, shoving her fear deeper into the pit of her stomach, where it rolled and threatened to spill over every time she opened her mouth. She gripped the post and peered in the direction Modius pointed.

The ground raced under them at a dizzying speed, but she managed to focus on the approaching grove. Just like the text had mentioned, the trees were planted in the shapes of the glyphs for "king" and "blessing". "I think that's it," she mumbled before closing her eyes.

"Good," Marcus said from the wheel. "I'll turn back to that last town we passed and drop you off there."

The short burst of joy was quickly washed away by a wave of nausea. She couldn't get off this airship fast enough.

Modius took her hands and pulled her against his chest. "Let's go back down until we land."

She didn't resist his offer. Since she'd spoken to Azurha this morning, she'd remained on the bridge, keeping a lookout for the grove that held the moon lilies and growing sicker with each passing mile. Her legs quivered as they crossed the deck and down the stairs to her room, but she made it back without collapsing.

Modius pressed his lips to her temple. "Would you like a bit of ginger? It works wonders for upset stomachs."

She nodded, not trusting her stomach enough to open her mouth until he held out a piece of the dried root. The sweet crystallized honey that coated it melted on her tongue, followed by a slow burn that went all the down her throat. By the time it dissolved, her nausea was beginning to fade. "Thank you."

"I wish I'd thought of it sooner. I hate seeing you with that sickly green color."

She probably looked like the epitome of health compared to what Azurha had shown her of the emperor. "Modius, do you think you can come up with an antidote?"

He paused from repacking his things, his expression solemn. "I don't know."

Izana refused to stand by and watch another emperor fade away. "If I can be of any help—"

"You already have." He resumed packing. "By tomorrow, we should have a flower, and I can begin extracting the oil from it to test my theory."

"But we'll have to find a Deizian to test it on."

He paused again, this time with a frown tugging at the corners of his mouth. "I don't suppose the emperor has a few Deizians hidden in the dungeon awaiting execution?"

In spite of the seriousness of the situation, Izana laughed. "No, but I could list several nobles his life would be easier without."

"This grows more complicated by the minute." He rubbed his face. "I'm more troubled knowing that the killer has managed to strike again, right under our noses. But how?"

"Once we know more about the poison, we can figure out the how." She handed him his gladius. "In the meantime, let's take it one step at a time."

"You're right." He stood and attached the sword to his belt as the ship decelerated. "It feels like we're landing. Are you ready to go?"

"I'll meet you up there in just a moment." Once she was alone, she removed the dagger her mistress had given her from the bundle she'd brought on board, and strapped it to her thigh.

The cold metal tingled against her skin, and the leather strap bit into her flesh. If any of the Alpirions tried to stop them, she was ready.

She came up on deck as the airship finished its final docking maneuvers. The mid-morning sun beat down on her shoulders and sparkled over the rolling blue dunes. Her breath caught. This was her ancestral home, the place her great-grandparents had once freely roamed before the Battle of Silbus turned them into slaves.

She ran down the gangplank and buried her feet in the warm sand. A hum vibrated through her body as though the land were singing a song of welcome. In the past, she'd dismissed Hapsa's tales of the old magic of Alpiria, but now she wondered if there might be some truth to them.

Modius came beside her, dressed in a billowing long-sleeved tunic that stretched to his ankles. Sweat streamed down his cheeks. "How could anyone stand to live here?"

She pointed the small settlement of light-colored tents and palm-filled courtyards. "My people adapted to the land centuries ago. You'll be more comfortable if we can get you to some shade."

"I doubt there's any shade out there." He pointed out into the desert in the direction of the oasis.

"Then we'll have to improvise." She pulled her spare dress out of the bundle and stretched it over his head like a canopy.

"You two will be much better off if you can convince one of the locals to sell you a droma," Marcus called from above. "Those beasts are bred for this climate, and one should be able to easily carry both of you."

Izana ran around the ship and spotted a pen full of the animals she'd heard of all her life but never seen. They appeared to be a cross between a horse and an ox with long faces, floppy ears, short horns, and a shaggy hump in the middle of the backs. Their fur varied from white to black, with shades of russet and brown mixed in, and thin tails whipped away the sand flies while they chewed on hay someone had imported for them to eat.

Marcus tossed a small purse of coins to them. "This should cover one, but don't accept their first offer. You'll be better off if you can talk them down."

"When should we meet you back here?" she asked.

He pressed his lips together. "It depends on how long I'll be in Silbus. If you finish ahead of time, keep going west, and we'll meet up along the way." He disappeared for a moment only to return with two leather bracelets. "Put these on, and I'll be able to find you when I'm done."

Modius caught them and passed one to her. She flipped it over and found a small ore disc sewn to the leather. She'd heard tales of masters using them on slaves before branding became popular, but they'd long fallen out of favor. "Tracking devices?"

Marcus grinned. "I hope they don't offend you, Izana."

"No, not for this reason." She buckled the leather strap around her wrist. "Good luck."

"You, too." He disappeared again, and the airship roared to life, rising up into the sky in a cloud of swirling sand that stung her skin and choked her nose.

Once the air cleared, Modius jingled the coin purse. "Ready to make a deal?"

She nodded and led the way to the pen of dromas.

***

Hours later, they spotted the hazy outline of the oasis on the horizon. The sun was low in the sky, but the air still carried the scorching blast of an oven. The only thing that kept Modius from melting was the shaded canopy which Izana had talked the farmer into including in the outrageous price of the droma. He sat deep in the back, Izana riding in front, but even that offered little refuge from the oppressive heat.

He dragged his damp sleeve across his face, tasting the salt of his sweat on his lip, and drained the last drops of water from his waterskin. Izana's sloshed beside her, still full and tempting him with each step the six-legged droma took. "How much further do you think it is?"

"Maybe an hour or two," she replied, her voice annoyingly chipper despite the extreme climate.

His tongue was already parched and begging for more water. "We should be able to find water there, right?"

She nodded. "The description mentioned a grotto with a waterfall."

Then they should be fine if he helped himself to some of her water. He grabbed her waterskin, only to hear the sharp slap of her hand on his.

"You could try asking first," she scolded.

He rubbed the back of his hand like a child who'd just been caught stealing a pie from a window sill. "How is that you are faring so well here?"

"Perhaps because I'm an Alpirion," she said with a shrug. "But if you can't wait until we reach the oasis, I suppose you can have a little of my water."

"Thank you." He opened her waterskin and took long a long swig. "You know how you felt on the airship? That's exactly how I feel here."

Izana laughed and looked over her shoulder at him. "I've heard tales that the ancient Alpirions built elaborate underground cities so they could hide from the heat of the day, only coming to the surface at night."

"That might also explain how they managed to fend off the Barbarians for centuries without the barrier."

"Perhaps, but now you can understand why they called themselves the People of the Moon. Everything about our culture revolves around the phases of the moon. When it's full, it's a time of celebration and fertility. Fields were planted, marriages took place, and children were conceived. When the moon was dark, we hid and prayed, asking the gods for mercy and protection."

He thought back to the night Izana left his chamber after kissing him. "Was that the reason you didn't join me in my bed the other night?"

"Yes," she paused and added, "and no. I knew what phase the moon was in, but I also was a little on guard after revealing so much to you that day."

He counted the number of days until the imperial wedding. "Do you think that's why Lady Azurha's marrying the emperor on a full moon?"

She cocked her head to the side. "Maybe, although I'm not sure if my mistress was aware of our customs when she chose that date."

The worry in her voice said far more than her words. *If the emperor lived long enough to make it to the wedding.*

"The moon should be waxing tonight," he said, diverting the conversation from the morose subject that hung over them. "Hopefully, it should give us enough light to make it back to the village. I'm all for avoiding the sun after today."

"We'll have to wait until the moon is high before we can find the flowers. After all, they're called moon lilies for a reason."

"And what shall we do in the meantime if we arrive early?"

"I'm sure we can think of something." She stroked his thigh, and his cock twitched to life. He might be sweaty and miserable, but all it took was one inviting touch from her to make him forget about it. "Perhaps we could take a quick bath in the waterfall?"

The mere thought of her naked body swimming around his, her long legs wrapped around his waist while he plunged into her, had him ready to whip the droma into a full gallop. "I'm looking forward to that."

A throaty laugh told him she was, too.

***

Izana climbed out of the small pool by the waterfall and stretched out on the warm sand. The sun was dipping below the horizon, and the first stars twinkled overhead through the palm leaves. The air around her still vibrated with the same song she'd heard this morning, enveloping her with its magic and mingling with the contended hum that flowed through her body. She'd never felt more alive in her life, and if the emperor's life wasn't fading away, she'd linger here longer.

Modius plopped down next to her, pulling her into his arms. His stubble scraped along her cheeks as he murmured, "We should take baths like that more often."

She giggled, remembering the frantic way they'd made love once they arrived at the oasis. Their clothes were still on the ground by the droma, who contentedly chewed on the tender green shrubs that surrounded the date palms. She rolled over, her lips seeking his again. The water had washed away the salt from his skin, but he still tasted delicious to her.

"Careful," he teased, catching her bottom lip with his teeth. "I don't relish the idea of getting sand in my sensitive areas, but if you keep kissing me that way, I'll be forced to make love to you again."

She sighed and ran her fingers through his wet hair. Making love. He made sex sound like something rare and special. When she'd been a *lupa*, she would've scoffed at the idea. But now, seeing the glow from his eyes as he looked down on her, feeling the warmth that flowed through her veins and serene contentment that filled her every time she was in his arms, she was starting to believe it was more than just sex with him.

He placed a playful kiss on the tip of her nose and got up on his knees. "I'll grab our clothes while you rinse off."

She dipped back into the pool and washed away the sand that clung to her skin.

When she climbed out, Modius stood at the edge of the water, holding out the dagger Azurha had given her. "Expecting trouble?"

"No more than you are." She snatched it and strapped it to her thigh. "My mistress ordered me to take it, and I won't disobey her."

His hand fell to the hilt of his sword. "Do you think I won't protect you?"

"Not at all." She slipped her dress over her head and cinched it around her waist. "But I refuse to be a useless burden."

"You do know that I'll protect you with my life?"

A lump rose into her throat, and her mouth went dry. His question tread upon a subject she didn't want to address. "Even though I'm nothing but a slave?"

"You are more than just a slave, Izana." His eyes glittered with a flood of emotions that mimicked the ones brewing in her chest, but like her, he didn't dare voice them. "The moon is rising. We should start looking for the flowers."

She blew out a breath of relief. It was difficult enough to admit she was developing feelings for him, especially when she knew nothing would ever come of them. Even if they managed to save the emperor's life, Modius would return to Madrena, and she would stay at the palace and try to forget how close to perfect things were with him.

But if they failed...

She shook that thought from her mind. They couldn't fail. There had to be a cure out there. How else did Tiberius survive in the legend?

Modius was already searching the area around the pool. It made sense to split up and scour the entire oasis separately. "I'm going to climb up to the top of the waterfall and see if I can find the moon lilies up there."

He didn't look back at her, his attention fixed on the shrubs. "Good idea."

The oasis was centered around a small outcropping of rock that jutted out from the blue sand. The warm brown stone seemed oddly out of place at first, but when she examined it closer, she found veins of metallic greens and blues along the surface. She scrambled up the steep side, digging her nails into the crevices to pull herself up to the top. There, a spring bubbled up from inside a grotto and flowed into the waterfall.

Delicate vines encased the stones of the grotto, holding them in place as well as any plaster and mortar. Long white thorns projecting from the stems kept her from coming closer to the source of the water, but she explored the rest of the outcropping. From this height, she could easily read the glyphs for "king's blessing" outlined by the trees and pluck the ripe dates from their branches. The vast desert stretched out around them as far as she could see, the blue sand sparkling under the stars and moon.

A sweet perfume filled the air, one she'd never encountered despite serving the empress for years. It was floral with a hint of citrus and ended with the notes of black pepper, completely intoxicating. She sniffed the air, trying to find the flower producing it. Her nose led her back to the grotto.

The moonlight fell on the vines, and she forgot to breathe. The white thorns had unfurled under the pale beams, revealing the delicate moon lilies she'd seen in the paintings. She reached out to touch one. A zing of magic raced up her arm, silencing any doubts she had.

"I've found them," she called down to Modius.

"Where?"

"Up here by the grotto." She ripped a strip of fabric from the bottom of her dress and laid it out on the rocks. With each flower she picked, she folded a bit of cloth around it to protect the petals. By the time Modius joined her, she'd already filled the strip with flowers and tucked it into her bodice.

His mouth parted, and he stared at the vines with awe. The grotto had disappeared under the cover of the lilies. Their surfaces shimmered under the moon like flawless pearls, and their perfume wafted on the breeze. "I don't believe it," he whispered.

Izana laughed and ripped another strip of fabric from her dress. "I hope you brought something to put them in, or I'll be without a dress."

He pulled out a small leather satchel. "In an ideal situation, I'd set the flowers out to dry before transporting them, but we don't have time for that."

"Neither does the emperor." She plucked several flowers from the vines and placed them in his pouch. "How many do you think you'll need?"

"Maybe a dozen more." The satchel was already half full as they both picked the flowers. "I'd like to have enough to distill a small amount of the oil you found the recipe for, but it wouldn't hurt to have some extra flowers in case I need them."

He was just fastening the top of the full pouch when the ground rumbled beneath them. A rising cloud of sand to the west raced toward them.

Sandstorms don't shake the ground.

Izana's heart jumped as she realized the cause. "Riders are coming. Hide."

She ran to the edge of the outcropping to climb down, but Modius pulled her back. "We're better defended from up here."

"Even though we're completely out in the open?"

He searched the area before dragging her toward the grotto. The icy water splashed along her legs as he pulled her inside and pushed against the back wall. He drew his sword and waited.

Voices filtered up from below. Izana leaned forward, trying to catch a few words. They were all men, their conversations completely in Alpirion.

Modius turned to her and whispered, "What are they saying?"

She placed her finger over his lips and strained to hear more.

After a minute, two things became very clear. The Alpirion men were looking for them, and they were prepared to kill them when they found them.

"Hide your satchel," she hissed. "If they find you've taken the flowers, they won't hesitate to kill you."

He slipped it under his tunic. "How many men are there?"

She counted the different voices she'd heard. "At least six of them, maybe more."

The voices came closer, accompanied by the scatter of loose pebbles. They were climbing the rock.

Modius tensed in front of her, shielding her completely with his body as he pressed her deeper into the shadows.

The first Alpirion appeared over the crest. He was bare-chested, wearing only a linen cloth tied around his waist. His muscles rippled in the moonlight. On the inside of his arm, he bore a tattoo of the glyph for freedom, and her pulse quickened. These men were part of the same brotherhood as the men who'd attacked them in the library, perhaps the very same group of men who'd massacred the imperial soldiers. And when the Alpirion spotted them, he grinned and drew his curved blade. "I've found them," he called down in his native tongue.

Modius shifted his weight and tightened his grip on his gladius.

"I wouldn't do that," the Alpirion mocked in the common language. "There are far more of me than of you."

As if to prove his point, eight more warriors appeared over the ledge. The largest of them all strode toward the Alpirion who'd found them. Instead of a simple cloth around his waist, he wore a fine linen skirt that fell over his thighs in intricate pleats. Silver and gold adorned his belt, and unlike the cleanly shaven heads of his comrades, a single thick braid ran from the top of his head to his shoulder. He was the very image of the kings of old, and he glared at Modius with thinly veiled hostility.

"Who are you, and why have you come to desecrate this site?" the leader asked.

Modius remained defiant. "That is none of your concern."

"Oh, but it is." The Alpirion leader came toward them, his sword still hanging from his belt. "This oasis is sacred to my people, and you have sought it out for a reason."

One of the men made a bet with another how much longer Modius had to live, and snickers flowed through the group.

Izana's mind raced to find a way to diffuse the situation, finally choosing to risk her own life to protect his. "Please," she said, stepping out from behind Modius, "he's only here to protect me. He knows nothing about this place."

The leader's eyes flickered from her head to her toes and back again. A cold smile rose on his lips. "And who are you?"

"Izana."

"And what are you doing here?" he asked, this time in Alpirion.

She remembered her mistress's warning and molded her features into a mask of confusion, even though she understood him. It was safer to pretend she didn't. Maybe then, they would talk freely around her, and she could learn more about them.

When she didn't answer, he repeated the question in the common language.

"My mistress sent me."

His smile warmed into one of amusement, and he crossed his arms. "And who is your mistress?"

Even if she lied, they would see the mark on her neck and know whom she served. She lifted her chin instead, adopting the posture she'd seen Empress Horatia carry for years, and stepped forward. "Azurha, imperial consort to Emperor Titus Sergius Flavus and future empress of the Deizian Empire."

Another murmur flowed through the men, this time more from shock than ridicule.

The leader's hooded eyes revealed nothing, however. "And why did she send you here?"

Modius growled a warning behind her, but she kept her gaze level with the leader. On the hierarchy of slaves, she was near the top. "Who are you to demand such information from me?"

He laughed, the lines of his shoulders easing. "You amuse me, little Izana."

"And you didn't answer my question."

His men remained on edge, their weapons drawn, but their leader appeared more relaxed that ever. "I'm known as Tuhotep."

It was the name of the Alpirion king who had first driven back the Deizians when they arrived on this planet. She kept her voice cool and detached, hiding the warning bells that rang in the back of her mind. "That's quite an arrogant name."

"Then you know the significance behind it." He stepped into the stream and froze when Modius tugged her back into the grotto. "Izana, perhaps you can reason with your bodyguard. This can be simple, or it can be bloody."

His men raised their swords and inched closer as though they hoped for the latter.

She shook off Modius's hand. "If you harm either of us, then you risk alienating yourself from my mistress's favor."

"And why should I care about that?"

"Because, when an Alpirion empress sits on the throne, she'll have the power to influence the emperor on a great many things, including freeing our people and lifting the restrictive laws placed on us. But, if you anger her, then expect no mercy."

"The dead reveal no secrets."

"But grateful servants whisper in their mistress's ear, who will in turn whisper to the emperor."

His stance hardened, and the amusement faded from his eyes. He reached for his sword, and a tremor formed at the base of her spine.

Have I pushed him too hard?

Then he called out to his men in Alpirion, "Should I kill them now, or shall we see what secrets they yield?"

The first two replies called for their deaths, but then several other men suggested Tuhotep let them live long enough to discover why they were there. One of the warriors asked him to spare her so they could pass her around for their amusement. In the end though, most of them voted to spare them.

Tuhotep unwound his fingers from the sword's hilt. "It seems my men find you as amusing as I do, little Izana."

A lump of fear still lingered in her throat, but she could finally swallow past it. "Oh?"

"Tell me why your mistress sent you here."

"Agree to spare our lives, and I'll tell you."

The cold smile returned. "Order you bodyguard to drop

his weapon, and I'll agree to your terms."

The tremor grew stronger, but she turned around and whispered, "Do as he says."

Modius's eyes narrowed. "I don't trust him."

"Please, Modius, I don't want to watch you die."

His expression softened, and he ran his thumb along her bottom lip. "Nor I, you."

"Then trust me." She leaned against him, pressing the dagger strapped to her thigh against his leg.

His brows rose ever so slightly, acknowledging her silent message, and he threw his sword into the stream.

She turned back to Tuhotep. "You agree to my terms?"

"I do, so long as you keep your end."

"I'll tell you once your men sheath their weapons."

Seconds ticked by, each one adding to the icy waves of apprehension that assaulted her, until he gave a sharp nod. The warriors sheathed their swords, but still seemed ready to attack on his command.

"My mistress sent us here to collect the moon lilies for her wedding bouquet."

Tuhotep laughed so hard, he doubled over. Then he waved his men forward.

The Alpirion warriors rushed at them, knocking her aside as they subdued Modius with their hands and fists. He tried to fight them off, but he was outnumbered. When they forced his face into the water, he went so still, her chest tightened with the fear they'd drowned him. Then one of them gripped him by the hair to pull him out, and she nearly wept with relief to see him coughing out a mouthful of water.

A hand clamped around her upper arm, and Tuhotep said close to her ear, "You are most certainly amusing, Izana. A liar, but amusing. And for that reason, I'll let you live to see another sunrise."

She forced every muscle in her body to remain still. "You agreed to spare both of our lives."

"So I did." He pulled her out of the stream, his grip

tightening to the point her hand tingled. "But I never agreed to let you go."

She struggled against him, but he was as unmovable as the stone beneath her feet. Two of his men came toward her, one of them pulling a rope from his belt.

The next minute passed in a blur. Tuhotep knocked her to the ground. Ropes bit into her wrists and ankles. A glance over her shoulder told her they were doing the same to Modius. Once she was bound, one of the men yanked her back up and held her in front of his leader.

Tuhotep's grin oozed malice. He held a strip of cloth in his hand and came toward her like a lyger stalking its prey. "You need to learn to negotiate better, little Izana."

He tied the cloth around her eyes, plunging her into darkness, and murmured in her ear. "There are fates worse than death."

18

Modius stopped trying to estimate how far they'd traveled. Once he'd been bound and blindfolded, the Alpirion rebels lowered him from the rock, taking care to add to his bruises along the way, and threw him on the back of a horse. He'd called out for Izana, his heart refusing to beat until he heard her answer him with surprising calm in her voice.

She'd asked him to trust her, but he hoped that she had a plan to get them out of this. But if she didn't, then he needed to find a way to get them free from their captors. If he could see them, he could start to figure out their weaknesses, something he could take advantage of. An old scar. Eyes heavy with fatigue. A sword that was within easy reach. Anything that would make them easier to overpower.

The cool of the night gave way to the heat of the sun beating on his back, the only clue to how much time had passed. His body ached from the constant jostling of the horse, and his skin burned from the sand that was continuously kicked into his face. He let his mind go numb and drifted into a semi-conscious level of sleep.

When he came around, the horses had slowed, and the air was cool again. His throat was drier than the desert they'd just crossed, but he managed a hoarse whisper. "Izana?"

"I'm still here," she said, her voice as parched as his, but still calm and reassuring.

Tuhotep's voice came from the same direction as Izana's. "Your bodyguard is remarkably dedicated."

A bolt of anger raced through Modius, erasing his fatigue. "Have they hurt you?"

"I'm fine." Her words carried an unspoken warning for him to be silent.

"Yes, do not worry, Elymanian," Tuhotep continued, mocking him, "I have every intention of taking very good care of her."

Visions of the Alpirion forcing himself on her assaulted his mind, stoking the fires of rage already burning inside him. He strained against the ropes binding his hands until blood trickled down his fingers.

Tuhotep's laughter echoed around him. "Such loyalty you inspire, Izana."

Modius froze, listening to how the sounds bounced around him. Echoes didn't occur in the vast, empty desert. The horses' hooves clomped against stone instead of swishing through the sand. Water dripped in the distance, and the damp air penetrated his aching joints. All the clues pointed to them being inside some kind of structure, like a cave.

His horse stopped, and two pairs of rough hands pulled him down. His knees buckled from under him, and the metallic taste of blood filled his mouth as his face connected with the hard ground.

"Put them in the cell for the time being," Tuhotep ordered. "When I'm rested, I'll start wrestling the truth from them."

The hand grabbed him again and dragged him down a flight of stairs before tossing him into a room. A smaller body crashed into him with a feminine grunt, followed by the clang of a metal door slamming shut. He writhed under the weight of the second person until Izana said, "Hold still a moment."

She rolled over until her icy fingers brushed against his. Once they made contact, he threaded them together, refusing to let her go.

"Are you hurt?" he asked.

"No, not really. You?"

"I've been better, but I'll survive."

"Did they break your ribs again?"

He chuckled in spite of himself, noting that it didn't hurt as much as the other day. "I'm going to be sporting some fantastic bruises, but as far as I can tell, nothing's broken." He remembered the innuendo in Tuhotep's promise to take care of her. "Did any of them force themselves on you?"

"No, we've been too busy riding. Of course, that didn't prevent Tuhotep from fondling my breasts along the way."

He tightened his fingers around hers. "He'll pay for that."

"I was just grateful he kept his hands there." She pressed her thigh against his, the scabbard of her dagger still hidden beneath her dress.

At least they had a weapon. "Do you think you can bring it to my hands?"

"I'll try."

His hands were numb and clumsy from the ropes. He strained for the hilt, but after a few minutes of struggle, he couldn't wrap his fingers around it. "Maybe we can try again after a few minutes."

A heavy sigh filled their cell. "I'm sorry I got you into this, Modius."

"Don't apologize. You did the best you could, and I think even your mistress would be proud of the way you handled things. We're still alive."

"But we're still prisoners, and I have no idea if Tuhotep will remain true to his word."

"Well, there's always Marcus."

She gave a half-hearted chuckle. "Yes, I suppose you're right."

They lapsed into silence, their fingers still joined, until he said, "I just wish I could see where we are."

"Hold still." Izana released his hand and pressed the back of her head against his, slowly moving it up and down until the blindfold lifted.

He shook it off and let his eyes adjust to the dim light. They were in a cell with one wall made entirely of rough granite and the others made of clay bricks. "What kind of place it this?"

"Help me so I can see."

He copied her maneuvers, catching the knot of her blindfold with the top of his head and pushing it up until she could slip out of it.

"It looks like a prison cell to me." She scooted closer to one of the clay walls and used it to raise herself into a sitting position. "There's Alpirion graffiti here."

"An abandoned building?"

She shook her head. "No, I think this might be one of the underground settlements I was telling you about yesterday."

He followed her lead and managed to sit up next to her. "If that's the case, Marcus might have some trouble finding us."

"We'll find a way out of this." She leaned her head on his shoulder. "Trust me."

"I do." He placed a kiss on her temple and listened the slowing of her breath as she surrendered to sleep.

***

Izana awoke to the sound of soft snoring coming from the man beside her. The light that filtered into the cell from the small window in the door remained unchanged from before, giving her no clue to how long she'd slept. She listened for voices outside, but heard nothing.

Her shoulders ached from her arms being bound behind her back for hours. She inched away from Modius so she could stretch without waking him. Once the tense muscles loosened, she tested the ropes.

They didn't budge.

What was the use of having a knife on her if she couldn't reach it? Maybe once Modius woke up, she could find a way to get the hilt into his hands, and they could take turns cutting the ropes. But after that...

She slumped against the wall. That was the problem. Even if she found a way to free them from the ropes, they were still locked in a cell in a secret underground city in the middle of the Alpirion desert. *That'll teach me to word my bargains more carefully.*

At least she hadn't given Tuhotep the truth.

But then, he'd called her a liar, which made her wonder how much he really knew of their mission. For all she knew, his men had already captured Marcus and extracted answers from him.

She laughed softly. Marcus wouldn't betray the emperor any more than she'd betray her mistress. However, she was definitely caught in a spider's web where she needed to tread lightly. Tuhotep wasn't a fool. She'd just need to outsmart him if she wanted to return to Emona with the precious flowers hidden in her bodice.

Modius stirred, jerking awake with a start. "Izana?"

"Right here." She fell to her side, landing in his lap. "Come up with any brilliant plans to get us out of here?"

"All I could come up with involves getting to that trinket Lady Azurha gave you, but my hands are even more numb that before."

"The same as me. But there's one thing I haven't tried yet." She arched her back and lifted her bottom off the cold stone floor, stretching her arms as far down as possible. Her left shoulder cracked. Pain shot down her arm, and a cry broke free from her lips.

A look of worry washed over Modius's face as he looked down at her. "Izana, stop before you hurt yourself even more."

She gritted her teeth and made the final push to get the ropes around her hips. From there, it was easy to slip her legs through her arms.

He waited until her breathing slowed before speaking in calm, reassuring tones. "Listen to me carefully, and I can help you get your arm back into place. Can you feel your fingers?" She nodded, and he continued. "Good. Now, bend your arm at the elbow and slowly swing it out."

"How do you know what I need to do?"

"I'm a healer—remember?"

She exhaled as she rolled her arm outward. The shoulder popped back into place, easing her pain.

Modius winced, his breath as swift and shaky as hers. "By the gods, Izana, why did you do that to yourself?"

"Because I can actually use my hands better now." She shimmied up her skirt to reveal the golden dagger. "Turn around so I can get to you."

She fumbled for the hilt, her fingers fat and clumsy from the restrictive hemp that cut into her skin, and her shoulder was still throbbing. Once she had it in her hands, she turned and started sawing at the ropes that bound Modius first instead of her own.

She was halfway through them when a door banged off in the distance. She flinched, and the dagger fell from her hands. Modius jumped to cover it with his body, sliding it between his back and the wall just as a shadow passed across the window.

The door opened, and one of the warriors came into the cell. He eyed Izana's bound hands in her lap and reached for his sword. "Tuhotep wishes to speak with you."

"Which one of us?" Modius asked.

"Her." He yanked Izana up by her wrists, reviving the throbbing ache in her shoulders. "You live only because she pleaded for your life."

"I'll be back, Modius," she said, more to herself than him. "Don't worry."

Her ankles still bound, she hopped behind the warrior as he dragged her out of the cell, falling to the ground once he slammed the door shut again.

"I don't have time for this." He drew his sword, and she forgot all about her pain in that moment of panic. But instead of running it through her heart, he swiped the blade over the ropes around her ankles. The steel nicked her skin as it passed, but the small trickle of blood was worth the freedom that followed.

He stood her up, leaving her wrists tied together. "Follow me."

Her feet were as clumsy as her fingers, slow and unsteady, but she stumbled after him from the prison to the long corridors that resembled city streets. "Where are we?"

"That's none of your business."

That didn't prevent her from memorizing every detail about the place. She'd been right to assume they were in one of the underground cities, although this looked more like a small village. Empty rooms lined the streets, their occupants long since gone. A small temple or palace stood at the end of the corridor, the façade much grander than the simple dwellings closer to the prison. The scents of wood fires and animal dung choked the air, but the sweet smell of incense mingled with it as she came closer to the palace. She counted the number of men she passed in the dim light, only reaching a dozen by the time she entered the palace.

Inside, the walls still retained some of their former glory. Cracked frescos depicted Alpirion life before the Deizians had conquered them, the metallic paint flashing in the torchlight. A bubbling spring beckoned in the distance. She longed to take a dip in it and wash the sweat and grime from her skin, but the hostile frown from her escort told her they didn't have time for that.

They passed a set of guards who stood by a doorway and entered the chamber where Tuhotep sat on a throne like the ancient king he longed to be. He grinned at her, but the glint in his eyes was anything but welcoming. "So nice of you join me, Izana."

"I didn't know this was an invitation I could refuse."

His grin faded. "You have quite an impertinent tongue for a slave."

"And you are not my master. You are an Alpirion like me. Therefore, I do not need to watch what I say or how I say it."

He chuckled and waved her escort away. The two guards

outside shut the doors behind him, leaving her alone with
Tuhotep.

19

Tuhotep rose from the throne with the slow, easy grace of a predator and pulled the knife from his belt. "It seems you've managed to free your arms part of the way."

Izana's pulse pounded in her ears. Experience told her that she'd have greater success bending her captor to her will if she employed her feminine wiles rather than her wits, but that didn't mean she couldn't use both. Tuhotep was dangerous, and one false move could end not only her life, but Modius's as well.

Izana lowered her voice into a sultry tone that usually left her clients begging for more. "I'm very flexible."

"Are you?" The curiosity in his voice told her he'd caught her innuendo. "Shall I find out?"

"It depends." She held up her bound hands.

He slipped the knife between her wrists and sliced through the ropes. "On what?"

"On how amusing I find you." She stepped away, her hips swaying as she moved toward the feast on the table. The only hunger she felt right now was the one in her empty stomach. "Is this for me?"

"No, it's for me, but you are welcome to join me." He tucked his knife back into his belt and pointed to the smaller of the two chairs. "Please, sit."

Again, even though the words implied it was an

invitation, the hard edge in his voice left little room for refusal. She lowered herself onto the chair, her eyes never leaving him. Until she found some weakness to exploit, she had no other choice but to obey.

He sat in the larger chair and opened a bottle. "Care for some wine?"

"How do I know it's not poisoned?"

"Are you always this suspicious?"

"My mistress taught me well."

He poured some into the two cups and took a sip from each. Once she assured herself the level was lower and he'd actually drank from hers, she raised the cup to her lips. The wine was sweet and cool and refreshing after the grueling journey from the oasis. It burned when it reached her stomach and revived her exhausted spirit.

"Are you going to ask me to prove that everything on the table is safe to eat?" Tuhotep asked, his eyes softening with laughter.

"No, I suppose not." But she waited for him to try a dish before sampling it herself. And if she caught him looking away, she'd try to smuggle some back to Modius. "Why did you summon me?"

"Can't a man wish to enjoy dinner with a beautiful woman?"

"Not a man like you." She studied him over the rim of her cup. He'd styled himself as a king, but his features were not like the sharp, angular ones she'd seen depicted in the paintings and statues of the royal family. His nose was beaklike, and his jaw too wide.

He speared the flank of roasted meat on the plate between, letting his knife linger there a moment before he cut a chunk off. "I want to know more about you."

"I'm just a simple slave performing her mistress's bidding."

"That's not what I've heard about you."

The base of her spine tightened. "And where would you

hear anything about me?"

He grinned and chewed the morsel in his mouth before answering. "I have eyes and ears everywhere, Izana, including the palace."

The tension climbed up her spine, but she managed to keep her shoulders loose and her voice flippant. "There are hundreds of slaves in the palace. I doubt your spies would find anything interesting about me."

"A whore who rose above her station to serve an empress?"

She pulled her hair over the mark on her neck to cover it, but Tuhotep only laughed.

"It's too late to hide that from me. I got a good look at it on the journey here. The imperial brand marks you as a member of the royal household, but I can still see the wolf underneath it."

She lowered her hand and resumed eating as though nothing were amiss. "Then, since you already know everything there is to know about me, why ask questions?"

"Why indeed?" He rested his elbows on the table and leaned forward. "What can you tell me about your mistress?"

She played the same game he had, taking her time chewing before answering him. "If you truly have eyes and ears in the palace, then you should already know as much about her as you do about me."

His face hardened. "You are far closer to her than they are."

"Yes, and I've worked hard to earn her trust."

"And what if I said you were finally free?" He pulled a delicate golden chain with a feather pendant from a box on the table and dangled it in front of her. "Now that you are here, you no longer have to serve your mistress."

She stared at the piece of jewelry that would proclaim her a free woman. For a brief moment, she coveted it and everything it stood for. She could read and write without fear of punishment. She could walk beside Modius on a city street and follow him back to Madrena.

Then her gaze drifted to the man holding it. "No, I would be trading one master for another. At least I know my mistress's motives."

"Such loyalty." He placed the chain back in the box. "Is it true your mistress is a *wa'ai?*"

She fixed her features into a mask of confusion. "A what?"

"Don't pretend you don't know what I'm talking about."

"Sorry, but we're forbidden to speak the Alpirion language." She refilled her cup, but didn't drink. If she was going to win this battle of wits, she didn't need hers dulled by too much wine.

He sat back in his chair, his black eyes glittering with hostility. "An Alpirion with blue eyes, a cursed one."

"Couldn't your spies confirm that for you?" She pretended to sip her wine. "I'm really beginning to doubt you're as powerful as you claim. For all I know, your pitiful little rebellion is confined to the group of men you rode up to the oasis with."

His fingers curled into his palm. "Do not toy with me, Izana. I am more powerful than you think."

"But you're not as powerful as my mistress."

"My pitiful little rebellion, as you called it, managed to kill an emperor."

Her heart hiccupped. She was just one question away from confirming the "who" part of the mystery, but if he was telling the truth, her chances of leaving here alive had shrunk to zero. "Are you claiming credit for Emperor Decius's death?"

His lips curled into a sinister smile, and he gave her one slow nod.

She tucked her hands into her lap before he saw the way they trembled. "Why do I find that hard to believe?"

"You were there, Izana. Do you really think he died of natural causes?"

The image of the former emperor's sunken face flashed in front of her. There was nothing natural about the way he had faded from this world. "Why?"

"Why not?" Tuhotep rose from his chair and stood behind her. "Now that you know I'm not to be trifled with, you'll tell me why your mistress sent you here."

The coarse linen of her dress scratched against her breasts, reminding her that the flowers she'd hidden were still there. "I already told you—she sent me to gather flowers for her wedding."

"And I don't believe you." He combed his fingers through her hair, balling them into a fist when he reached the base of her skull, and yanking her head back.

Tears sprang into her eyes. She looked up into his face and found no mercy there. The game was coming to an end, and she only had a few chances left to come out alive.

"Tell me, Izana."

"Why are you so interested in my mistress?"

His mouth twisted into a snarl as his fingers twisted in her hair. "You were found at a site sacred to our people, it's location a secret. Yet you knew exactly where it was and what was hidden there. Tell me why."

She closed her eyes and prepared for the knife's sting across her throat. She'd rather die than tell him the truth.

When she didn't answer, Tuhotep pulled her from her chair, his hand still gripping her hair by the roots, and dragged her to the doors. "Perhaps watching your companion suffer will loosen your lips."

"You gave your word not to kill us."

"And I told you there are fates worse than death." He pulled her against him, his hard muscles as unyielding as his will. "Tell me, how would you like to watch my men cut off his fingers, one by one?"

Her chest rattled when she inhaled, but she didn't reply.

"Or maybe I'm trying to extract answers from the wrong person." His free hand roved over her breast, squeezing it until she cried out. His breath bathed her ear. "What if I made him watch while I fucked you like the whore you are? What if I then

171

passed you around to each of my men, all in front of him? How would he like that?"

He'd hate it. He'd probably reveal their secret to protect her from such a fate, only to be forced to watch as Tuhotep carried it out just to assert his power over them.

But she hardened her expression to the one she'd worn years ago which betrayed none of the turmoil raging inside. "What makes you think he'd care?"

"I've seen the way he looks at you." He ran his finger up her neck, pausing at the brand. "He'll probably thank me when he learns the truth about you."

"What makes you think he doesn't already know it?"

"Because no man wants to give his heart to a woman who'll sell her body for the right price. Such women are never faithful."

An ache formed inside her when he confirmed what she'd known all along. She struggled against him, balling her hands into fists and pounding them against his stony chest, but his arms tightened around her until it hurt to breathe.

"No more games, Izana. All it takes is one word from me, and they'll fetch him."

She bit her bottom lip. The gods mocked her, offering her no way out. "If I answer your questions, will you set him free?"

His muscles slackened, and both brows shot up. "Just him?"

She nodded, fighting back tears. Modius was the one person who could unravel this mystery, not her. He was the one who would find the cure to save Emperor Sergius. She'd played her part already, and he would be happier without her when all was said and done.

"You would plead for his life and freedom, but not value your own when it was offered to you?" His snicker was as sharp as any blade piercing her heart. "This is why love is for the weak."

In the past, she would have agreed with him. But she'd

seen how strong the love was between her mistress and the emperor, how it turned them into better people and stronger rulers, how it defied all the odds. She wanted something like that for herself. Maybe Modius would reject her once he learned the truth about her former life, but right now, she was willing to barter her body and her life to save him. Hopefully, he'd remember that and not the sordid details of her past.

She rolled her hips, grinding against him and grinning when his cock hardened. Her years as a *lupa* taught her how to awaken desire in a man, to pretend to enjoy his touch when everything inside recoiled, to make him feel like he was the only man she wanted. "Perhaps you're right. Perhaps love is for the weak. But lust…"

She left the suggestion open as her voice trailed off and her fingers hooked under his belt.

One by one, the signs appeared. The widening of the pupils. The licking of the lips. The shallow breaths. Tuhotep was no different than any other man. She cursed her arrogance for not stooping to this sooner, but some part of her had hoped she would never have to lie with a man to survive ever again.

Because now, she knew what it felt like to have a man of her choosing make love to her, to look down at her with adoration shining from his eyes when he sent her over the edge. If Tuhotep agreed to her proposition, she'd close her eyes and imagine it was Modius inside her, not him.

Tuhotep's mouth thinned. "Oh, you're good, little Izana. For a moment, you almost had me convinced you wanted me."

"What makes you think I don't?"

"Because I see it in your eyes. You'd always be thinking of him." His grin was as cruel as the words that followed. "Tell me—if your positions were reversed, would he give up his freedom for you yours, especially once he knew what you were? What you just proposed to me?"

A wail rose into her throat. She clamped her mouth closed to keep it from escaping.

"Or better yet, let's invite him to watch a demonstration

173

of your skills on me. I'd be willing to set him free afterward, provided you never told him why. One peep out of you, and my men would kill him. He'd leave seeing you for the whore you really are."

Izana looked away, her eyes burning. No matter what she did, Modius would be hurt.

"So you see," Tuhotep murmured, "there are fates worse than death. But you can change all that by telling me what I want to know."

Her conscience wrestled with her heart. As much as she wanted to remain loyal to Azurha, she wanted Modius's love more. Reveal a secret to protect a secret.

But that didn't mean she couldn't manipulate the truth a bit.

She let one tear fall and willed her body to slump in defeat. If he believed she was surrendering, perhaps he'd be more willing to believe what she was about to tell him. "My mistress heard the story of Ausetsut and Tiberius."

A triumphant gleam filled his eyes. "And?"

"It didn't take long for her to figure out that the moon lily was used to poison the emperor."

He unwound his fingers from her hair, massaging her scalp in a way that made her flesh crawl. "Go on."

"She sent us to find the source."

"And you did." He released her and stepped back as though he were about to take a bow for his part in the emperor's murder.

"But now I'm curious how you pulled it off. I've been in the palace for two years and have never seen you there."

"A member of my brotherhood carried out the deed for me, right under the noses of everyone there. Captain Galerius of the Legion. That insufferable steward, Varro. Empress Horatia. None of them even knew what we'd done until it was too late." He rested his hand on his sword with an arrogant tilt of his jaw. "Perhaps now Emperor Sergius will take our requests seriously, or he'll suffer the same fate as his father."

His threat was meant to intimidate her, but a spark of hope flared inside her when she heard it. He didn't know about Emperor Sergius. "Ah, but you know the trouble with allowing your minions to carry out deeds in your name? Sometimes they assume too much power and try to take control from you."

His brows drew closer, and his confidence wavered. "What are you talking about?"

"I'm surprised your eyes and ears haven't told you."

He grabbed her arm, pulling her until his face hovered inches above her own. "Told me what?"

Her heart beat in her chest like an agitated bird in a cage too small for its wings. Now was her chance to gain the upper hand on Tuhotep. "It seems your assassin decided to take matters in his own hands and poison Emperor Sergius, too."

"You lie." He spat the words out at her, but his fingers trembled around her arm.

"Think, Tuhotep. My mistress can do nothing about a man who's already dead, but she will do anything to save the man she loves. That's why we're here—to find the source so we can find a cure."

He shoved her back in a howl of rage. "I can't believe my man would act without my permission."

Her heart beat faster. Perhaps if she aroused his anger enough, he would let slip the name of his accomplice. "I'd say the emperor has a week left to live, maybe less, meaning you'll never see an Alpirion empress on the throne."

A stream of Alpirion curses poured from his lips as he dug his fingers into his scalp and paced the length of the room.

Now it was her turn to laugh. "And you don't know the best part of it."

He stilled, his face contorted in anger. "And what's that?"

"If the emperor dies, the Rabbit will be coming for you." She sauntered toward him, praying her show of cockiness would be the final blow that sent him over the edge and revealed what she needed to know. "I hope you can sleep with one eye open, because you'll spend the rest of your days wondering when my mistress will come to end your life."

He paled for a moment before the ruddy glow returned to his cheeks. He flung the doors open. "We leave for Emona now," he instructed his men in Alpirion. "If what she says is true, there'll be no mercy for my brother."

The guards ran off, calling out to the other men in the abandoned settlement, but the warrior who'd brought her from the cell remained. Tuhotep pointed to him. "Take her back to the cell. I want her and her companion alive when I return."

Then he turned to her. "If you are lying, I will make you wish for death a hundred times over."

She lifted her chin. "I have nothing to fear, but you do."

The thunder of hooves echoed off the walls of the underground street. The dozen men she'd counted on her way over charged toward them on horseback, drawing to a stop a few feet away from the entrance of the palace.

Tuhotep mounted the riderless horse in the front. "We won't rest until we reach Emona," he shouted to the men. Then he kicked his horse forward and galloped up a steep side street that vanished above the rooftops.

Izana dug her nails into her palm to make sure this wasn't a dream. Tuhotep had taken all but one of his men with him, and now she knew the way out of this underground city. If she could somehow make it back to Emona before Tuhotep, she'd be able to turn him over to her mistress and maybe even discover a cure for the emperor.

The warrior who was left behind stepped behind her and shoved her forward. "It's back to the cell for you."

"You'd be wise to treat me with care."

"Don't get all uppity with me, slave." He drew his sword. "All Tuhotep said was that you had to be alive when he came back. He didn't mention anything about you needing to be in one piece."

She walked in the direction he indicated with his blade, keeping her lips shut. She'd managed to outwit Tuhotep. Now, all she had to do was find a way to slip past the guard.

But the opportunity never presented itself on the way back to the cell. He kept his sword drawn the entire way, making any sudden moves risky. When they entered the prison, he grabbed the key ring from the hook by the entrance and unlocked the door. "Get in there."

Modius sat where she'd left him, his feet still bound and his arms behind his back, but the hint of a smile on his lips told her he might have found a way to finish what she started.

"I assume you'll bring us food and water while we're here," she said, refusing to move.

He growled and muttered something in Alpirion about how they should've left them in the middle of the desert, before nodding. "Yes, but don't expect the feast you enjoyed tonight."

She took a step, then paused. "My bodyguard must be famished and parched from the journey. He could do with at least a drink of water and bit of bread."

"You'll be thankful for what you get." He pushed her into the cell and slammed the door shut behind her.

20

Modius reached out to catch Izana, not caring if the guard saw that his hands were unbound. She landed against him with a soft thump. The slamming door concealed them in the shadows, but he waited several breaths before he dared to move.

Once he was certain the guard was gone, he examined her for any injuries. "Did he hurt you?"

She shook her head. A shaky grin played on her lips, but never reached her eyes.

He pulled her to his chest, hoping it would comfort her. "I was worried sick about you."

"I'm fine, really, but I—" She stopped and sat back. "You cut yourself free."

It was the first bit of joy he'd heard in her voice since they'd been captured, and his fears abated. He held out his hands for her. "I just finished maybe two minutes before he brought you back, right around the time I heard what sounded like thunder."

"It wasn't thunder—it was Tuhotep and his men leaving on horseback." She searched the floor around him, grabbing the knife where it had fallen from his hands, and began cutting through the ropes on his ankles. "They're on their way to Emona, but—"

"Hold on a moment. I feel like I'm only getting half the

story. Tell me everything that happened after you left."

She froze, her gaze still fixed on his feet, and his gut knotted. Whatever she was going to tell him, it would be censored. She'd asked him to trust her, and yet, she still didn't trust him enough to be completely honest with him.

"Tuhotep placed a member of his brotherhood in the palace. That's who poisoned Emperor Decius."

A curse fell from his lips, but Izana shushed him by placing her finger over them.

"Wait, there's more. The reason he left was because I told him Emperor Sergius had also been poisoned."

"Why did you do that? If he knows his enemy is weak, he'll finish him off."

"Maybe, but it was a risk I had to take." She went back to work on the ropes. "He was furious to find out that Emperor Sergius had been poisoned, saying his brother had overstepped his bounds. He's on his way to Emona now to punish whoever his spy in the palace is, but I'm hoping we can get back before him and catch both him and his assassin."

The ropes gave way, and his feet burned from the blood rushing back into them. He took her hands and stood. The first steps made him wince after hours off his feet, but after a minute, he was able to cross the room without too much pain.

He rubbed his chin. "Do you have a plan to get us out of this cell?"

She nodded, her eyes dull in the beam of light that came from the window. "Why else do you think I demanded food and water for us? When he brings it, we'll overpower him and escape."

"And then?"

"Then we go to the surface and pray Marcus finds us quickly." She slipped the dagger back into the sheath on her thigh.

"What about the others?"

"Tuhotep took them with him. It's just the guard, as far as I could see. And I found the way out, so we shouldn't get lost

179

in the tunnels." She leaned back on her heels. "If my estimates are correct, it will take them a good week to reach Emona on horseback. Unless they have someone with Deizian blood in their ranks, they won't be able to fly there or use a communication orb. We have time to escape, find Marcus, and get home to warn the emperor."

It sounded too easy, which set him on edge. Nothing was ever as easy as it seemed, especially when he knew there was information she was hiding from him. But even though she didn't trust him, he had to trust her. He saw no other way out.

"By any chance, you didn't happen to find my satchel with the flowers in it?"

She smile faded, and she shook her head. "But I might have enough."

She reached into her bodice and pulled out a swatch of cloth. Inside were twelve delicate moon lilies.

His hope returned. Thank the gods for Izana's foresight. "Yes, that should be enough."

***

Azurha paced behind Titus, listening to his conversation with Marcus through the communication orb and wishing her insides didn't feel so hollow.

"Any sign of Izana or Modius?" he asked.

Marcus shook his head. "I barely have the ship airworthy after that ambush. Worse, I can't detect the signals from the tracking devices I gave them."

Azurha paused. "But the tracking devices would still work, even if they'd been killed?"

"By the gods, you're morbid." Marcus rubbed his nose, then his cheeks. "But yes, they would work, even if the person were dead, which is why the complete loss of signal is so baffling."

"If those Alpirion rebels are as wily as their ancestors, I'm sure they've found a way to hide the signal." Titus's shoulders slumped a bit lower, the conversation draining what little energy he had. The poison continued to eat away at him, wasting the once-strong muscles that rippled under his skin until he looked like a man half-starved. "Keep looking for them. I'll call you back if I need you to return sooner."

He didn't need to say why. All three of them knew his days were numbered unless they found a cure.

Marcus's face faded from the orb, and Titus let it fall from his fingers onto the cushions around him. He raked his fingers through his hair and pressed his palms against his temples. "I hate this. I hate feeling so useless, so weak."

Azurha sat beside him and wrapped her arm around him. "You're not useless, and you're not weak."

"I can barely walk to the throne room without being on the verge of collapsing."

"And yet you do it every morning so you can restore the barrier. That's not being weak or useless."

He lowered his hands and stared straight ahead. "But how much longer will I be able to do that?"

She closed her eyes and willed back the tears that threatened to spill over. She had to remain strong. For the millionth time since she'd realized he'd been poisoned, she wished she could switch places with him. This had to be some cruel punishment from the gods for all the lives she'd taken with poison. Now, she was forced to watch death slowly claim the one person she treasured above all else, and there was nothing she could do about it.

The ache in her chest intensified, stealing her breath, but she had to push it aside. She took his hand and stood. "Shall we tend to the barrier now?"

"Might as well." Titus rose to his feet and wobbled, leaning on her more than he had the previous day. Together, they made it down the long hallway to the empty throne room. The grey of dawn still filled the windows, and only the earliest of slaves stirred at this hour. It was the best time of day to make the trip. They'd have little worry of someone spying the emperor in his weakened condition.

The red glow of the barrier filled the throne room,

181

casting sinister shadows on the walls. It was weak, but it still held.

Titus shifted his weight from her to the floating globe, the massive structure barely shifting from the new burden. He closed his eyes and drew his brows together. Beads of perspiration broke out along his forehead, but the barrier remained unchanged.

Worry tumbled inside her stomach. If anyone felt useless, it was her. Titus was the only one who could protect his people, and if he failed, they'd have an even greater problem to deal with. Alpirion rebels could be reasoned with; the Barbarians couldn't.

A new sensation mingled with her fear, growing stronger with each beat of her heart. It pounded against the confines of her body like a prisoner trying to break free, and clouded her vision with a hazy blue light. Her hands trembled from the intensity of it. She'd felt something like this before—the night she had saved Titus—but she doubted she'd need it to bust down a door.

Instead, she reached for his hand and released this strange power into him.

He cried out, more in surprise than in pain, and laced his fingers through hers. And in that moment, they were one being. Their hearts beat in time, their breaths flowed in and out together, and their souls blurred into each other. She couldn't tell where she ended and he began, but she didn't want to let go.

It ended far too soon. The strange power inside her faded, and her consciousness retreated back into her body. But when her vision cleared, the barrier sparkled like a string of diamonds.

Titus squeezed her hand and smiled at her. A bloom of health appeared in his sickly pale cheeks, and some of the weariness had faded from his eyes. "See what your magic can do, Azurha?"

She looked at the globe, trying to remember every detail about what had just happened so she could grab the magic again, then back at him. "If it would cure you, I'd gladly pour every ounce of it into doing so."

His smile waned, taking her hope with it. "I am feeling a bit better, but..."

But he still felt the poison ravaging his body.

She guided his arm around her waist and kissed him. His love filled the void left behind by the wild power she'd given him, but it never reached the bliss she'd enjoyed moments before. "Perhaps I need to practice more. In the meantime, the barrier should hold for a few days."

He nodded and let her take him back to their quarters.

With each slow step they took, she tried to capture that power again, but found nothing. Not even the intensity of her fear for him could trigger it. By the time they reached their bed, she wondered if it had been nothing more than a dream.

21

The slap of sandals against stone jerked Izana from sleep. The clang of keys followed. She reached for her dagger only to have Modius grab her wrist.

He crouched in the darkness beside her like a lyger ready to spring, his eyes focused on the door. The lock clicked, and he shifted his weight to the balls of his feet. A beam of light fell on his face as the door swung open, highlighting the bruise that bloomed along his jaw. He rushed at the guard with a blur of motion.

A soft grunt filled the cell, followed by the blinding light from the room outside. Izana crawled forward, blinking rapidly until things came into focus. When they did, she found Modius wrestling with the guard. Their bodies rolled across the floor in a series of blows and kicks, twists and turns, each one trying to gain the upper hand over his opponent.

It soon became very clear, however, that the guard was winning. Modius had the lean frame of a scholar, not the bulging muscles of a warrior. Nor did he possess the dangerous curved blade that hung from the guard's belt. Once the guard pinned Modius to the ground, he reached for his sword, his eyes showing no hint of mercy.

Izana's heart skipped a beat, and time seemed to slow. Modius strained against his captor, the cords of his neck bulging.

The guard's hand crept closer to the hilt, his back to her. If she didn't act soon, the guard would end Modius's life with one quick slice.

Her pulse returned with the fury of galloping horse. She reached under her skirt for the dagger and raced toward the guard as he drew his own blade. She didn't think. She didn't feel. She didn't stop until her dagger was firmly planted in the soft flesh under his ribs.

The guard gasped, and the sword fell from his fingers. He started to roll to the side to throw her off.

Izana yanked the dagger out and swiped it across the front of his throat as he turned toward her, his back to Modius. Blood sprayed her face, coating the look of shock on the guard's face in a sea of red. He reached for her. She screamed and backed away just out of his reach until he fell at her feet.

Blood. So much blood.

The sticky red liquid covered her hands, her arms, her dress. It dripped from her hair and ran down her cheeks. Horror chilled her insides and rattled her bones. She glanced down at the dagger still her hand and dropped it with a shudder.

"It's all right, Izana," Modius said, rising from the ground, but his words sounded like they were miles away.

Warm liquid pooled around her bare feet. She screamed again and retreated from the blood that seemed to chase after her even though its owner had passed into the afterlife.

Blood. So much blood. Too much blood.

She didn't know she was speaking the words until Modius took her in his arms and said, "Shh, Izana. We can wash the blood away."

Could they? She'd never dreamed of taking a life. How could her mistress have taken so many in her past and not felt the same shock, the same disgust that rolled through her now? And yet, she couldn't take her eyes of the fresh corpse she'd created.

Numbness took over as Modius led her away from the scene of her crime. He paused long enough to retrieve her mistress's dagger and the guard's sword, but didn't stop until they were in the main street of the underground village. "You said there was a way out."

She nodded, her eyes burning. Her breath hiccupped, and the tremor inside her intensified. He tried to pull her along, but her feet refused to move.

"Please, Izana, I know you're upset, but this is no time to freeze up on me. Remember our mission. We only have a small window of time to save the emperor, and every second counts."

Yes, we have to save the emperor. She focused on that instead of the life she'd just taken, of the blood that covered her and marked her as a killer, and willed her body to move forward.

Eerie torchlight illuminated the abandoned city. This time, she saw no one in the houses they passed. The Alpirions had all gone with their leader. When they reached the end of the street, she pointed toward the incline Tuhotep and his men had taken up to the surface.

The trickling sound of water grew louder as they pressed on, growing into the shower of a small waterfall. Modius stopped beside it when they found it. "Take a moment to wash off."

Izana closed her eyes and stepped right into the heart of the stream. The icy water sent shivers down her spine, but it washed away the sticky evidence from her skin into the pool below and then downstream. Unfortunately, it couldn't remove the stain of guilt from her heart. She stood there until her teeth stopped chattering and her soul grew as numb as her body.

"Better now?" Modius asked, pulling her out from the waterfall.

She would've said yes, but he handed the dagger back to her, and a new wave of memories assaulted her. She fought her way through them, squeezing the hilt until her fingers tingled, and finally slipped the blade back into the sheath along her side. "I'm better now."

"Good. Now, let's fill this waterskin so we have something to drink out there."

Tuhotep and his men had taken all the good skins,

leaving behind the ones that dripped water along the side of her skirt when she slung it over her shoulder. But they needed water if they were going to survive in the desert long enough for Marcus to find them.

The passage led to an opening hidden between two boulders. The sun was high in the sky when they reached the surface. Heat rippled off the sand dunes in waves, drying her wet clothes in minutes. Modius went directly for the shade provided by the cluster of four palms trees to their left, but otherwise, they were left open to the vast expanse of nothingness as far as she could see.

The hot sand bit into her feet as she crossed the space between the underground city and the palm grove. She glanced down at the leather strap on her wrist. After this long, would the tracking devices still work?

Modius took a long drink from his skin. "We'll stay here until nightfall. That way, if Marcus is nearby, he can find us. Once it's cooler, we'll refill the waterskins and start walking."

"Which way?"

A muscle tensed along his jaw, indicating he was just as lost as she was. "I'll try to figure that out as the day goes on. In the meantime, let's rest."

She sat beside him, but every time she closed her eyes, she saw nothing but red.

***

Modius finished the last drops of water from his skin and stared out into the desert. The sun hung low on the horizon like a glowing orange shield. Night would be on them soon, and then they'd have to make their move. Izana had managed to get them out of the city, but now it was up to him to get them home.

The safest bet would be to go north. Emona was that way. But he had no idea how far it was from here to the next source of water. The only person who might have known was lying dead in the prison below.

He slid his gaze over to Izana. She'd been silent since they'd come up to the surface, her chin resting on her knees and her normally bright eyes flat and dull. The death of their enemy weighed upon her conscience. He'd give her time to cope with it, but he wouldn't let it interfere with their mission. Eventually, she'd have to come to terms with killing the guard and accept it was take a life or lose one.

He ran his fingers along her cheek, gently coaxing her attention to him. "I never thanked you for saving my life."

She started and stared at him. "You're welcome," she mumbled before slipping into the realm of her thoughts.

He bit back a curse. He had a strong body, a sharp mind, but he lacked the words to soothe her soul and help her find peace with her actions. And until she accepted what she'd done, she would remain distant. He'd have to give her time for that, but that didn't mean he couldn't ask her about other things. "What else did you learn about Tuhotep?"

She lifted her head and blinked. "Why do you want to know about him?"

"Because if he's our enemy, then we'll be more successful if we can spot his weaknesses."

She chewed her lip, the haunted haze clearing from her eyes. "I don't think his real name is Tuhotep. I think he goes by that to rally the people behind him, but he probably doesn't have a drop of royal blood in him."

"What makes you think that?" he asked, relieved to engage her thoughts on something besides her act.

"He doesn't have the royal look about him." She chuckled. "I know that sounds silly, but if you can remember the statues and the paintings hidden in the library, the old kings all had a certain shape to their face—a straight nose, high cheekbones, a sharp chin and angled jaws. Azurha looks more like a descendant of the royal family than he does."

He stretched his legs out in the sand and leaned back on his hands. "Wouldn't it be funny if Lady Azurha was descended from the royal family?"

A ghost of a smile played on her lips. "Yes, it would be, but we'll never know, will we?"

"What about the fact she's a wa-wa like the princess?"

This time, she genuinely laughed. "It's *wa'ai*, and I have no idea if that's something confined to the royal blood or not. Maybe we can ask Hapsa about that when we get home."

His spirits lifted. *When we get home.* He had no idea if he'd be able to find a cure, but he wasn't going to stop searching until the emperor drew his last breath. "Did Tuhotep confirm that the poison was the moon lily?"

She pursed her lips together. "Yes, and no. I mean, he didn't deny it when I confronted him about it, but he could've been playing games with me, too."

"What I wouldn't have given to see you take him on."

Her face hardened. "No, be thankful you weren't there."

Her reply prickled his mind like a swarm of mosquitoes. "What did he do?"

"It's not what he did."

Her words slammed into him like battering ram. *It's not what* he *did.* All this time, he'd assumed her guilt had been over killing the guard. What if it was due to something else? "Izana, what—"

"I don't want to talk about it." She stood and shook the sand from her skirts. "Do you hear that hum?"

He opened his mouth to accuse her of changing the subject, but then he heard it, too. It came from behind him and grew louder with each passing second. He turned around and saw a cloud of dust approaching from that direction. "Take cover."

She started toward the boulders that hid the passageway to the underground city, but halted. "No, it's not a sandstorm. It's a ship."

He followed her finger and caught the gleam of the setting sun on the bronze hull. "You don't think it's Marcus, do you?"

"Do you know of anyone else who'd be flying an airship through the Alpirion desert?" She pulled her bodice up over her mouth and nose and ran out from the shelter of the tree, her arm waving.

Modius offered a quick prayer to the gods that she was right and followed her.

The airship slowed as it approached, calming the blusters of sand that billowed up around it. The hull bore recent damage, with some of the ore plates missing to reveal singed wood underneath, but there was no mistaking the grandeur of the emperor's ship. The air whooshed out of his lungs, and his spirits started to rise.

The ship stopped a few hundred yards in front of them, hovering a good twenty feet above their heads. Marcus appeared over the railing. "Thank the gods you two are alive. You won't believe the grief Azurha's been giving me since we lost you."

"You won't believe the adventure we've had since you left us at the village." Modius caught the end of the rope ladder that someone tossed to them and lifted Izana up until her foot slipped into the first rung. "Looks like you had a bit of fun yourself."

"Damn Alpirion rebels had a catapult hidden in one of those palm groves." Marcus patted the side of the hull. "But it will take more than a few rocks and fireballs to take this ship down."

Modius jumped and pulled himself up by his arms until his feet reached the bottom of the ladder. His muscles burned from the effort, and his new bruises throbbed, but he made it up to the deck. "How quickly will she carry us to Emona?"

"Maybe an hour or two slower, but we should get there within two days."

"Good, because we have a rebel leader to catch."

22

A bath and change of clothes had removed the evidence of the murder, but it couldn't erase the guilt that clung to her heart.

No man wants to give his heart to a woman who'll sell her body for the right price. Such women are never faithful.

Tears stung her eyes, threatening to spill over. Tuhotep was right. She couldn't be faithful. Not to her mistress. Not to Modius. She'd betrayed them all to protect herself. She'd even been willing to sleep with Tuhotep to protect Modius from both her past and from their captors.

Wetness streaked down her cheeks. She wiped it away with the back of her hand and cursed. Crying wouldn't solve anything. They had only a few days left to save the emperor. And once they did, Modius would return to Madrena, where he'd be much better off without someone like her.

She released a sardonic laugh. During all her years as a *lupa*, she'd never known the shame that haunted her now. She'd been forced to lie with men she abhorred, but it was never her choice. She did it because her mistress ordered her to. And sometimes, it was actually pleasurable. But last night had been her choice. Last night, she'd become a whore in the truest sense of the word by offering herself to Tuhotep. Even though she never carried out the act, she had been willing to do it.

191

The door to her cabin opened, and she turned away before Modius could see she'd been crying.

"You changed your dress," he said softly.

"You can burn the old one." Her voice was hoarse from the tears. "There's no way I can get the bloodstains out now."

He stood behind her, the warmth of his skin permeating her own as he wrapped his arms around her. "Does his death still trouble you?"

It would be all too easy to lie and tell him yes, but she remained silent. She wasn't ready to confess her sins just yet.

He turned her around and tilted her chin until her eyes met his. "Never be ashamed of something you have to do to survive. You did what you had to do, and if you hadn't, we wouldn't be alive."

His words acted like a balm to soothe her raw soul. "Do you really mean that?"

He nodded, tenderness softening the hard lines of his face. "If our situations had been reversed, I would've killed a hundred men to save you."

She let herself believe he would forgive her of everything long enough to lean into his embrace and listen to the steady throb of his heart. But the moment fled as her past crept back along the edges of her mind. If she ever wanted to feel safe with him, if she ever wanted to know if what they had was real, she needed to reveal her secrets to him. She drew in a breath and asked, "Is there anything about your past you wished would just disappear?"

He tensed, and she got her answer. She wasn't the only one guarding a secret. Perhaps if she trusted him with hers, he'd reveal his secret with her.

"Why do you ask that?"

"Because of something Tuhotep said to me." She stepped back and pulled her hair back to reveal the mark on her neck. "There's a reason why I don't wish to talk about my former mistress with you. Do you see the tattoo under the brand?"

He came closer to study it, his thumb running across the

192

gnarled scars.

She stiffened her spine, preparing for the worst. Would he hit her? Yell at her? Recoil in disgust?

"Is that a wol—" His breath hitched, and his eyes widened.

She didn't look away as she gave him one solemn nod. "Yes, it is a wolf."

He stumbled back a step. "But that means you were a…"

His reaction was no different than she expected. It stung like a thousand lashes of the whip, ripping apart any hope that she might have a future with him. She gritted her teeth and closed her eyes until she found her voice again. "Yes, Modius, I was a *lupa*. My former mistress was Calpurnia," she explained, naming the owner of the most exclusive *lupanar* in Emona. "When she died, her daughter didn't have a need for me anymore and sold me to the empress. But it still doesn't change my past and what I've done."

The shuffle of footsteps told her he had moved even further away from her. When she opened her eyes, he was sitting on the edge of the bed and staring at the wall. Minutes dragged out into the most painful torture she could imagine, and yet all she could do was stand there and wait for him to order out of his sight.

"So was it that for me, too?" he asked at last, his question barely more than a whisper.

"No, never." Panic sharpened her voice. If she didn't explain her heart now, she risked losing him. "No money was exchanged. My mistress never ordered me to pleasure you. I came to you because I wanted you, but I understand if you no longer want me." She went to the door, her shoulders squared and her head held high. If this was the last he'd see of her, she didn't want him to know how much he'd hurt her.

"Izana, wait."

She froze when he called her named, her attention focused on the door. Her pulse fluttered with an erratic beat. Would he mock her and sneer in her face as he called her a whore? Or would he be willing to look past her former life and accept who she was now? "Why?"

"Look at me when I'm talking to you."

It was an order, one she was bound to follow as a slave, even though his words were as soft as a caress. She turned around, but kept her eyes downcast more as an act of defiance than an act of shame.

"I meant what I said earlier. You should never be ashamed of what you had to do to survive."

She lifted her gaze so that she peered at him through her lashes. "Even that?"

He gulped and nodded. "Even that."

Her brain was warning her to stop now while she still had his acceptance, but her conscience wouldn't let her rest until she'd told him the entire truth. "And would you still feel the same way if I told you I had been willing to sleep with Tuhotep to protect you?"

His jaw opened, then snapped shut. A wave of red rose into his cheeks. "And did you?"

"No. I found another way to placate him by telling him about Emperor Sergius." *And by betraying my mistress in the process.*

He stood and rocked back and forth on his feet, rubbing his hand across his face while he struggled to respond to her confession. An exasperated sigh stilled him, and it was his turn to stare at the floor. "Why would you consider doing such a thing?"

She watched him, the ache in her chest becoming almost unbearable. She loved him—she knew that now—but she refused to show him how much he was hurting her now. "Because I'm a fool."

"Don't say that," he snapped, anger flashing in his eyes when he looked up.

"But it's the truth. I'm nothing more than a stupid slave whose only talent lies in making men come." Bitterness choked her words, but that didn't stop them from spilling forth. "And when I was faced with a life or death situation, I fell back on what I do best."

"Stop that right now." He crossed the space between them in three long strides and grabbed her by shoulders. "You are smart and clever and far more courageous than most of those women who call themselves nobles. When those Alpirions surrounded us, it was you who saved us. It was you how found a way out of that prison, and it was you who discovered how Tuhotep poisoned the emperor. And each and every time, you relied on your wits, not your body. So don't you stand there and tell me you're nothing more than a stupid whore because you're not."

Hope and pride pounded through her veins, but ended when she witnessed the continued torment on his face. "And yet it's still not enough to make you forget about my past, is it?"

"No, it has nothing to do with your past." He released her and stepped back. "It has more to do with mine."

"Tell me."

A cynical chuckle answered her. "If I did, you'd probably wonder why you'd risked so much to save a monster like me."

A chill rippled down her back and lodged in the pit of her stomach. "What have you done that you wished would disappear?"

"Are you certain you wish to know?"

She braced herself for whatever he was preparing to unleash on her and nodded.

"My father always considered my interest in medicine and healing to be unnatural. He discouraged it by forcing me to join the army when I was barely old enough to handle a gladius, but all it did was whet my curiosity more. The wounds, the injuries, the illnesses—they all fascinated me. And when my term of enlistment was up, I returned to Emona and spent days in the library, learning more about the workings of the body and how to heal it."

He paused and rubbed the back of his neck, his face pinched in pain. "Three years ago, I discovered a way to further my studies in a way the library couldn't. The emperor had just hosted several days of gladiatorial games to celebrate his thirtieth year on the throne, and I—" His voice broke. He swallowed and continued, "And I bribed a gravedigger to bring the bodies of the fallen to me so I could use them for research."

A knot formed in her stomach, tightening to the point of nausea. She'd heard a rumor years ago about a crazy young man who'd mutilated corpses, but she never would've believed it had been Modius.

"I spent the next week working like mad to dissect them before they began rotting, hardly sleeping in my attempt to catalog every muscle, every vessel, every organ. But eventually, someone noticed the stench and called the city guard. And when they found me…" He paused and gave her a wry smile. "Well, let's just say I made your dress look immaculate. I hadn't slept, hadn't bathed, hadn't shaved in days. I don't think there was an inch of me that wasn't covered in blood. I looked like every peaceful citizen's worst nightmare come true."

The stories from that event surfaced to the forefront of her mind. She'd heard everything, from that he was drinking their blood as part of some occult ritual to that he was eating their flesh. Whispers of horror had floated through the streets of Emona for days. But the man before her would have never done those things.

"They arrested me and took me to the palace dungeon. I remember hearing the crowds outside demanding my head, and I already felt the executioners axe slicing through my neck before I'd been sentenced. But then, my fate changed."

"How?"

"Emperor Decius." This time, his smile was humble. "He came down to my cell and asked me why I'd done what I'd done. I pleaded for him to just look at my notes, to see for himself the discoveries I'd made, and—" he choked again, "and I was surprised to learn he had.

"He told me he was impressed with my research, unorthodox as it was, and said he needed men with minds like mine. So he spared my life and sent me to Madrena, where I became the steward of his palace and oversaw the gardens there.

It was exile, but it got me out of Emona and kept me alive until the uproar died down."

Izana wrung her hands together, not knowing how to take this news. The Modius she knew was nothing like the man in those stories.

"So to answer your question, Izana, yes, there is something in my past I wish would just disappear. But I can't change it. It's part of me, of who I am, and why I'm here today. I can't separate it from me any more than you with your past. But, if you can find it in your heart to accept me as I am…" He held out his hand to her.

Her lungs refused to move. He still wanted her, even though he knew what she'd done. And he'd even shared his secret with her. But instead of making her recoil in disgust, it made her love him all the more. He understood what it was like to have people judge him, even though his intentions bore no malice. He knew what it was like to hide from the scandal of the past and try to make a fresh start. And, she realized as she reached for his outstretched hand, he was willing to entrust his heart to her and make a future together.

The moment her fingers touched his palm, he pulled her into his arms and covered her lips with his own. The kiss was as searing as though he wanted to brand her as his own and bind her to him permanently. She followed his lead, returning his intensity with her own. He was hers as much as she was his, and she never wanted him to doubt that.

They left a trail of clothes behind them as they stumbled toward the bed and fell onto it. Desire overwhelmed any shame, any guilt, any fear that lingered. All Izana knew was the physical need that throbbed through her body, augmented by the love that radiated from her heart. She wanted to cover him with kisses, to taste every inch of him and drive him wild with lust until he could no longer take it. Then he'd enter her and send her over the edge like he had done so many times.

She broke her lips away from his and placed a nip at his jaw. Her tongue glided over the rough stubble, removing the salt that clung to his skin, and continued lower along his neck. His breath hitched when she came to his flat nipple and rumbled out in a moan as she continued to tease it with her mouth the same way he'd done to her breasts before.

She reached down and wrapped her hand around the base of his cock, hard and tense and beckoning her to come lower with her mouth. And she wanted him in her mouth. She wanted to take him all the way inside her, to suck away the drop of liquid that already beaded at the tip, to run her tongue up and down the length of him until he surrendered to his release.

But as soon as her lips wrapped around its head, he pried her away and rolled his weight on top of her. "No, not tonight. You've seen to a man's pleasure too many times. It's time someone saw to your own."

In the times they'd been together, he'd probably kissed every part of her body. He'd even made her come with his tongue that first night to prove his point, but this time was different. He started by lacing his fingers through hers and raising her arms above her head. Then, ever so gently, his lips grazed hers in kisses as light as butterfly wings.

The soft sensations startled her. She was so used to sex being fierce and intense, about finding that release she and her partner both sought. She'd never dreamed something delicate and tender could arouse the same desire she'd indulged in with him before. In truth, these light kisses magnified the throbbing inside her far more than his earlier kisses. The tension in her muscles melted, and she surrendered to the sensation of being loved.

His lips fluttered across her cheek, and his warm breath bathed her ear. "Tell me what you want, Izana. Tell me how to please you, how to make you happy, and I'll do it."

Her body knew what it wanted. Her hips rolled under him, seeking the erect cock that pressed against her stomach. Her fingers squeezed his with unspoken need. But when her gaze locked with his, all that was forgotten.

The gold flecks in his eyes seemed to glow with an

emotion she both feared and welcomed. He wasn't just asking for instructions on how to please her now in bed. He was asking what she wanted from him, now and forever.

A pressure burned in her chest, steadily increasing until it exploded and spilled into the rest of body. It was different from the physical ecstasy she'd experienced, but the aftereffects still left her with that warm, contented glow. And she finally knew what she wanted. "I want you, just as you are, wanting me, just as I am."

A slow smile spread on his lips, reigniting the glow inside her. "And I do."

He released her hands as he kissed her again, this time slow and full as though he'd poured every ounce of his being into the flicks of his tongue. When he finally pulled away, just as breathless as her, he lowered his head and pressed his lips to the brand on her neck.

Her breath caught. It was the one place on her body she'd hidden from him so long, the one thing that could potentially drive them apart, despite his sweet words. And yet, he treated it with the same reverence as he did every other part of her body.

His words vibrated against her skin in a silken hum. "I love you, Izana, just the way you are."

Her reply rushed to her tongue faster than she could gather the words, but somehow, they came out clearly. "I love you, too."

She heard a happy sigh, but she had no idea if it came from her or him. He moved lower, his mouth caressing the sensitive parts of her body between her neck and her thighs with the same gentle passion he'd started with. Every place he touched, he awakened some new facet of her awareness, claiming it and making it his.

She ran her fingers through his hair, along his arms and back and shoulders with light strokes, matching the pressure of his kisses. Words of endearment—both in Alpirion and the common language—tumbled forth from her lips. Every fiber of her being encouraged him to continue, to never stop making love to her.

By the time he got to the place between her legs, she was primed and on the edge. With one swipe of his tongue, she dissolved into the weightless rush of orgasm. He could've stopped there, but he didn't. Over and over, he teased the recess of her sex, drawing out her release until the pleasure turned into pain. When she cried out for him to stop, he cradled her in his arms until the last violent shudders ceased.

"Should I continue?" he asked, the hard ridge of his cock against her hip reminding her of his unfulfilled need.

Had Modius been any other man, he wouldn't have bothered to ask. He would've just taken, justifying his actions because he'd let her come first. But with Modius, she knew that if she said no, he'd still continue to hold her like he did now. He wouldn't accuse her of teasing him or force himself on her.

Not that it mattered, though. She wanted him all the more for asking. She shifted beneath him, opening her legs to him.

He slid in with one graceful stroke, his eyes closed tight as a moan vibrated through his chest. He stilled, letting his lungs draw in three long, deep breaths before opening his eyes. He looked down at her with a grin. "I can't think of anything more perfect than this."

"What? Being inside me?"

"That's nice, too, but I was thinking about the way you're staring up at me like you are now, so happy, so content—"

"And yet so desperate for more." She writhed under him, impatient for him to start moving inside her again.

He laughed and pressed his hand against her hip, stilling her and withdrawing until he was barely inside. "Are you always this bossy?"

Now it was her turn to laugh, remembering how he'd asked her that same question their first night together. She ran her fingers through his hair and along his neck, her eyes never leaving his, and savored the moment for as long as she dared. "Only with you."

"Yes, only with you," he murmured.

He made love to her with his eyes open, starting slow and easy, gradually increasing to the quick thrusts that set off a series of small explosions inside her body. She clung to him as she came, her gaze locked with his the entire time. And when he followed her over the brink, she saw nothing but love shining from his eyes.

As she lay beside him afterward, her body curled along his, Izana forgot about the fear and guilt that had plagued her earlier that night. Modius loved her, and her heart belonged to him.

23

No matter how much crystalized ginger Modius gave her, Izana's stomach still lurched as the airship descended into the palace's docks. At least now, though, she could enjoy the scenery of Emona from above without the fear of losing her last meal.

"He was a smart one," one of the sailors said behind her, "bringing along a little entertainment for the trip. No wonder he barely left his cabin."

She stiffened and pulled her hair over her shoulder to hide her brand, refusing to even acknowledge him.

The sailor snickered behind her. "Don't try to hide what you are from me. I can still see Calpurnia's mark on you."

The wood creaked behind her, and her pulse jumped. She ran her hand along her skirt, wondering how quickly she could draw the dagger still strapped to her thigh. Before this trip, she would have never found comfort in a weapon, but now, she understood why her mistress liked to wear the dagger under her dresses.

The stench of sweat and cheap wine filled her nostrils. "How much did he pay for you, *lupa*? I've been saving my money, and I'd love to have a little something like you on our next voyage."

She kept her eyes fixed on the rooftops below while her

fingers curled around the hilt of the dagger.

But she never had the chance to draw it.

Modius's voice sliced through the silence. "Leave her alone."

The sailor took a step away from her and turned to Modius. "I was just asking her how much she charged you."

The crack of a fist against bone sounded behind her. She whirled around just as Modius delivered the second blow, sending the sailor sprawling across the deck.

Modius stood over him, his hands still clenching into fists, his nostrils flaring, and his cheeks red. Anger flashed from his eyes and seeped into his cold threat. "Don't you ever talk to her that way."

"Why are you defending her?" The sailor sat up, leaning on one arm for support while the other acted as a flimsy shield. "She's nothing more than a whore."

Modius yanked him up to his feet with a primal growl that sent shivers down her spine and delivered another punch that knocked the sailor back to the edge of the railing. Then Modius grabbed him by the hair and pushed him down so that all the sailor could see was the hundred yards between him and the ground. "Next time you insult her, I'll toss you overboard."

He released the sailor and came to her. "Are you all right?"

She slipped her hand through his arm and nodded. "You didn't have to threaten him."

"Yes, I did. I don't want anyone thinking they can get away with calling you that." He nodded to Marcus as they crossed the deck. "I hope you don't mind that I disciplined your man."

The ship's captain cracked his knuckles. "Oh, believe me, he got off easy compared to what I'm about to do to him. I apologize for my man's behavior, Izana."

"Apology accepted." A new wave of confidence surged through her. For the first time in her life, she didn't feel like a slave. They were treating her as well as they did her mistress.

She leaned her head on Modius's shoulder. "Thank you for defending me."

"Anytime." He pressed his lips to her forehead. "You deserve to be treated with respect, and I'll have words with any person who doesn't give it to you."

The ship sank into the docking bay, and the gangplank rolled out. Izana disembarked with her arm still looped through Modius's, ignoring the conventions which dictated she walk behind him. For the next few moments, she was his equal.

All that ended when saw Varro frowning at her. Just like that, she was reminded of her place and moved behind Modius. He reached for her hand, but she ducked out of his grasp and nodded to his father.

"Lady Azurha wishes to speak to you both," the steward said with stiff formality. "Let's not keep her waiting, shall we?"

Modius cast one more inviting glance over his shoulder, but when she didn't come alongside him, he sighed and followed his father.

She trailed behind them, keenly aware of the stares her fellow slaves were giving her. Her gaze darted around the main courtyard and fell on one face in particular.

Farros frowned at her from the second story landing of the old barracks, his jaw as tight as his grip on the railing. He turned and whispered something to the person standing in the shadows beside him, his sleeve rising just enough for her to glimpse the edge of a tattoo on his inner arm.

Sweat prickled her skin, despite the chill that raced down her spine. *Of course. Why didn't I see it sooner?* The tattoo wasn't a feather like the others, but it was still in the same place.

Farros grinned at her with pure malice before fading into the shadows with his companion.

"Izana?" Modius's voice jerked her away. "What's wrong?"

She looked back at the landing, but both men were gone. "I thought I saw someone on the balcony."

"There's no one suicidal enough to go in the old

barracks, Izana. That building is on the verge of collapsing." He placed his hand on her forehead, then her cheek. "You're probably just exhausted from everything that's happened. Let's give our report to your mistress and then let you get some rest."

One final glance at the landing told her it was still empty, and she questioned what she'd seen. Had Farros even been there at all?

***

Modius stood inside the private quarters of the emperor and finished his account of their adventures in Alpiria by producing the small vial of moon lily oil he'd extracted on the way back to Emona. "This was all I was able to extract from what Izana managed to get past the rebels, but I hope it's enough to help us find a cure."

"And the source." Azurha took the vial from him and sniffed the contents. Her lips parted. "I think I may have smelled something like this before."

Emperor Sergius took it from her and sniffed, too. "It must be something leftover from your training, Azurha. I don't recall ever smelling something like that."

She shook her head. "No, it's not something Cassius taught me." She stood and paced the length of the room, her brow furrowed. "It's something recent. Something I've come in contact with since arriving at the palace."

Modius took the vial back from the emperor and inhaled the scent. It started out deceptively sweet before finishing with a peppery spice that burned his nostrils. He'd never smelled anything like it before, but if Azurha recognized it, then perhaps she'd be able to help him discover how the emperor was poisoned.

He studied Emperor Sergius, noting the ravaging effects of the poison on him already. Barely a week had passed since he'd seen him last, and emperor looked like he'd hadn't eaten in over a month. His cheeks were pale and sunken, and his bones protruded like sharp knobs under his toga. One silent nod from Izana told him this was the exact same thing that had happened to the prior emperor, and his stomach knotted.

Marcus leaned forward and motioned for the vial. "Are you certain this is the poison?"

"Yes," Izana answered, lifting her chin. Since they'd returned, he'd noticed a subtle change in her. She was no longer the timid slave. She was a woman who had a new sense of worth, and he hoped he'd been able to play a small part in her newfound confidence. "Tuhotep confirmed our suspicions when admitted to plotting Emperor Decius's death."

Marcus gave him the vial back, disbelief tugging at the corners of his mouth. "But I find it hard to believe something as simple as a flower could be so deadly to one person and not to everyone else who might have come in contact with it."

"It's because the Deizians are from another planet," he answered. "There are several plants I could name that have different effects on Deizians than they do on Elymanians and Alpirions, along with some plants from the Deizian home world that have no effect on the native races."

"Such as?" Marcus asked, one brow cocked in a challenge.

Modius mentally scoured the contents of the healing garden back in Madrena. "The purifico root. If you grind it into a paste, it's caustic to Elymanians and Alpirions, but it works very well at drawing out infections from Deizian wounds."

"Fine, you've named one plant."

"I can name a dozen more, if you'd like."

"Enough," the future empress ordered, still pacing. "Arguing gets us nowhere. Two things have become very clear to me. One, there's a good chance the poison is still somewhere in these chambers. And two, we still have an assassin in our midst who needs to be caught."

Modius nudged Izana. "Can you draw a sketch of the rebel leader and give it to Captain Galerius? That way, we can alert the Legion to him when he arrives."

Izana nodded. "May I use some of the paper in here?"

Azurha waved her toward the desk and then came to

him. "Do you recognize the scent?"

"I know it well enough to be able to recognize the oil should I smell it elsewhere."

"Then go with your father and try to find the source."

He looked over shoulder to see if the emperor had anything to add, but Emperor Sergius slumped against the cushions with his eyes closed in sleep.

Azurha met his gaze. "Now you see why I'm so desperate to find a cure. He's fading right before me."

"I'll do my best, my lady."

"As will I," his father said from where he'd stood by the door the entire time. "Come this way, Modius."

He followed his father into the emperor's dressing room.

"Let me smell that," Varro ordered. After one sniff, the old soldier wrinkled his nose. "Lady Azurha's right. I have smelled something like this before, although not as strong."

"Can you tell me the emperor's daily routine? We can start by ruling out things he'd normally come in contact with day to day and then move onto other possible sources."

"Very good." A hint of praise warmed his father's reply before the imperial steward took over. "Emperor Sergius is odd in that he starts his mornings with a bath."

"In addition to the normal bath in the afternoon?"

"Yes. Says it wakes him up. This way." His father moved swiftly, exaggerating his limp even more. "We can start with the baths and go from there."

Modius had been to some of the finest public baths in the empire, but none of them compared to the opulence of the emperor's private baths. Gold tiles shimmered through the intricate mosaics and sparkled underneath the water. Steam from the caldarium filled the air with humidity that infiltrated his clothes and mingled with his sweat. Exotic scents filled the air—sandalwood, jasmine, orange blossoms—but none of them matched the moon lily.

His father crossed the room to the small alcove containing a massage table and pulled a bottle out from the drawer under it. "This is the oil Emperor Sergius prefers."

He found the source of the sandalwood perfume in the air, but he didn't detect the sweet peppery notes of the moon lily oil. "Did Emperor Decius use this oil, too?"

"No, he didn't." Varro placed the stopped back in the bottle and retrieved a different one. "This is what Emperor Decius preferred."

At first, Modius only caught the heavy scents of leather, amber, and cedar. Then, at the very end, he caught the pepper. He inhaled it again, searching for the sweet floral notes of the moon lily scent. His stomach dropped when he found them. "I think I can smell the poison."

"Don't be ridiculous. Emperor Decius used this same oil for years, and—" He paused as he sniffed it. "Let me smell the poison again."

Varro went back and forth between the two oils, his face paling with each pass. "By the gods, I think you're right. But that doesn't explain how Emperor Sergius was poisoned."

"But it gives us a start." He took both the bottle and the vial from his father and ran back to the chambers. "Lady Azurha, I think I discovered how Emperor Decius was poisoned."

Upon hearing his father's name, the current emperor stirred and sat up. "How?"

"I believe someone tainted his massage oil." He handed the two oils to the emperor. "If you sniff carefully, you can smell a hint of the moon lily oil mixed in with it."

Emperor Sergius repeated the same back and forth process as Modius's father had, but Azurha covered her mouth and sank into the cushions beside her future husband. "By the gods, it was me," she said in a breathless whisper.

Modius blinked, wondering if he'd heard her correctly. The stony glare on his father's face told him he had.

Emperor Sergius froze. "What do you mean, Azurha?"

"That night, when I gave you the massage. You said I'd used your father's oil." A sob choked her words, preventing her from continuing.

The emperor set the vial and bottle aside, taking her into his frail arms. "Don't blame yourself—you didn't know."

"But that doesn't change the fact that I was the one who did this to you." No tears fell from her eyes, but the anguish in her voice spoke volumes. "I'm sorry, Titus, so sorry."

His father tapped his shoulder and jerked his head, indicating they should leave. He retreated, waiting half a breath for Izana to join him before leaving the room with Marcus and his father.

The deep shadows of the corridor only added to the gloom. For a moment, no one said anything. Then Marcus stood a bit straighter, a new look of determination on his face. "I'm going to find out how that oil got there in the first place."

"I'll come with you," Varro said, his limp almost vanishing. "I know where the shipment records are kept."

They disappeared down the hallway, leaving him alone with Izana.

She held up her sketch. "It's still rough, but I think I'll be done soon."

He stared at the remarkable likeness of the rebel leader. Izana had managed to capture the arrogant tilt of his chin and the fearless determination in his eyes. He even caught a glimpse of the haughty snarl in his upper lip. All things he'd remembered about Tuhotep during their brief interaction, now brought together in one drawing. "I think the Legion will have no trouble spotting him when you're finished."

Her attention reached past him to the door. "Do you think I should check on my mistress?"

"Let them be for now." Even though it had been an accident, he doubted anyone could soothe Lady Azurha right now. He wrapped his arm around her waist, wondering if he'd be as calm and forgiving as the emperor had been if he'd been in his place. "You can check on her in the morning."

"May I use your desk to finish my drawing?"

"Yes, but only if you agree to stay the rest of the night with me."

Her smile chased away the gloom with its brightness. "There's nowhere else I'd rather be."

And right then, he knew he'd forgive her just about anything so long as she looked at him that way.

24

Izana lay next Modius, her body cradled by his, and listened to his slow, even breaths that were so at odds with her racing thoughts. She replayed the story of Tiberius and Ausetsut over and over again, but every time, she failed to discover how he survived. She punched a pillow, and Modius stirred.

"Is something wrong?" he asked, sleep still lingering in his voice as he tightened his arms around her waist.

"I know there has to be a cure, but I can't find it."

She'd played her part in all this so far. Captain Galerius had her drawing of Tuhotep and had his men on the lookout for him. She'd found the moon lilies and saved enough for Modius to extract the oil from them and discover how the emperors had been poisoned. But she couldn't rest until she finished answering that one last question.

"If Tiberius was poisoned like his father, how did he survive?"

Modius rested his chin on the top of her head. "I wish I knew. Do you remember anything from the story?"

She shook her head. "All I know is that from the Alpirion accounts, he was struck with the same illness as his father, but the painting of Ausetsut mentioned she saved his life." She chewed her bottom lip. "I wonder if that fact she was a *wa'ai* played a part in his cure."

"What do you mean?" Modius sat, his eyes alert despite the early hour.

"The tale mentioned that she was in love with him, and that she saved his life. What if she used the magic she had as a *wa'ai* to do so?"

"I still find it hard to believe the Alpirions have magic like the Deizians."

"Hapsa said it was different, that it came from the moon and could be only be used to heal or protect." She jumped out bed, her hair swishing around her bare hips as she paced the room. "She sent us away before she reached the ending, but I bet it will answer our question."

"Shall I trouble my father for a bottle of wine from the emperor's personal stash?"

She nodded, already knowing what he was planning. "And fresh berries. Perhaps even a bit of sweetbread and honey. Hapsa loves that."

He caught her and pressed a kiss on her lips. "What time shall I meet you at the gates with our little picnic?"

"The tenth hour of the morning will be fine. That will give me enough time to ask my mistress if she would like to come with us."

He raised both brows. "You want to bring Lady Azurha with us."

"Hapsa might be more willing to reveal the secrets of the *wa'ai* if she has one in front of her, don't you agree?" She found her dress and pulled it over her head before trying to comb her hair into some sort of obedience. "Besides, there's one more thing I want to investigate before we leave."

"What's that?"

She paused, her fingers still caught in her tangled curls. "I have no evidence other than a gut feeling, but I think I might know the Alpirion who slipped the poison into the emperor's massage oil."

"My father and I reviewed the logs last night. Very few people had access to it, and none of them bore the feather tattoo."

"Perhaps, but what if the assassin managed to slip past them and add the oil? And he has to still be here." The uneasy churning in her gut told her as much. "I just want to ask some of the slaves about a suspect."

Modius reached for his tunic. "I'll come with you."

"No, no, that's not necessary. It's one of those things that will be easier if I ask the other slaves alone. You, on the other hand, will silence any slave from speaking."

"Fine," he said with a sigh of resignation. "But can you at least give me a name of your suspect?"

"I think it might be Farros. He has a tattoo on his arm in the same place as the others, but from what I can remember, it's not a feather."

"And what if he tries to hurt you?"

The warnings Farros had given her over the last few weeks echoed through her mind. "I promise I won't engage him. I'll just go in close enough to see what his tattoo is."

"And if it's something that links him to the rebels?"

"Then I'll go straight to Captain Galerius."

Modius lowered his head. "I don't like the idea of you putting yourself in danger like this."

"I still have this." She held up the golden dagger her mistress had given her and strapped it to her thigh. "If I need to defend myself, I will." Even though she inwardly cringed at the idea of drawing more blood from another victim.

The wariness didn't fade from his expression. "Just be careful. If you aren't at the gates at ten, I'll come looking for you and have every member of the Legion looking for this Farros."

"I'll be fine." She placed a quick kiss on his cheek before slipping out of his room and crossing the palace to the imperial quarters.

She found her mistress at the emperor's bedside while he slept, holding his hand as his ragged breaths echoed through the chamber. "Do you need anything from me, my lady?"

Azurha looked up. Dark circles framed her eyes,

amplifying the guilt that clouded the bright teal irises. "No, Izana, I'll be fine."

It was a dismissal, but Izana chose instead to come closer and kneel beside her mistress's chair. "Modius and I are planning on going back to the lorekeeper today to see if she can finish the tale of Ausetsut and Tiberius, and I was wondering if you would like to join us."

"My place is here."

"Yes, but what if I told you that Hapsa might be able to reveal how Tiberius was cured from this poison?"

Her breath hitched, and a brief glimpse of hope washed over her weary face. "But why should I come?"

Izana smoothed her skirt, searching for the most delicate way to say this. "Because the princess who supposedly saved Tiberius was a *wa'ai* like you."

Azurha pinched the bridge of her nose and turned away, focusing her attention on the man who lay dying in the bed. "And why would the fact that I have light colored eyes mean anything?"

"Because according to Hapsa, it means you have to ability to channel the moon's power."

Her mistress gave her a bitter laugh. "More talk about magic that I can't call upon when I truly need it."

"Are you so certain, my lady?"

Azurha went still, her eyes still fixed on her future husband. "Do you think this lorekeeper might be able to help us?"

"If anyone can, it's her."

She covered the emperor's hand with her other one. "Then it's a risk I'm willing to take. What time are you planning on going?"

"At the tenth hour of the morning."

"Then I will arrange for Empress Horatia to take my place at the vigil during that time." She turned to Izana, her teal eyes shining once again. "I'm willing to do anything to save Titus, and if there's something we can glean from the story, then

I will try it."

"I pray to the gods we'll find our answer through Hapsa." She stood and bowed. "If you do not need me now, my lady, I will follow up on something else that needs attention."

"Please have Varro send for Empress Horatia before attending to that other matter."

Izana paused at the doorway and watched the tender way her mistress pressed a cool cloth to the emperor's head. No one who saw them together could ever doubt their love for each other. She added a silent prayer that when their wedding day came, it would be a day of joy and not a day of mourning.

After she relayed the message to Varro, she asked several slaves if any of them had seen Farros. All of them said the last time they'd seen him was yesterday afternoon. None of them had wanted to report him late for his morning duties and cause him to get ten lashes.

She went back out into the main courtyard and scanned the balconies for the place where she'd thought she'd seen Farros. It was a building which had once housed the Legion, but was currently being remodeled into a school of some sort, from what she'd heard. Right now, though, it looked as though the slaves had abandoned this project. Scaffolding lined one wall of the building, and the balconies that she'd seen him standing on last night now appeared rickety and unstable.

Maybe I did dream it up. How could they have supported a large slave like him without collapsing?

But she came closer to the empty building, noting how the plaster walls had been demolished in some areas to reveal the wood and brick underneath. Inside, the stairs to the second floor lacked a railing and wobbled as she climbed them. Her heart jumped more than once from the cracking wood beneath her feet. Faint squeaks down the hall told her the rats had already made a home here, but those were the only signs of life she detected.

She crept down the hallway, one hand braced against the wall in case the floor decided to give way from under her. The room she'd thought she'd seen Farros in was at the end of the building. Unlike the other rooms, that door was closed. A scream of warning rang through her mind. He had to be here.

Her promise to Modius not to engage Farros echoed through her mind. She turned around to alert the Legion only to find a familiarly arrogant Alpirion blocking her escape.

A blade poked her ribs, and Tuhotep grinned at her with the same malice his brother had the day before. "Well, well, well, how nice to see you again, little Izana."

25

Azurha dashed through the open courtyard, her palla pulled low over her face so no one would recognize her. Her heart pounded in her chest like an executioner's drum, sending new waves of guilt through her with each beat. She almost wanted to laugh at the irony of her situation. She'd been sent here to kill Titus, and somehow, inadvertently, she may have succeeded in doing just that.

You'll never find a knot you can't unravel.

The words of the soothsayer from years ago stopped her dead in her tracks. She always heard them in her mind whenever she felt hopeless, and by some chance of fate, she always managed to rise above the situation. She prayed the soothsayer was right once again.

Modius stood by the palace gates alone, a basket hanging from his arm and a look of worry on his face. When he spotted her, he did a double take. "Lady Azurha?"

She grinned and held a finger to her lips. Her chiton and palla were made of coarse linen, not the fine silks she'd become accustomed to wearing since she'd arrived at the palace. "I thought I'd draw less attention in this outfit."

He nodded, although the tense cords in his neck told her he wasn't quite comfortable with her disguise. "Have you seen Izana?"

"Not since this morning."

"She was supposed to meet me here at the tenth hour, but I don't see her anywhere."

A jolt of panic skidded through her stomach. Titus seemed to have worsened overnight, and every second she was away from him meant one less she could spend with him. "I haven't much time, Modius. If you can lead me to this lorekeeper now, I'm sure Izana will catch up."

"But—"

"Modius, I'm ordering you to take me to the lorekeeper now." She softened her voice and added, "Please, we don't have a moment to lose."

The tension didn't ease from his body when he heard her plea. He cast one more glance over his shoulder, his face tight with worry, before nodding. "You're right, but please give me a moment to alert the Legion about Izana. Then we can go and see if Hapsa can tell us how to save the emperor."

After he took a moment to speak to a member of the Legion, he led her into the heart of the city, to a street where the homes were barely livable and barefooted Alpirion children dressed in rags played. For once, she wasn't the object of everyone's attention. The freed slaves who lived in this area all stared at Modius, the lone Elymanian who dared enter their neighborhood. When she caught a group of young men curling their hands into fists and glaring at him, she lowered her palla enough to reveal that she was one of them and flashed her golden bracelets. They might not recognize her as the future empress in her simple attire, but they would at least know she was a free member of their race.

They arrived at a small house with a blue door at the end of a narrow street. Modius knocked, and a thin woman with a nervous gleam in her dark eyes answered. "You again?" She scanned the street behind him. "Where's Izana?"

"She couldn't make it."

"I'm not letting you in without her." The woman attempted to close the door, but Modius wedged his foot and gave Azurha a sheepish smile.

"Baza was this hospitable last time, my lady."

The Alpirion women jerked her attention from Modius to her, and her mouth gaped open. "A *wa'ai*."

Azurha had been called that for as long as she could remember, but time hadn't softened the blow of those fearful words.

Modius took advantage of Baza's shock and opened the door. "This way, Lady Azurha."

The Alpirion woman pressed against the opposite wall, her gaze never leaving Azurha. "Why did you bring her here?"

"Because I ordered him to," Azurha replied, assuming her authority as the future empress. "I wish to speak to Hapsa."

Baza pointed on tremulous finger toward the back of the house.

Modius led her to the small room that smelled of incense and quieted her doubtful thoughts. Despite the cool reception from Baza, this space welcomed her.

The old woman sitting on the pile of cushions smiled as they entered, even though her clouded eyes couldn't see them. Her voice was soft and frail as she greeted them. "You've returned, Elymanian from the sea and friend of Izana."

"You have a good memory of my scent, Hapsa." He knelt beside her and unpacked the basket, pouring the old woman a cup of wine. "Izana couldn't make it today, but she sent someone else with me."

The old woman sniffed the air. "An Alpirion, but one who sits far above us." She gave Azurha a toothless grin and sipped her wine. "One who brings me wine fit for an emperor."

She came closer and sat in front of Hapsa, sensing something vaguely familiar about the old woman. "You have a very accurate sense of smell."

The old woman's laugh sounded more like a cackle. "You are more than just an Alpirion who shares the emperor's bed. I can smell the power of the moon on you."

She sent a questioning glance to Modius, who just shook

219

his head in a way that meant he'd try to explain later. "My maid, Izana, was telling me the story of Tiberius and Ausetsut, but she couldn't remember the ending."

"Are you certain you wish to hear it? It has a tragic ending."

Her throat tightened. What if the tale didn't give her the information she desired? What if it ended with Tiberius's death? She steeled her courage and said, "Yes, please. I know the part about her falling in love with him and how he fell ill from the moon lily, but what happened after that?"

"Ausetsut's heart grieved, for she was watching the one man she loved more than life itself dying in front of her. When none of the People from the Sun's healers could stop the poison's progress, she went to the temple and prayed to the moon."

Azurha dug her nails into her palm. She doubted praying to the moon would do anything to help Titus. "How did she save Tiberius?"

Hapsa's eyes widened. "You are getting ahead of the story, my child. Patience. There is a reason why I didn't finish the story the other day. It takes time to unravel a knot."

You will never find a knot you can't unravel.

Azurha gasped. Years had passed since she'd offered an old blind soothsayer a drink of water and had received the cryptic fortune that had haunted her since then. The memory of that day slammed into her with enough force to drive the air from her lungs. She'd been a child when she'd first met Hapsa, but now there was no mistaking the woman in front of her. It was the very same soothsayer.

The old woman grinned and ate one of the ripe berries Modius had brought, chewing it thoroughly before finishing her tale. "The gods reminded Ausetsut of her duty as a *wa'ai*. She was bound to protect her land and her people. But as she prayed to them, she saw that by saving her love, she might prevent war between their people. The magic inside her awoke and flowed through her veins. She returned to the palace and used it to draw the moon lily oil from her lover's body and save him from the clutches of death."

Azurha's heart skipped a beat. It all came back down to magic—magic she couldn't call upon or control. "How would I be able to follow her example to save my lover?"

Hapsa pursed her lips. "Why do you wish to save him? For your own selfish purposes?"

"No," she paused, trying to a picture a future without Titus, "and yes. I love him with all my heart and want him to live, but it's more than just my happiness on the line. Titus is the only one who can maintain the barrier that protects our people from the Barbarians. He wants to bring much-needed change to the empire, from making sure resources are evenly distributed to building an academy of learning on the palace grounds to freeing the slaves. And if he dies, all his dreams die with him, and our people are in danger from invaders."

Hapsa gave her a smile and nodded. "As a *wa'ai*, you have the power to protect and heal, but only if it's for the good of your people. "

"But how? How can I call upon this magic and use it to draw the poison out from Titus's body?"

The old woman closed her eyes and drew in a long breath through her nose. She held it, her lips silently moving as though she were having a conversation with the gods themselves.

Seconds ticked by, and the anxious twitching of the muscles in Azurha's body grew stronger. She was so close to discovering the cure. And if the old woman wouldn't tell her, she feared what her temper might do.

At last, Hapsa opened her eyes. "Leave this room, Elymanian. This is not for your ears."

Modius rose and bowed to both of them. "I'll be just outside if you need me, Lady Azurha."

Once they were alone, the soothsayer's voice lost its frail edge. The old woman spoke with the same power of a high priestess as she had all those years ago. "This was why I didn't tell Izana the ending the other day—because it wasn't meant for her ears, either. I knew when I met you years ago that this tale was for you, Azurha. Tell me—have you ever felt the magic inside you?"

"Yes," she whispered. "It's wild and chaotic and seems to want to explode from within me when it appears, but is never there when I try to call on it."

"When it has appeared, what was the situation?"

"The first time was when I trying to get to Titus to save him from his cousin. The magic burst from my hand and blew away the doors."

"And the second time?"

She toyed with her fingers, uncertain if she should reveal the emperor's weakness with the barrier. "When I was helping Titus restore the barrier."

"Do you see anything similar about both instances?"

Azurha sucked in a breath, her mind racing back and forth between the memories. "Both times, Titus was involved."

"And both times, you used the magic to protect someone. In the first instance, you wanted to protect him from death. The second instance, it was to protect the empire from the Barbarians."

"But how was the first instance any different from now? I still want to save his life."

"You answer that question. Was there something different that night you blew away the doors?"

The cold shiver of death reminded her of the one difference. That night, she was the one who was poisoned and dying. She didn't care if she ever saw him again. She just wanted to make sure he lived. "Yes, something was different, and if I could, I'd place myself in that same position again if it meant I could cure him."

Hapsa gave her a gentle laugh. "There is no need for that. But you failed to notice the other important aspect of your magic. Just like the People from the Sun require the use of their ore to conduct their magic, your magic has limits. It can only be used to augment what's already present."

The old soothsayer preferred to talk in riddles, and the assassin within her was growing impatient. But Azurha managed to keep her voice calm as she asked, "What do you mean?"

"During the first instance, were you the only person trying to knock down the doors?"

And suddenly, it became clear. "Both times I've felt it was when someone near me was on the verge of failing."

"Now can you think of a way to heal the emperor?"

She stood, her mind already forming a plan, and took the old woman's hands in her own. "Yes, I think I have an idea. Thank you from the bottom of my heart."

Hapsa squeezed them. "I wish you and your emperor a happier ending than Tiberius and Ausetsut. His mistrust drove them apart, but I can sense that your relationship has already overcome that hurdle."

Azurha grinned. Yes, if Titus could still want her after learning she was sent there to kill him, then she had little to worry about.

She opened the door to find Modius at an uneasy standoff with Baza. "You consider yourself a healer, don't you, Modius?"

"Yes, my lady. Why?"

"Because I'm going to need you to help me." She strode through the house, ignoring its occupants, and continued up the street. "What was the name of that root that can draw out infections from Deizians?"

Modius jogged behind her to catch up. "The purifico root."

"We need to get some on the way home."

26

The slant of the shadows from the window told Izana it was past noon, but she dared not move from the corner Tuhotep had shoved her into.

Her captor sat in front of her, his blade still drawn and pointed at her. Their staring match had lasted for hours, neither of them speaking. Farros stayed by the window, watching the action below. She could've sworn at one point she heard someone say his name below, but no one had ventured into the building all day.

Sweat dripped down the side of her face. Looking back, she wished she'd waited to look for Farros after they'd returned from Hapsa's.

But maybe by now Modius already was looking for her with the help of the Legion, just like he said he would. That faint hope gave her the courage to try to pull more answers from Tuhotep. "How did you get here so quickly?"

His lips quirked into a mocking grin. "You aren't the only person who can ride on an airship. For the right price, I can easily bribe a Deizian captain to take me anywhere I want."

"How did you slip past the guards and gain entrance to the palace?"

He waved his sword in front of him like a wagging finger. "You're asking too many questions."

"What do you plan to do to me?" she asked, undaunted by his threat. She'd wasted too much time being afraid of him. The firm pressure against her thigh reminded her she still had a weapon of her own once she was ready to escape.

"I'm still trying to decide."

"You should make your mind up soon. My mistress will be quite upset if I'm not there to fix her hair for dinner."

Farros pulled back from the window. "The Elymanian that was with her just returned with the *wa'ai*."

Tuhotep pointed his blade at her. "Any idea where they went, Izana?"

She kept her face blank. "Nope."

"You're lying."

"What makes you think that?"

He stood and closed the space between them, the tip of his sword inches from her chest. "Because you are the only connection between them."

She forced herself to remain calm. Men like Tuhotep fed on fear, and she refused to fall into his trap. Eventually, someone would notice she was missing and would look for her. "Actually, you're mistaken. My mistress summoned him first, then asked me to spy on him."

A cold leer twisted Farros's face. "Does that include fucking him?"

"No. That was an added bonus, completely by my choice." She couldn't resist adding one more jab. "And you should know that Elymanian men are much more well-endowed than Alpirion men."

She studied them side by side, noting the same jaw line, the same nose. "Are you two related?"

They exchanged menacing glances with each other, but neither gave her an answer.

"I figured as much. Of course, this confirms my assumption that your name really isn't Tuhotep and that you're just a slave pretending to be above your station."

Tuhotep turned his attention back to her, his blade

gazing her bodice. "Like you?"

"I've never pretended to be royalty." She flicked her finger on the sword like it was a pesky mosquito. "I'm just the empress's maid."

"This isn't a game." He leveled the sword with the tip of her nose. "People can and will die."

"Let's hope it's you who dies, then."

His brow furrowed as though her flippant response puzzled him. Then a cruel grin curled his lips. "Ah, I see where you're going with this. I've been playing you all wrong. You don't fear death, but you do fear your lover finding out your little secret."

She shook her head. "No, we've already gotten that out into the open. He doesn't care about my past."

The grin twisted into a snarl. "Then how would you like to watch him slowly die?"

Her heart slammed into her chest, knocking the air from her lungs. "You'd have to catch him first."

He snorted with laughter and turned to his brother. "Farros, go fetch the Elymanian and bring him to me. Then we'll see how brave little Izana can be."

She curled her fingers into her skirt, fighting to keep all emotion from her face as Farros left.

Tuhotep crouched in front of her, leaning on his sword. No mercy glittered in his eyes when they met hers. "Remember what I told you. There are fates worse than death."

***

Azurha raced through the courtyard, the steady echo of footsteps telling her Modius was close behind. She shed her palla as she entered the throne room and checked the globe. The barrier still shimmered from the reinforcements she'd helped Titus erect the other day. A remnant of the wild, chaotic magic wound up her arm when she touched it. She closed her eyes and tried to capture that sensation for later.

Modius stood beside her. "I need to go to my room for a mortar and pestle to make the paste."

"Then get it and meet me back in the imperial chambers." She offered a quick prayer that this would work. If what Hapsa told her was correct, she could use the magic to augment Modius's healing efforts and save Titus. But first, she had to create a means where the Elymanian could heal the Deizian.

She turned around only to have Hostilius Pacilus block her path. The governor of Lucrilla sneered at her rough clothing. "I was hoping to have an audience with the emperor about the state of affairs in Lucrilla."

"The emperor is not to be disturbed." She tried to pass him, but he cut her off, fury flaring in his cold blue eyes.

"I hope you're not responsible for his recent confinement. After all, an emperor has a duty to his people."

"Which he is tending to." She pointed to the globe. "See, the barrier is stronger than ever."

"For now." Hostilius wrinkled his nose as though he smelled something unpleasant. "Please inform the emperor that I need to return to Lucrilla as soon as the wedding is over to deal with various matters, and I'd prefer to speak to him before then."

By various matters, she wondered if that included his daughter. "Please give my regards to Lady Claudia when you return."

His expression darkened, and for the first time, Azurha understood Empress Horatia's fears for the other woman.

Modius returned to the throne room before anything else could be said. She pressed her hand against the key pad, watching the governor to make sure he didn't try to slip past them. It wasn't until she heard the locks close behind her that she turned to the healer. "Do you have everything you need?"

"I think so." His arms were full, juggling more than just the mortar and pestle he'd gone to fetch. "I grabbed a few more items that could be used as expectorants."

She led the way, offering a quick prayer to the gods this would work. The coil of magic from the globe swirled inside her chest, a light breeze compared to the tempests she'd experienced before.

Inside the chambers, the scene remained unchanged from this morning. Titus lay sleeping on the bed where she'd left him, his mother sitting at his side. Marcus paced the length of the sitting room.

She nodded to Modius. "Get started on that paste now."

"Yes, my lady." He laid out the ingredients, and a few moments later, the grinding of the pestle filled the room.

"Any change?" she asked as she came into the bedroom.

The empress shook her head, her eyes glistening. "No. It's like watching Gaius fade all over again."

"I won't let that happen." She cradled his cheek and kissed his forehead. "Titus, can you hear me?"

His eyelids fluttered open. "What time is it?"

"Afternoon." Uncertainty drummed through her, threatening to douse the fragile tendrils of magic that still swirled inside her chest. "I think I might have found a way to cure you."

"Oh?"

She nodded. "But I need to know you trust me."

He covered her hand with his own and gave her a weak smile. "You know I do, Azurha. Do what you need to do."

"Then let's remove your tunic and have you lie on your stomach like you did when I gave you the massage." Once that was done, she held out her hand behind her. "Marcus, I'll need that little knife you have concealed in your bracer."

"What are you—?" he started in mock innocence before ending with a groan. He pulled out the knife and gave it to her. "I should've known you'd be able to spot it."

"You need to find a better hiding place for it, and for the other blade you have hidden in the sole of your sandal."

Another wave of sputtering came from Marcus, triggering a chuckle from Titus. Her chest tightened as she listened to it. It was the first laughter she'd heard from him in days. Hopefully, it would not be the last.

"Is that paste almost done?"

"Just finishing it up." Modius came beside her with the

228

pale yellow paste that smelled of vinegar.

"Then let's create a wound."

Titus hissed as she drew the blade across his upper back and shoulders, pressing hard enough to break the surface of the skin and leave a line of blood in her wake. Once she'd covered the area she'd massaged, she turned to Modius. "Apply the paste to the wounds."

He did as she said, smoothing the paste on with the pestle. "Care to share your reasoning?"

"Yes, please enlighten all of us why you saw fit to injure Titus in order to cure him?" Marcus asked from the foot of the bed.

"The purifco root draws out infection from wounds in Deizians." She gulped past the lump of doubt forming in her throat. "If you think of infection as a type of poison, then I'm hoping it will also draw out the moon lily oil."

Modius paused from applying the paste. "That may take days, my lady."

"If it works at all," Marcus added.

"It has to," she whispered, her heart beating erratically. She was the only one who could save him now, and she'd sooner die than fail.

The power inside her flared as though it heard her plea. Azurha closed her eyes and let the wild chaotic force build. It pulsated through her limbs and shimmered through her mind like the very beams of the moon itself. Her fingers tingled as it demanded release, but she curled them into a fist. *Not yet. Not until it's strong enough to reverse this curse.*

The power roared at her attempts to contain it. It pounded against her chest, twisted through her gut, blinded her vision with the bright blue light. Her hands trembled. She locked her jaw and stiffened her arms, holding the magic back until it was ready.

Modius laid a steadying hand on her shoulder. "Lady Azurha, are you ill?"

"Stay back," she panted, holding on long enough to

press her palms against Titus's skin.

The paste burned her hands like boiling water, driving the breath from her lungs as her skin blistered. Somewhere behind her, she heard Modius shout a warning, but she didn't care. The ancient magic roared like a caged lyger. She released it into Titus with a scream and surrendered to it.

27

It was as though the painting of Ausetsut had come to life.

Modius stepped back as Azurha had ordered, shielding his face from the bolts of blue magic that forked down her arms like lightning. His heart pounded from the storm that raged in the emperor's bed chamber. Hot wind blasted the room as though she'd called it up from the Alpirion desert. The curtains whipped their faces, and her scream echoed liked thunder.

Then, as suddenly as the storm hit, it vanished, leaving Azurha to crumple in exhaustion.

Modius caught her before her head hit the floor. Her eyes stared past him, her lips moving to silent words. But the thing that worried him the most were the red blisters rising from her hands. "Get me some water, quickly. We need to get the purifico paste off her hands."

He grabbed a sheet and traced the rims of bubbled skin, removing as much of the paste as he dared without breaking the blisters. The empress ran to fetch the water while a man crouched next to him to cradle Azurha.

"She'll be fine," the man said.

He looked up into the sharp blue eyes of the emperor and froze. Gone were the pale sunken cheeks and wasted muscles. Gone was the man who labored to breathe and drifted in and out of sleep. In his place was the strong, virile man he'd met a week ago.

His tongue tripped over itself. "It worked."

"By the gods, he's right," Marcus said behind him. "I don't know what she did, nor do I care to endure that moment of terror again, but it worked."

"That still doesn't change the fact her hands need attention." Emperor Sergius held her wrists as his mother poured a decanter of water over them.

Azurha hissed and stiffened, her gaze returning to those around her. A tear streaked down her face. "Titus?"

The emperor pulled her back against his chest. "Right here, my love."

She let out a shaky breath, then another until laughter rose from her throat. "I found the magic."

"You've had it there all along." Emperor Sergius placed a kiss on her cheek. "Modius, do you think you can heal her?"

"I can make a poultice that would ease her pain and aid in the healing, but it would take a week or two."

"Not good enough for her." He scooped her up in arms and laid her in the bed he'd formerly occupied. "Fetch me a healing rod."

Marcus dashed out of the room while the emperor and empress fussed over Azurha.

Modius used the distraction to study the paste that still clung to the emperor's back. It had hardened and dried to a muddy brown color. He still caught a faint whiff of the vinegar he'd used to thin the mashed purifico root, but the floral peppery scent of the moon lily overwhelmed it.

"Your Imperial Majesty, I hate to take you away from Lady Azurha, but I need to remove the dried paste before the moon lily oil finds its way back into your system."

Emperor Sergius retreated from the bed long enough to let Modius scrape off the paste with the sheet and wash the underlying skin. The lines Azurha had cut remained as faint scars, but otherwise, no other damage was noted.

Marcus returned with Varro and an entourage of slaves to attend to the imperial couple.

Modius scanned their members for Izana, but couldn't find her. He sent a questioning glance to his father, who shook his head. No one had seen her since this morning, and a thread of fear twisted along his spine.

It quickly turned into a rope tightening around his throat when he saw the murderous glare in one of the slave's eyes. The man was massively built, more a warrior than a common slave, and had the same beaked nose as Tuhotep. A tattoo peeked out from under the sleeve of his tunic, and Modius's pulse jumped. It wasn't a feather like the others, but this had to be the slave Izana suspected.

The Alpirion met his gaze and curled his lip up into a snarl, daring him to call him out.

Modius pointed at the slave. "Stop him—he's one of the rebels."

The slave's eyes widened a split second before he threw his tray at Varro and ran.

Modius dropped the sheet and gave chase, not pausing to help his father. His gut told him this was the man who'd poisoned the emperor, and his heart told him he knew where Izana was.

The slave ran toward the baths. Beyond them lay a small courtyard and the only chance the slave had at escaping, as the door to the rest of the palace was locked. Someone in the room called for the Legion, but Modius knew the slave would be long gone before Captain Galerius and his men arrived.

The air was humid and foggy as he entered the baths, choking him and obscuring his vision. A hiss filled the air, followed by more blinding white steam. Modius slowed down and listened for the slave's location. Tuhotep's assassin was no fool. Another gurgling hiss told him the Alpirion had opened up the vents to the fires under the caldarium and was pouring water on them.

Modius crept through the room, his muscles tense as he

233

strained to hear any movements from his enemy. He'd shed his sword when he'd returned last night, but now he wished he'd kept it. The slave may have been unarmed, but his size was weapon enough.

A shadowy figure darted past him. Modius ran after it, not seeing the marble statue hurling toward him until it slammed into his gut.

Stars danced in front of his eyes, and his lungs burned for air. He fell back, his head cracking against the floor. He rolled over to his side, praying he wouldn't lose his attacker again. By the time he got to his knees, he managed to catch his breath long enough to say, "There's no way out for you. You can surrender peacefully, or you can die."

"There is freedom in death," a low voice said behind him.

Modius whirled around to catch the slave's fist squarely in the jaw. The impact sent him sprawling, and his attacker vanished back into the steamy mist. Blood filled his mouth. He spit it out. "The Legion is coming for you."

"Let them come," the voice said from his left. "But know this, Elymanian—when I do not return, my brother will kill Izana."

His throat closed, and icy dread clawed this veins. "Where is she?"

The voice laughed, this time from his right. It echoed off the smooth tiles that lined the baths and mocked him. "Tuhotep has your little *lupa*."

A dozen more questions filled his mind, but none of them mattered more than finding her. He stood and stilled, trying to place his attacker. "How did he get her?"

"Who's to say she didn't seek him out?"

Modius ignored his taunt and focused on the subtle slap of bare feet against the tiles. The Alpirion was circling him, perhaps preparing to deliver the next blow. "What does your brother want with Izana?"

"She's a traitor," he growled, now in front of him. "She

revealed our secrets to save the tyrant who enslaves us all."

He pulled himself up into a crouch, tracking his attacker's movements. "What if she helped you to gain your freedom by helping him?"

"Lies, all lies. The only way to ensure our freedom is to bring the entire empire down to its knees, starting with the emperor."

Voices filtered in from the imperial chambers, the sharp orders of Galerius rising above them all. "The Legion is here," he warned the Alpirion.

"Then they'll all die, starting with you."

The Alpirion burst through the cloud of steam, his hands open and ready to grab whatever he could. Modius leaned to his left and straightened his right leg, dodging the force of the attack while tripping up the slave. Now it was the Alpirion's turn to go sprawling across the floor.

Modius jumped on the slave's back, not wanting to lose the brief advantage he had, and hooked his arm around the man's thick throat. But unlike his opponent in the library, the Alpirion was not as easily subdued. He staggered to his feet and scrambled backward, ramming Modius into a wall.

He gritted his teeth and tightened his hold on the slave's neck. "Where's Izana?"

The slave gasped for a breath, releasing it with a cold laugh. "Already dead."

"You're lying!"

"Am I?" The slave slammed him into the wall again, although with less force this time, and dug his fingers into Modius's arm. "By the time you find her, her body will already be cold."

The voices of the Legion came closer just his grip started to slip. "I have the emperor's killer here," Modius called.

Footsteps pounded toward them. The slave's muscles coiled, and he fell forward, somersaulting Modius over his head in the process. The first members of the Legion tripped over Modius and gave the slave a chance to escape back into the steam.

Galerius picked Modius off of the floor. "Which way did he go?"

"That way." He pointed to the right just as a grunt came from that direction, followed by the clang of metal.

Galerius drew his sword and ran into the swirling mist. "No quarter."

Modius's heart squeezed when he heard the call for the slave's death. If the Legion got to him first, he'd carry the secret of Izana's location with him to the grave. He ran after them. "No, let him live. He knows where the rebel leader is."

A fierce cry rang through the baths, followed by scrape of blades engaged in battle. Modius halted, staying back in case one of the members of the Legion mistook him for the Alpirion. Then a wheeze ended the battle, followed by the thump of a body falling to the floor.

"We got him," Galerius preened.

"You fool!" Modius followed the sounds until he came to where the members of the Legion gathered around the slave's corpse. "You killed him before you learned what secrets he held."

Galerius faced him. "It was kill or be killed."

"But now we'll never find out where the rebel leader is hiding within the palace walls."

One of the members of the Legion came toward him with his blade still drawn, an argument forming on his lips, but Galerius halted him with a raised hand. "What are you talking about, Modius?"

"While you were on your way here, I got him to confess that Tuhotep is here, and he has Izana."

"Ridiculous. No one could've slipped past my men."

He lifted the dead slave's sleeve high enough to reveal the feather tattoo. "And yet you failed to notice the rebel posing as a slave here the entire time."

Galerius stared down at the Alpirion, his nostrils flaring and his jaw clenched. His hand tightened around his sword.

"Alert all the men. I'm not going to rest until I have Tuhotep's head."

He turned on his heel and disappeared back into the steam, his men following.

Modius knelt beside the fallen slave, hoping he might squeeze one more confession from his lips, but dead men didn't speak. His stomach knotted. Somewhere out there, Tuhotep had Izana, and his chances of finding her alive grew smaller and smaller with each member of the Legion who hunted him down.

Footsteps came from behind him, the familiar sound of one foot dragging behind the other dousing any alarm. "Farros has been here for almost a year. I should've suspected him, even though he had rare access to the imperial quarters." His father laid a hand on his shoulder. "Is it true he has Izana?"

Modius nodded, fear gluing his lips together.

"Then let's find her before the Legion marks her as expendable."

28

Modius followed his father through the maze of hidden hallways that ran through the palace and led out into the courtyard by the slave quarters. Shouts from the Legion rang from those buildings, but Varro only shook his head. "They're never going to find him that way."

He took a torch and headed for the armory. "Modius, you've met this rebel leader. What are your thoughts of him? Is he intelligent, or is he blinded by his own power like Galerius seems to be tonight?"

"Very intelligent." Wily came to mind. "So, if he's not hiding in the slave quarters, where do you think he'll be?"

"Someplace safe where he's probably watching all this and laughing."

"I'd rather he be doing that than harming Izana."

"Ah, that girl's got her claws into you good, hasn't she?" He grabbed two swords and handed one to Modius.

He didn't take it right away. His whole life, he'd fallen short of his father's expectations. Why should his choice in a woman be any different? "You disapprove?"

His father appeared to study him, the wrinkles in his face finally drawing up into a grin. "No. I have a feeling you two are well-matched." He offered the gladius to him again. "You'll need this for when you'll find him."

He took the sword and went back into the main courtyard, studying the structures. "If I were a rebel war load, I'd want to be in a defensible position."

"Good thinking." His father came alongside him and scanned the area. "The walls are not a good choice—too many members of the Legion patrolling them."

"And like you said, I doubt he'd be hiding in the slave quarters—that would be first place the Legion would go to search for him."

"So we're looking for a place high, defensible, and yet relatively isolated." Varro pointed to the old barracks. "If I were a rebel leader, that's where I would be."

The chill raced down his spine. The abandoned and partially demolished building would be the perfect hiding place for the Alpirion rebel and was the same place Izana had been staring at when they returned yesterday. He tested his grip on his sword and checked its balance. "Are you coming with me?"

His father raised a brow. "If you think I'll be of any use."

"I do." His gaze didn't fall on the scar that wound around his father's bad leg. It fell on the way the torchlight flickered off the deadly blade in his hand. An injury may have ended Varro's military career, but that didn't mean his skill with a sword was diminished. "Let me go in first, though."

"Lead the way."

Darkness shrouded the old barracks. Silence accompanied it, and as they entered the front door, Modius doubted his intuition. This place appeared uninhabitable, much less defendable. Holes gaped in the ceiling, exposing the floor above. The floor creaked under his feet, and the remnant of a staircase looked ready to collapse.

He was about to turn around and tell his father they'd made a mistake when he caught a feminine gasp from above. His blood burned with the thousand unspoken curses that raced through his mind. Izana had to be up there, and he was going to fight until his last breath to save her.

He glanced at his father, who nodded and waved him

239

forward. They climbed the stairs with their swords drawn, testing each step before moving up. The firelight bounced off the broken beams and shattered walls, creating menacing shadows that danced across the hallway when they came to the top.

Sweat beaded along his forehead and ran down the back of his neck as he chose his movements with care. One false step could send them crashing to the floor below. One squeaky floorboard could alert Tuhotep. One second's delay could end Izana's life.

Only the door at the end of the hall was closed, but that didn't stop him from checking each room when he passed it. He'd learned never to underestimate his opponent, especially one like Tuhotep. But when he came to that final door, his swallowed his nerves and fixed his courage into place.

Varro stood next to him in nodded. They were going together.

Modius wrapped his fingers around the handle, mentally counted to three, and flung the door open.

A muffled squeal from the dark greeted him. When the torch illuminated the room, his heart raced from both fear and relief.

Izana was alive.

And Tuhotep held her with his hand over her mouth and a curved blade pressed against her ribs.

"Ah, Modius, I was wondering when you'd join us." The rebel leader grinned down at Izana. "We've been anxiously awaiting your arrival."

Izana's wide eyes fixed on him. Blood covered her dress and dried in streaks along her bare arms.

Fury curled inside his gut. "Let her go."

"Why?" Tuhotep asked with a sneer. "What do you want with a whore like her?"

He bit back the angry growl and inched closer. "The game's up, Tuhotep. The Legion has already killed Farros, and they're coming after you."

A flicker of remorse over his brother's death registered

on Tuhotep's face before hiding under a mask of defiance. "If they can find me."

"I did."

"Yes, and look who you brought with you—an old man with a bad leg." He pulled Izana closer to him, forcing another muffled cry from her. "Which one should I kill first, little Izana? The old steward who thinks he can order us around, or your lover?"

Modius took a step toward them, drawing to stop when Izana gave him a frantic squeal. A fresh splotch of red appeared on her dress.

Tuhotep shook his head, dragging her closer to the balcony. "Be careful, Modius, or she will be the first one to die."

It was all a game to the Alpirion. It didn't matter what Modius did, Tuhotep had the upper hand as long as he had Izana. Violence wasn't the answer to this riddle. He lowered his sword. "What do you want?"

"Giving up so soon?"

"More like trying to figure out what you're trying to accomplish by holding a slave hostage. She must be of some use to you or you would've killed her hours ago."

"Perhaps I wish to punish her by killing you first."

Modius shook his head. "Something other than revenge is motivating you. You need her for something, and you need her alive."

A slow grin appeared on his father's face. "He needs Izana to gain access to the emperor."

A muscle rippled along the Alpirion's jaw, but he neither confirmed nor denied Varro's accusation.

But that wasn't what caught Modius's attention. It was the slow way Izana was hiking up the left side of her skirt to reveal the golden dagger strapped to her thigh. He snapped his gaze to her face, trying to read what her plan was. An almost imperceptible nod urged him to continue.

He tightened his grip on the sword's hilt, but kept it lowered. "Of course. Why didn't I see it sooner? Not can only

Izana read and write both languages, but she is one of the most trusted servants of the imperial family."

"And one of the few slaves who has unrestricted access to the imperial quarters," his father added, his sword still level with his hip. "Without her, he can't enter the emperor's room."

"And he can't get close enough to threaten him again. After all, Farros is dead."

Izana paused with her hand around the dagger's hilt, her face flinching as Tuhotep jerked her closer to him.

"And I'll make them pay for killing my brother."

Modius exchanged a glance with his father, hoping he saw the same thing.

Varro's attention remained fixed on the rebel leader, though. "He died quite like a coward, you know, begging for mercy."

"You lie!"

His father chuckled and slid a few inches closer, exaggerating his limp as he moved. "Of course, Captain Galerius knew exactly how to end his life so he'd have no peace in the afterlife. He cut out his heart."

Tuhotep's breathing quickened, and his fingertips dug into Izana's cheek. A stream of Alpirion words poured from his lips, all tainted with rage.

And that was Modius noticed that Izana had managed to draw the dagger completely out of its sheath. She stared at him, waiting for his signal.

He raised his sword. "And that was just the start of his desecration."

The lie broke Tuhotep's restraint. His sword left Izana's side and turned toward them. The break gave her the space she needed to jab her elbow under his ribs. Tuhotep's curses ended with a grunt. His hand loosened around her mouth just enough to allow her to spin around in his hold. She plunged the dagger into his chest.

Modius watched everything play out with shielded excitement. They were going to win. They were going to get out of this alive.

Tuhotep grabbed Izana's hair and flung her out onto the balcony. A loud snap overpowered his cry. A look of panic washed over her pale face as she continued to fall backward.

His heart stopped beating as the timbers supporting the balcony cracked under her slight weight. He tried to run to her, but his feet seemed to be made of marble.

Izana reached for him, her lips forming his name.

A crash rattled the room, but nothing could drown out her scream. She disappeared over the edge.

A sickening thud of a body hitting stone followed, and Modius forgot how to breathe.

Voices faded into the distance, and his body slowed as though a hundred chains bound him. His pulse rushed past his ears, doubling in speed with each beat. Rage boiled over with grief and pounded through his muscles. A sob inflated his chest, straining to break free.

And when it did, it came out as primal battle cry.

Modius raised his sword and charged Tuhotep.

The Alpirion warrior deflected his blow and spun around, backing away from the collapsed balcony. His laughter mocked the pain burning inside Modius's heart. "I win."

"No, you die." He swung again, but even injured, Tuhotep blocked him and added his own attack.

"You are no soldier."

"But I am." Varro flanked the Alpirion, and together, they circled the rebel leader.

"You can kill me, but it won't bring her back."

Modius's breath caught, and his vision blurred.

When it came back into focus, Tuhotep was running toward him, the point of his sword aimed for his heart.

Modius had only a split second to analyze his opponent. He knew he couldn't overpower him. But he could outwit him.

Tuhotep had his arm raised high, exposing the fragile nerves and tendons that ran through his armpit into his arm. Instead of trying to resist the Alpirion's attack, Modius waited until the last moment, turned to the side, and ran his sword through the vulnerable area.

The increasing resistance of his blade slicing through flesh told him he'd hit his mark. He continued to rotate, letting Tuhotep brush by him before pulling his sword back and shoving it between his ribs.

The Alpirion stiffened, the curved sword falling from his hand.

Then Varro delivered the killing blow along the throat, severing the rebel leader's neck with a shower of blood.

Modius yanked his sword out and leaned on it, his chest heaving as though he'd been the one who'd been stabbed. The rage flowed out of him as quickly as Tuhotep's blood, leaving only anguish in its wake. He didn't want to peek over the edge and see Izana's crumpled body below. He didn't want to see her eyes staring up at him in death. And yet, he wouldn't know peace until he knew for sure that she was dead.

He pushed off his blade and dashed down the stairs, not caring if they collapsed the same way the balcony did. He shoved past the members of the Legion who swarmed the old barracks and were fighting their way up to the room where Tuhotep had been hiding. He kept running until the humid night air bathed his face and stung his eyes.

He rounded the corner and found a group of people gathered around the place where Izana had fallen. He wedged past and fell to his knees by her side.

She lay motionless, her eyes closed, a pool of blood forming around her head.

Her hand still felt warm in his. Reflexively, he sought out the place where her pulse throbbed at her wrist and gasped when he discovered a slow beat there.

His eyes went to her chest. After what seemed like an eternity, her chest rose to take in a breath.

Izana was still alive.

Modius squeezed her hand and offered a quick prayer of thanks to the gods. But as swiftly as the ecstatic joy swept through him, it faded, and the healer in him took over. Both her pulse and her respirations were dangerously slow. He scratched his nail down her palm and watched with grim uncertainty as she balled her hands into fists and curled her arms into her chest. A quick peek at her eyes showed one pupil that was much larger than the other.

All signs of severe head injury, one she may not ever wake up from. And even if she did, there would be lasting effects.

His father's voice rang out across the courtyard, asking for a healer, but Modius already knew what he had to do. He'd seen this injury on the battlefield and in the gladiators he'd examined. If he didn't relieve the pressure around her brain, Izana would die in a matter of minutes to hours.

He reached behind her head, taking care not to move her neck as he felt for any depressions in her skull, any boney fragments. When he discovered none, he dragged his fingers along the side searching for the thin plate of bone above the temples. "I need a drill."

His father looked at him as though he'd lost his mind. "What are you talking about?"

"I need to drill a hole in her skull to relieve the pressure."

"Are you mad?"

"No, I'm a healer, Father, and I know what I need to do. Now get me that drill."

The crowd around him dispersed, either to look for the item he needed or to stay far away from the man who talked of drilling holes into people's heads. It didn't matter to him. He kept one hand over the place he'd marked for the burr hole, and the other fixed over the slow throbbing artery along her neck.

A few minutes later, his father held out a crude hand drill. "Will this do?"

"It has to." He took it and placed the bit perpendicularly to the weak spot in Izana's skull. Then he offered one more prayer to the gods before cranking the handle and boring down

245

into her flesh.

29

Modius strode into the throne room and dropped to one knee. "You summoned me, Your Imperial Majesty?"

Azurha smiled at him from her new throne beside Emperor Sergius, already taking her place by his side even though their wedding was still a week away, and gestured for him to rise. "How is Izana?"

He stood and rubbed the thick stubble on his cheeks, wishing he could erase the exhaustion from his body as easily as his beard. Since the night of her fall, he'd rarely left Izana's side. "Better, Lady Azurha. She doesn't remember what happened that night, and despite the efforts of the Deizian healer you sent, she is still unable to speak. Otherwise, she's finally feeling well enough to eat a little bit this morning."

"I'll continue to send my healer to her until she makes a full recovery." The emperor's voice was rich and strong, so very different than it was a few days ago.

And so very different from the woman who struggled even to say one word in another part of the palace.

A ball of anger rolled through his gut. "Thank you, Emperor Sergius, but I get the distinct impression your healer has done all he can for her." *More like all the healer wanted to do for her.*

The imperial couple exchanged glances, and the emperor

shifted in his throne. "Is there something I need to know about the treatment he's been giving her?"

"He did enough to pull her back from the brink of death, but he basically told me that healing her other injuries was a waste of his magic since she was only a slave."

Emperor Sergius's eyes darkened, but they paled in comparison to the murderous gleam in Azurha's eyes. "Perhaps we should speak with him," she said, her words cold and merciless.

"Indeed." The emperor's face then eased into something akin to embarrassment. "I apologize for my healer's behavior, and I promise I will personally see to her healing from now on."

Modius opened his mouth to say that wasn't necessary, but the words failed to reach his tongue. He wanted Izana fully healed. He wanted to see her eyes bright with mischief again, not dulled by pain. He wanted to hold her in his arms and hear her murmur his name as he made love to her again.

"Let me come with you, Titus." Azurha grinned, and he could've sworn he saw a glimmer of blue light dance around her fingers. "I might be able to augment your efforts."

Modius took a step back. "Are you planning on using your magic on her?"

"More like it's decided to help her."

He barely understood the Deizian magic, much less her strange power as a *wa'ai*, but after witnessing what she'd done to save the emperor, he'd never doubt its existence. "Thank you, Lady Azurha," he replied, his head bowed. "I know Izana would appreciate seeing both of you."

"We will deal with her shortly." The emperor took his future wife's hand in his and squeezed it, his love for her as bright as the lines of the barrier that glittered around the globe in the center of the room. "We were wondering how we could repay you for saving my life and the empire."

The air whooshed from his lungs, leaving his tongue paralyzed. A dozen ideas raced through his mind, but in the end, he only wanted one thing.

"You may have heard that I'm building a community of scholars that would reside here in the palace," the emperor continued. "I only want the best and the brightest in the empire to advise me and to make new discoveries about our world and our people. Your knowledge of medicine would be an ideal addition to it."

Once again, he struggled for words. After years of being in exile, he was being offered a chance to return home. "You wish for me to become one of your advisors?"

"Despite what my healer may have thought about tending to Izana, he was quick to tell me your burr hole saved her life. You have a sharp mind, and a heart courageous enough to take risks, Modius. My father saw that in you, which is why he sent you to Madrena. He knew that you needed time for the scandal to die down, time to hone your skills and expand your knowledge, and space away from your father to become your own person. Now that I've seen how far you've come, I'm humbly asking you to return."

His stomach dropped, and he stared at the tiles making up the grand mosaic on the floor, grounding himself. He'd be back in Emona, in the center of the imperial world, with access to everything a person could want. And yet, he'd grown so accustomed to the solitude of Madrena, to the sound of the sea and the scent of the clean air. It would be the perfect place to build a new life with the woman he loved. "I appreciate your offer, Emperor Sergius, but after the excitement of the last two weeks, I miss the boring home I've built in Madrena. If it pleases you, I only ask that Izana joins me there."

Azurha's shoulders dropped, and the corners of her mouth fell. "I'm terribly sorry, Modius, but we cannot give her to you."

"Why not?" The question rushed out before he could stop it. His fingers curled into his palm to prevent him saying something else that might cost him his life.

"I will explain once she is well enough to hear our reasoning."

He turned away from Azurha before she saw the anger in his face and mistook it for a challenge. Disappointment lodged in his throat, forcing him to swallow it before speaking. "I can think of nothing else I want, Your Imperial Majesty."

"And my offer to join my advisors?"

It tempted him. If he stayed here, he could remain close to Izana. But, if they refused to allow her to be with him, his hope would slowly turn into agony. He couldn't stand to be this close to her and not be with her. "Thank you, Emperor Sergius, but it would be better if I continued my studies in a place where the crowds wouldn't call for my execution." *And allow me to mend my wounded heart.*

The emperor turned to Azurha, both brows raised as though he wished for her to say something, but she shook her head. "It is not my decision to make, Titus," she murmured.

He let out a sigh that sounded like one of defeat. "Very well." He turned back to Modius. "If you think of anything else…"

"Thank you, Your Imperial Majesty, but I must return to my patient." He bowed and left the throne room, his chest still aching from their decision.

***

Something cool and wet pressed against Izana's lips. She opened her eyes to find Modius leaning above her. She tried to form his name on her tongue, but it refused to obey. Frustration welled up inside her, mingling with all the things she wanted to say but couldn't. She reached for his hand, the pain from the movement driving her breath from her chest, and squeezed it.

He brushed her hair back and offered a sympathetic smile. "I know you're hurting, Izana. But the emperor said he'd come by later today to heal you himself."

The pain she could deal with. It was the not being able to tell him everything that her heart wanted to say. She had no idea what had happened to her—her memories ended with the night she'd drawn a picture of Tuhotep to give to the Legion—but she believed Modius when he told her she'd almost died. And now

250

that the gods had shown her how fragile her own existence was, she never wanted to take a moment for granted.

She moved his hand to breast and pressed his palm over the place where her heart beat. With her gaze locked with his, she gave him a smile and hoped he'd understand what she was trying to tell him.

His lips rose, and fine lines crinkled around his eyes. "I love you, too."

And just like that, her pain lessened and her frustration ebbed. They knew each other so well, words were not needed, which was why the sudden wave of grief on his face doused those happy feelings. She opened and closed her mouth, her breath quickening from trying to force a simple word to the surface and ask him why, but it never came.

He shushed her and placed a chaste kiss on her forehead. "Don't get yourself worked up, Izana. You'll only cause yourself more pain."

His refusal to share what upset him caused her more pain than the protests of her battered and broken body. She clamped her hand over his, grinding it against her chest in order to wrestle the truth from him.

"I'll tell you more once Lady Azurha has a chance to explain things." A muscle rippled along his jaw before he added, "To both of us."

"And I shall," her mistress said from the doorway, the emperor at her side, "once I'm assured Izana is well again."

She released Modius and tried to sit up out of respect for them, but what felt like a sharp knife jabbed through her lower back and numbed her lower legs.

Modius eased her back down. "Please, Izana, try not to hurt yourself."

Tears stung her eyes from more than just pain. She balled her hands into fists until the sensations waned.

"Izana, do I have your permission to use my magic on you?" The emperor held a small staff with an orb at the end, made of the same ore that conducted the Deizian magic. It was more ornate than the one the healer had used on her, but she understood its purpose.

She nodded, thankful she could still do that to communicate.

"Thank you," he said so humbly, it seemed as though their roles had been reversed.

The metal was cold against her forehead. Izana closed her eyes, preparing for the sting of the foreign magic as it coursed through her body. The magical healing process may have been faster, but it was also almost as painful as the injuries themselves.

The first pulse of golden magic burned into her skull like flaming torch, forcing her to grit her teeth together to keep from crying out. But then the heat vanished as a new wave of magic overtook it. It was as cool and blue as the distant oceans and sparkled through her mind like the moonlight on the Alpirion desert. A hum of music flowed through her, reminding her of the tune she'd heard when she'd been there. Her soreness slipped away as she surrendered to it.

When she opened her eyes again, she saw Azurha's hand on the healing rod next to the emperor's. This time, her words flowed as freely as the ancient power from her homeland. "The magic of a *wa'at?*"

Her mistress smiled, the light glowing from her teal-colored eyes more comforting than the rage she'd seen in the painting of Ausetsut. "Yes. Hapsa showed me how I could use it to protect and to heal."

The magic retreated, taking with it every ache she'd known since waking up in this room. "Thank you."

"You are most welcome, Izana." The emperor removed the healing rod from her forehead and kissed his future wife. "Now that I know she is better, I'll leave you to explain yourself to them."

Once he left, Azurha sat in the chair Modius offered her and arranged her skirts before speaking. "It seems I have caused a problem for you two."

"I don't understand." Izana sat up and reached for Modius's hand, knowing exactly where he was without looking for him.

"When the emperor and I asked Modius what he wanted as a reward for his part in solving in the mystery of Emperor Decius's death and saving us from Tuhotep, he asked for the one thing we couldn't give him—you."

A flush stole through her when she realized the significance of his request. He could've asked for riches and palaces, but all he wanted was her. "I'm your slave, my lady. You have the power to do as you chose with me."

"No, Izana, I don't." One corner of her mouth rose into a teasing grin. "Do you remember the gift I gave you before you left for Alpiria?"

Izana's brows bunched together as she tried to see where her mistress was going with her question. "You gave me your dagger to use."

"Yes, and do you recall what it was made of?"

"It was gold."

And then it hit her. She gasped, wondering if she understood her mistress correctly. "You gave me the dagger to wear."

Azurha laughed, but the lines of confusion on Modius's brow only deepened as he said, "I'm failing to get the meaning of this."

Izana laced her fingers through his. Her heart fluttered with the joy and excitement. "Modius, my owner presented me with something made of gold to wear. It means I'm free."

"Which is why we couldn't give her to you." Azurha rose from her chair. "We can no longer decide these things for her. The decision is hers to make. But in the meantime, Izana, think of something you would like to wear instead of the dagger, and I will see that you get it. I doubt you want to display that to everyone you meet."

Modius sank onto the edge of her bed as Azurha left the room, his hand still linked with hers. He stared at it, his voice low. "Are you offended that I asked for you?"

"Am I the only thing you really wanted?"

He nodded, and the warm contentment she'd discovered from his love flowed through her veins. "But I didn't want you as my slave."

"What did you want me as?" She tilted his chin up and ran her thumb along his bottom lip, resisting the urge to kiss him before he had a chance to answer.

Desire flamed his eyes, brightening the gold and green flecks in them. He pulled her closer to him, his face inches from hers, his fingers tracing paths up and down her spine. "You, just as you are."

His mouth covered hers in a kiss that whetted a craving for more. She rose to her knees and straddled his lap, only pausing long enough to realize how lucky she was to be able to do so after her injuries. A tendril of the Alpirion magic swirled inside her, reminding her never to waste a moment. She cradled his face in her hands, thanking the gods for giving her another chance with the man she loved.

His hands stopped in the middle of her back, and his face turned serious. "I lied."

Her pulse hammered in her ears. "What do you mean?"

"I want you to be more than you already are, Izana. I want you to be my wife."

A laugh mixed with a sob as they both fought to flee her throat, giving voice to the emotions that churned inside her. She covered her mouth and nodded as a single tear fell. For the first time in her life, she was completely free to choose her own destiny, and she couldn't think of a better future than one spent with him.

Modius wrapped his arms around her and tucked her head under his chin. "I didn't mean to make you cry."

"I didn't mean to cry." She sniffed back the next tear that threatened to fall. "I think I know what to ask Lady Azurha for, though, as a marker of my freed status."

"And what's that?"

"A golden wedding ring, so everyone will know I'm yours."

30

Azurha strolled into the throne room with Titus, the gold and diamond band on her finger still sparkling as brightly as it had when he placed it there yesterday. The wedding had been a grand affair that left her exhausted by the end of the day, but as she fell asleep in her new husband's arms last night, she knew it was all worth it.

The room was surprisingly empty for this time of the morning, but she suspected the celebrations had gone on long after she and Titus had retired.

He pulled her to the globe. "Care to help me with the barrier?"

"I'd be honored." Since the day she'd saved him, she'd managed to hold on to some of the magic flowing within her. Once she finally learned to recognize it, she could constantly feel it swirling through her veins. It never reached the wild, chaotic level of that day, but it was always there, waiting for her to call on it at the right moment. It stirred inside her chest, lazily streaming down her arm and into Titus as he reinforced the barrier.

He leaned and murmured so only she could hear, "I could get used to having you help me with protecting the empire."

"As your empress, it's a duty I'll gladly assume, so long

as I have you by my side."

"Lucky me." His arm circled her waist and pulled her close to him, the hard planes of his body reviving all her lustful thoughts. "Perhaps we should return to our chambers and hide there for a few more days."

She chuckled and leaned in to kiss him. She'd need more than just a few days to quench the desire raging inside her.

A door banged open before their lips touched, followed by the sounds of heavy footsteps. They pulled away just as Captain Galerius stopped short, a hint of red rising into his ears. He looked to his side. "Your Majesties, may I have a word with you in private?"

"Of course, Galerius." Titus still kept his hand on the small of her back as he led them into the small antechamber off of the throne room. He waited until she sat down in one the chairs before taking his own. "What is it?"

The Captain of the Legion refused to meet their eyes. His chest rose and fell like a man caught in the throes of battle, his cheeks flushed. Then he drew his sword and laid it on the floor before Titus.

Her husband pressed his lips together in a grim line. "What is the meaning of this?"

"I have let one emperor be murdered under my watch and have failed to protect you twice, Emperor Sergius. I'm no longer fit be to called a member of the Legion, much less its captain. Please accept my resignation."

"And if I don't?"

Galerius snapped his head up, his grey eyes full of indignation. "Why would you want a failure like me?"

"Because you are still an effective leader of men, one I do not wish to lose."

His hands curled into fists, and he glanced down at the sword. For a moment, she thought he would pick it back up and slide it back into the scabbard that still hung from his belt. Then his fingers uncurled, and he squeezed his eyes closed. "Forgive me, Your Imperial Majesties, but I cannot accept your offer."

He turned on his heel and was almost to the door when Azurha jumped out of her chair and called out his name. Disdain simmered in the clench of his jaw, but he stopped.

She slipped off her bracelet to show him the tattoo on her wrist. "You made a vow."

"And I have proven myself unworthy of such an honor."

"Once a member of the Legion, always a member of the Legion."

The knob in throat bobbed as he stared at the emblem. He took a deep breath and lifted his gaze to her face. His wounded pride sat close to the surface, still too raw to see the repercussions of his actions. "The emperor is blessed to have someone like you to watch over him. He doesn't need me."

He continued for the door.

Behind her, Titus stood and came toward them. Azurha moved between the two men, allowing Galerius to escape. "Let him go, Titus," she whispered, pressing her hands against his chest. "He needs time to lick his wounds and remember what's important."

"So I should just let him go?"

She cast a glance over her shoulder at the door. "Yes, because men like him will always remain true to their duty. He'll be back."

Epilogue

No amount of crystalized ginger could ease the rolling in Izana's stomach as the airship descended into the landing docks of the emperor's palace in Madrena. She peered at her new home and breathed in the salty sea air.

Modius leaned on the railing beside her. "What do you think?"

The song of a gull bleated above them, harmonizing with the crash of the waves. A cool breeze pulled a few stray curls down from her pins to dance around her face. "It's very different from Emona."

"I hope in a good way." He slid his hand over hers so their matching gold bands touched.

She leaned into him and forgot all about her airsickness. "I don't care where I am, as long as I'm with you."

"You two lovebirds are almost as nauseatingly cute as Titus and Azurha," Marcus said behind them. "It makes me want to drink until I'm numb."

"Perhaps you should try harder for Sexta," she teased, remembering all the times Marcus had come to the *lupanar* seeking the attentions of her former mistress.

A wry and somewhat wistful grin rose from the corner of his mouth. "A man can only take so much rejection." He held out a sealed scroll. "Titus and Azurha made me to promise not to give this to you until we arrived."

Modius took the scroll and waited until Marcus walked away before opening it.

Izana skimmed the contents and gasped. "Am I reading this correctly?"

"I'm asking myself the same thing."

She read it again, slowly this time, but still not believing the words.

Dear Modius and Izana,

We are humbled by your simple requests, but felt they fell short of the magnitude of your brave actions in discovering Tuhotep's plot and stopping him. Furthermore, we do not wish to lose the knowledge each of you possess, as they are both important assets to the future of the empire. Therefore, we wish to give you our imperial palace in Madrena as a wedding gift and ask you to use it wisely to pursue your studies.

--Emperor Titus Sergius Flavus and Empress Azurha

Izana's vision blurred as she read the letter over and over again. When she finally tore her eyes away from it, she saw the same shock mirrored in her husband's expression. "The palace is ours?"

"So it says," he said with a strangled laugh. "I wonder how we should use it."

"Be careful with those statues—the emperor will be pissed if one of them breaks," a rough voice barked below, drawing them back to the railing.

Izana's heart skipped a beat as the likeness of an ancient Alpirion king rolled out onto the gangplank. "It's from the vault under the library."

A section of a fresco followed, the gold paint in the glyphs flashing under the sun.

She crossed the deck to Marcus. "Why is there Alpirion art on board?"

He gave her a devilish grin. "You tell me, Izana."

She laughed, finally understanding the last line in the letter from the emperor and empress. "I think I know what I'll be doing here in Madrena."

"And what's that?" Modius asked as he joined them.

"Lady Azurha said she wanted to learn more about the Alpirion language and culture. I think I'll be spending a lot of time translating the glyphs."

"And I suppose I'll continue with my medical studies." He offered her his hand. "So, are we in this together?"

She took it, savoring the warmth from his touch and the love shining from his eyes. "All the way to the very end."

A Note to Readers

Dear Reader,

Thank you so much for reading *Poisoned Web*. I hope you enjoyed it. If you did, please leave a review on the site where you purchased this book or on Goodreads. I'll be giving away ebook copies of the next book in the series, *Deception's Web*, to the first 50 people who email me with a link to their review.

I love to hear from readers. You can find me on Facebook and Twitter, or you can email me using the contact form on my website, www.CristaMcHugh.com.

If you would like to be the first to know about new releases or be entered into exclusive contests, please sign up for my newsletter using the contact form on my website, www.CristaMcHugh.com. Also, please like my Facebook page for more excerpts and teasers from upcoming books.

--Crista

DECEPTION'S WEB
THE DEIZIAN EMPIRE: BOOK THREE

A soldier looking for redemption falls into the arms of the empire's Black Widow...

Galerius, former Captain of the Legion, is honored to be given a chance to redeem himself by discovering who is behind the failing barrier. A series of anonymous letters all point to Hostilius, governor of Lucrilia, but Galerius thinks he'll learn more about the plot by seducing the governor's thrice widowed daughter, Claudia. Although he warns himself not to fall into snare of the empire's most deadly temptress, one kiss leaves him begging for more.

Claudia has spent years as a pawn in her father's political games and longs to break free of his rule, even it means betraying him to the emperor. When Galerius arrives in Tivola, she's not sure if he's there to aid her father or stop him. She willingly submits to his seduction, despite their class differences, in order to find the truth. What she doesn't expect to find is a man who indulges her secret fantasies, satisfying her in a way none of her previous husbands did, and treats her as something more than a conquest. As time runs out to thwart her father's plans, she must decide if she can trust Galerius not only with her life, but her heart.

Excerpt to follow

Excerpt from *Deception's Web*

As soon as Claudia Pacilus heard the engine of her father's airship die down, her pulse quickened. He'd sent her back to Tivola weeks ago, his displeasure at her inability to capture the attention of Emperor Serguis evident without him saying a word. Now, the emperor had married that Alpirion, Azurha, and she was left to deal with the punishment for her failure.

She pulled her palla tighter around her chest as though it would drive away the chill forming in her soul. Her gaze travelled to the cliffs on the far end of the moonlit garden. *Will I be the next person tossed over the edge for my father's pleasure?*

The waves crashed against the rocks in reply, and a shiver coursed down her spine. Her mind screamed for her to run and hide, but pride kept her feet planted firmly in the center of main atrium. She was a Deizian, and such cowardly behavior was beneath her. She would greet her father like a dutiful daughter and pray to the gods that his ire had lessened during the weeks of imperial wedding festivities.

Her father, Gaius Hostilius Pacilus, provincial governor of Lucrilla, strolled into the villa with a regal bearing that could rival the emperor himself, surrounded by slaves carrying torches to illuminate his way. Fine threads of silver shimmered in his golden fair, hinting at his age, but his body remained as well muscled as any member of the Imperial Army. He fixed his cold blue eyes on her, his mouth pressing in a tight line.

Claudia lowered her head and dipped into a curtsey. "Greetings, noble Father, and welcome home."

He stopped in front of her, but said nothing. She could feel his eyes upon her, dissecting each of her flaws from the loose strand of hair that had slipped free in the ocean breeze to the wrinkle creased where she'd gripped her palla moments ago.

A tremor worked its way into her bottom lip, but she dare not move from her position of subjugation. She stared at his sandals and waited for him to give her permission to stand. She was little better than the slaves that served them. Her father owned everything, from the jewels she wore to her freedom. If she left, she'd have to leave everything behind. It was far better to try and appease him than to be cast out with nothing but her name.

Another step of footsteps approached her with quick strikes on the tiled floor. Her body tensed a second before the back of a hand connected with her cheek, knocking her to the ground. Blood filled her mouth. She wiped it away and glared at her younger brother, Asinius.

"Washed up whore," he growled before he kicked her in the stomach, knocking the air from her lungs and leaving a burning ache behind that made her wonder if death wasn't far behind. "If you had done what you were supposed to do, you would be empress now instead of that slave."

He raised his foot back to deliver another blow, but froze when their father said, "Patience, Asinius. The emperor will fall in due time."

Then Hostilius peered down at her as if she were puzzle for him to unravel rather than his flesh and blood. Seconds passed in silence. Claudia gulped in a breath, but other than that, remained as still as a statue.

"Pity," he said at last as though he'd just discovered a smudge on his pristine white toga. "It seems like she has outlived her usefulness to us."

Anger tempered the fear chilling her blood. How dare he not show any concern for her welfare! She, the daughter whose three marriages helped him gain control of the province and elevate him to governor with the death of each of her husbands. Her jaw tightened, and she reached to pull her palla back over shoulders.

"What should we do with her?" Asinius asked as though she were a disobedient slave. The perverse note in his voice hinted that he would love to be the one who flung her over the cliffs. Even though he was the favored son, he'd always borne a grudge against her, especially when she reminded him her father's rise to power was due to her, not him.

"Time will tell." Hostilius continued past her on the way to his study. "Come along, son. We have much to discuss before we act again."

Her brother followed him like an eager puppy offered a juicy bone to chew on. Whatever they were planning, blood would be spilled when they carried it out. The slaves followed them with the torches, leaving her alone in the darkness.

Claudia spat out the last of the blood and pulled herself off of the floor. So, it had come to this. She had lost her father's favor, and her life hung on the thin string of his mercy. For years, she'd been a pawn in his political games. She'd warmed the beds of three men she loathed to strengthen her family's position, hoping for the day she'd satisfy her father's thirst for power long enough to be allowed to live out the rest of her days at country estate. She'd watched her father claim her widow's dowry each time and add it to his coffers, leaving her with nothing more than his approval and the ever tightening noose of guilt from association. She'd even agreed to lower herself to level of a concubine as part of her father's plan to gain imperial favor. And now she was left wondering when her body would slam against the rocks below and be carried off to sea.

The muffled voices of her father and brother floated out from under the closed doors of the study, fueling her anger. If they wanted to cut her out from their plans now, so be it. But that wouldn't keep her from discovering their plot. Perhaps she could use it to her advantage.

She moved to the gardens, keeping her steps silent as she crept closer to the open window of her father's study. She clung to the shadows and listened.

"Pontus was arrogant to think he could kill Sergius," Asinius said.

"Pontus had hired the Rabbit. He thought she would succeed as she has numerous times before. None of us imagined Sergius would succeed in seducing her."

"And now that she has her lips wrapped around his dick, it's only a matter of time before she convinces him to free all the slaves, even after that slave uprising in Alpiria last month."

"Emperor Sergius is too cautious to make such a sweeping change. He'll start slowly because he knows that such a drastic measure will crush the economy of the empire." Hostilius's chair creaked like it did every time he leaned back in it. Claudia pictured him steepling his fingers together and pressing them against his lips as he thought. "His marriage to the Alpirion has endeared him to the lower classes."

"All the more reason to destroy him as quickly as possible." Her brother's sandals slapped against the tile floors as he paced. "Who's the next best assassin in the empire?"

"You're not thinking clearly. The Legion will be guarding Sergius more tightly than ever, and even if an assassin gets past them, the Rabbit will already have placed measures to protect him. You forget that she knows many ways to kill a man, and she will have made sure that another assassin would not gain access to him."

"Then how are we going to get the throne?"

Her father's chuckle caused her gut to clench. It was too cool, too collected, too calm. "An emperor is only safe as his popularity. If the people fear he is placing them in danger, they will demand his head."

A pause filled the room, followed by Ansinius's laughter. "The barrier."

"It will take careful planning. Sergius has outwitted us once, and the barrier appeared stronger than ever when I was there. This time, I will not act until I am certain I will succeed."

Claudia bit her bottom lip to keep from gasping. She'd heard rumors that the barrier had been weakened after the death of the prior emperor, but she had no idea her father was behind it. Why would he risk having the empire over run by the Barbarians? Those creatures knew only death and destruction. They could not be reasoned with, and if the barrier fell, thousands of lives would be lost.

"How shall we start?"

"Slowly. I need to make sure the device is at its maximal potential."

"That will mean more ore."

"What do you think I was discussing with Minius last week? The first shipments should start arriving in less than a month. But we must be discreet. If the emperor catches wind of our plan, we'll suffer the same fate as Pontus."

"I doubt that, Father. You are far more cunning than him."

"As you can see, there's no need to bloody our hands. The masses will do it for us."

"And when we save them from the Barbarians, they will demand we assume the throne." Asinius's laughter drifted outside again, this time with a musical note of insanity in it. "It's perfect."

"Would you expect otherwise from me?" The chair creaked again, followed by footsteps. "Remember, patience is the key here. We wait until everything is ready." Their voices waned as they left the study.

Claudia slid along the wall and rubbed the chill from her arms. How long would her father allow the barrier to fall before he restored it? Hours? Days? Weeks? How many lives would be lost in the process? Whatever his plans included, they didn't include her. What was to keep him from selling her to Minius in exchange for more ore? Or worse, for him to shift the blame on her should they fail?

I refuse to be his pawn any more.

She took a deep breather, cleansing her fears from her mind. Her father made a mistake when he called her useless, and he would pay for it. If he feared the emperor would discover his plan, then perhaps she should capitalize on that.

She stood, straightened her clothes, and went to her room. In careful block letters to disguise her handwriting, she wrote, *If you wish for the barrier to remain intact, you should monitor the ore shipments from Gracchero.*

There. Nothing too exact. A hint, and no more. Just a clue of her father's plan that would hinder his efforts without giving everything away. No one would ever suspect the note would be from her. And when her father's face turned red from frustration, she would have the start of her revenge.

"Zavi," she called to her slave, "Could you please fetch Kafi. I have a task for him that requires his unique talent for discretion."

Books by Crista McHugh

The Soulbearer Trilogy
A Soul For Trouble
A Soul For Chaos
A Soul For Vengeance

The Elgean Chronicles:
A Thread of Magic
The Tears of Elios

The Deizian Empire:
Tangled Web
Poisoned Web
Deception's Web (coming Dec 2013)

The Kavanaugh Foundation:
Heart of a Huntress, Book 1
Angelic Surrender, Book 2
"A High Stakes Game", Book 2.5 (a free read)
Kiss of Temptation, Book 3
Night of the Huntress (Print Anthology of Books 1 and 2)

Other titles by Crista McHugh
The Alchemy of Desire
"A Waltz at Midnight"
Cat's Eyes
"Danny's Boy"
"Provoking the Spirit"
Eight Tiny Flames (part of *A Very Scandalous Holiday* Anthology)

Praise For Crista McHugh

A SOUL FOR TROUBLE

"Book one in the Soulbearer trilogy, this fantastical romance is completely different from the myriad of others out there. It's a great book that pits Trouble against Chaos — two characters that all readers will want to visit again and again!"
— 4 1/2 STARS, RT Book Reviews

TANGLED WEB

"Crista McHugh's **Tangled Web** is sinfully delicious! This erotic feast features one fascinating couple and a killer plotline. It's impossible to turn away from this story after reading the first few pages!... **Tangled Web** is a keeper!"
— Recommended Read, Joyfully Reviewed

THE TEARS OF ELIOS

"The first thing that came to mind upon finishing this book is, 'Holy Crap! Is that it?!' I did not want this book to end."
— Starcrossed Reviews

A WALTZ AT MIDNIGHT

"I love this story! I didn't expect it to be so entrancing and captivating... A WALTZ AT MIDNIGHT is a great romantic story with engaging characters that I didn't wish to end... A must read for romance lovers!"
—The Romance Reviews

HEART OF A HUNTRESS

"Warning: you will not want to put this book down once you start."
— Happily Ever After Reviews

ANGELIC SURRENDER

"The author did such a great job creating my ideal hero that I found myself thinking about him for days."
— Whipped Cream Reviews

KISS OF TEMPTATION

"As Ms. McHugh moves on with her writing of *The Kavanaugh Foundation*, I found this story even more spell binding than first two books."
— Literary Nymph Reviews

CAT'S EYES

"…an excellent plot with oodles of action and suspense. I could not put it down."
— Just Erotic Romance Reviews
"This is a well-paced, enjoyable read complete with action, suspense, humor, and hot sex."
— Night Owl Reviews

THE ALCHEMY OF DESIRE

"Crista McHugh did an incredible job of drawing me into the world of magic, steampunk, and old west that she created."
— Wakela Runen's World

MORE THAN A FLING

"What I liked most about this short story is the fact the main characters, Danni and Ryan, are "real" people… highly engaging and enjoyable."
— Whipped Cream Reviews

PROVOKING THE SPIRIT

"I loved the twists and turns the author threw at me while I was reading and felt my heart racing in my chest numerous times as I was flipping the pages… Overall, this is a fantastic story that's worth picking up!"
— Night Owl Reviews

Author Bio:

Growing up in small town Alabama, Crista relied on story-telling as a natural way for her to pass the time and keep her two younger sisters entertained.

She currently lives in the Audi-filled suburbs of Seattle with her husband and two children, maintaining her alter ego of mild-mannered physician by day while she continues to pursue writing on nights and weekends.

Just for laughs, here are some of the jobs she's had in the past to pay the bills: barista, bartender, sommelier, stagehand, actress, morgue attendant, and autopsy assistant.

And she's also a recovering LARPer. (She blames it on her crazy college days)

For the latest updates, deleted scenes, and answers to any burning questions you have, please check out her webpage, www.CristaMcHugh.com.

Find Crista online at:

Twitter: twitter.com/crista_mchugh

Facebook: www.facebook.com/CristaMcHugh